DEADLY DIAMONDS

Jeweltown Murder Mystery Book One

DEADLY DIAMONDS

DENISE RODGERS

Deadly Diamonds
Jeweltown Mystery Book One

Creative Writing Press
Troy, Michigan
Copyright © 2015 Denise Rodgers
ISBN 0-9708382-2-0

This is a work of fiction. Any resemblance to any person, living or dead, is purely co-incidental. While the city of Royal Oak, Michigan does, in fact, exist; all businesses and people mentioned therein are purely fictitious.

Contact Denise Rodgers
Email: deniserodgersbooks@gmail.com
Facebook: https://www.facebook.com/DeniseRodgersBooks
www.DeniseRodgersBooks.com

Interior designed and formatted by E.M. Tippetts Book Designs
www.emtippettsbookdesigns.com

Dedicated to fellow voracious readers everywhere. And to my husband, Peter, who hasn't read fiction for pleasure since he read Old Bones: The Wonder Horse *in elementary school, and yet is my number one support. They say opposites attract . . .*

CHAPTER 1

When I was a little girl in Detroit, I used to love playing with my Barbie. She had long, flowing, brown hair and the most amazing, hard plastic boobs. Her legs, while not terribly flexible, were long and lean, making her look terrific in every outfit my mother could afford to buy me. But it wasn't the clothes that made me want to play with Barbie. The exciting thing was that my Barbie had a Ken, her one and only true love that would last till the end of time, beyond the landfill and into eternity.

Go figure. I was a romantic at eight years of age. And though you wouldn't know it to look at me now, I still have that heartfelt wish for a lifetime 'someone.' Even if I'm fifty-four and my husband divorced me exactly one year ago to marry a sweet young thing who looks a lot more like my old Barbie than I do. This home-wrecker is a scant five years older than our oldest son, Vic. Her name, unbelievably, is Barbara.

My new problems started with a phone call on a Monday afternoon, just as the whole brouhaha over my divorce started to be old news. I'd been working like Santa in July to create some new jewelry pieces to sell. The Royal Oak Art Fair was coming up in just six days. Boodles, my miniature Bichon, nestled on my lap. Shelley, my assistant and right-hand younger sister, worked at the counter, showing rings to a woman who looked like she lived in one of the new upscale lofts on Main Street. Business was picking up. Things were finally going well. Best of all, it was a year to the day since the cataclysm, and I was just starting to be able to say the name Robert Blumer out loud, without swearing that one of these days I was going to kill the lying-cheating-womanizing dirt bag. Did I mention that I've been more than a little bitter?

But back to that phone call. It was my son, Vic. He's the second-in-command at Blumer Fine Jewelers and has managed to remain as neutral as Switzerland about his parents' divorce. For all my married years, I worked at Blumer's. It's a street-level store on Washington, below one of the few high rises in Royal Oak, a suburb just two miles north of Detroit. My ex-husband's father, Lou, started the business some forty-five years ago, and he promptly died in a burst of joy on the golf course in Boca, just a month after he and my mother-in-law, Myrna, retired and left the business to my husband.

"Hi, Honey." I felt the breeze of the store air conditioning on my face. "I'm kind of in the middle of an amazing pendant right now. Can I get back to you?"

There was no response, and that got my attention.

"What is it, Vic?"

Vic is not normally that talkative, but still his silence was deafening. He took a deep breath. "Dad is missing."

I took the message in stride; I wasn't about to start worrying about Robert Blumer. Not at this moment in time. "Your father is a grown man. What do you mean 'missing'?" I didn't want to sound edgy. But what the hell did he want *me* to do about it?

"He was supposed to be back from lunch more than four hours ago. He doesn't answer his cell." Vic paused. Was he trying to gain his composure? "And he was carrying two, three-carat diamonds in his suit pocket."

Now the silence was on my side of the line. I took a deep breath and asked the obvious. "What does Barbara have to say about this?" It had been a lovely family business until we hired her. She looks something like a young brunette Morgan Fairchild and apparently "Robbie," as she liked to call him, noticed. Because just six months after she arrived, "Robbie" had me served with papers at work, with absolutely no notice. I had been too blind and trusting to suspect anything. I had been so numb and nauseous over the whole thing that I'd asked for nothing more than a cash settlement — and I got it.

"She went to lunch with Loozie," said Vic. Loozie was Barbara's best friend; a tall, blond, hottie CPA who liked to carry a red leather briefcase and wear matching spike heels. "She told me that she was going to take off for a few hours because Loozie's going through a tough spell and needed a shoulder to cry on."

Well, boo hoo. Couldn't Barbie-girl and her blond counterpart do their crying after-hours?

I was so glad I didn't work there anymore. Exactly one year ago, I took my divorce money and moved out of our enormous home on Hendrie Boulevard, into a small bungalow near downtown. Best of all, I opened a small jewelry boutique of my own. I call it Bella's Baubles. It's down the road from my new home on Fourth Street, and just around the corner from Blumer Fine Jewelers on Washington.

"So if he isn't with Barbara, where is he?"

Vic cleared his throat. "He left the store at ten this morning and said he'd be back in by twelve-thirty, give or take a bit for lunch. He hasn't answered his phone once."

I looked at my Minnie Mouse watch; it was nearly three o'clock. "What's with the diamonds?"

"Dad's been hush-hush about it. Maybe they're for someone who doesn't want to be seen in the store." His voice trailed off.

Back when I actually worked at Blumer's, we did sell jewelry to other cheating-lying kind of guys who didn't want their wives to know what they were buying. But those were usually diamond-clad trinkets, not ginormous rocks. Three-carat was big, even for Robert Blumer's standards. Most Blumer Fine Jewelers diamond sales were in the one- to two-carat range. My thirty-one-year-old engagement diamond — now gathering dust in my Bank of Royal Oak safety deposit box — was a carat-and-a-half. Barbara-Baby had a two-carat princess. I stifled a groan.

"Will you come with me to the house?" Vic asked.

I froze. "Why the house?" The last place on earth I had any intention of visiting was my former home.

"Because that's where he goes sometimes." Vic had an edge to his voice. "He goes home and takes a *nap*." Vic's voice got even edgier, like maybe he was angry with his father. "I know his routine. But he's not answering any calls, and that's just not like him."

I paused. "Why me?" I really didn't want to go.

"I'm worried."

"Take Gramma." That was my knee-jerk response. Robert's mother, Myrna, still worked at the store. Myrna's all right. She still loves her son. After all, she gave birth to the big cheat and changed his diapers and all that. My guess is that she shares my disgust at his behavior. She doesn't come right out and say it, because Barbara is her new daughter-in-law, after all. But I know she doesn't approve of Robert's behavior, and I'm pretty sure she doesn't care for his new model any more than I do.

"I need Gramma to stay and watch the store." Geez, Vic wasn't giving me any slack here.

"What about Janine? Isn't she there?" I thought of the hefty redhead that sat at the back of the store, forever doing bookwork on the ancient PC.

Vic whispered, "Yeah, she's back from the dentist's, but you know I can't leave Janine alone at the counter. She's useless up there."

I sighed. "I have a business, too." I could hear the weariness in my voice, and maybe a little whine.

"C'mon, Mom. Aunt Shelley's there with you."

He was annoyed with me. I could hear the knitted eyebrows in his voice. For some reason, he was totally oblivious to the hurt caused by the divorce. He actually thought I should be concerned about his dad. Well, I wasn't.

What if Barbara wasn't with a "friend"? What if she was lying and Robert was lying, just as they had back when I was the real wife and she was the new-hire? The last thing I wanted permanently imprinted on my brain was the vision of my Rob enjoying a nooner on what used to be my bed, in what used to be my house, with that man-stealing, scruples-free, low-life tart.

Did I mention that I'm not that fond of Barbara either?

"I'm really worried, Mom, or I wouldn't ask you."

I sighed, carefully placing the peridot in my hands back

onto the beadboard. "When can you get here?"

"I'll be there in five minutes."

I stood beneath the "Bella's Baubles" sign on my storefront on Fourth Street. It was delightfully breezy for mid-July, and I could feel my gauzy yellow skirt ripple against my ankles. Vic pulled up in his brand new, red and white Mini Cooper. I scooped up Boodles and held all five pounds of him in my arms as I bent over and slid into Vic's impossibly small car.

Boodles and I are accustomed to my silver-white Escalade, and the hell with gas mileage. We are, after all, in metro Detroit, Motown, home of the Big Three, which aren't all that big anymore, but my ride is my ride.

"Did you even try to call Barbara?" I was still more than a little annoyed with the interruption in my business day — for Robert Blumer, no less.

"Yeah, I've been calling her all day." Vic shifted into second. Why he learned to drive a stick shift is one of those mysteries of the deep. "She never picked up."

I thought that was odd, but I keep my mouth shut about her when I'm with Mr. Neutral Switzerland who refuses to take sides — or hear anything from me about the divorce. And that really takes a lot of effort. I'm used to speaking my mind.

"Are you sure this is such a big deal?" It did seem like Vic was over-reacting.

"I'm worried about Dad." Vic looked straight ahead. "Cash flow's been pretty bad, and I think he's taking it hard."

I stiffened. "What do you mean cash flow is bad!" Robert Blumer was many things—generous, debonair, and a little bit bad-boy and dirt bag—but one thing he wasn't was fiscally irresponsible. Blumer Fine Jewelers supported not only Robert and his Barbie girl, but also Vic and his wife Marcy; the bookkeeper Janine; as well as Robert's mother, Myrna. The bank account was one place where he didn't think with his zipper. At least he never had before. But why would he be sharing that concern with Vic, if Robert had anything to do with being in the red? It didn't make sense.

"How could that possibly be?" I asked Vic. "Has business been down?"

Vic straightened his sunglasses. "No, not really. I've been trying to figure it out, and so has Dad. But so far, all we know is that the bank balance isn't what it should be."

I bit my tongue. Chances were that Barbie-girl had something to do with a drooping bank account, but I wasn't going to say a word. Not to Mr. Switzerland.

Vic crossed over Woodward and turned onto Hendrie Boulevard. Our house—pardon me, Robert and Barbara's house—is just a half-mile from downtown Royal Oak. It's a yellow-brick, center-entrance colonial, built in the early fifties, before they had the good sense to make a master bathroom big enough for two people at one time.

Vic turned into the driveway and slowed to a stop. I took a long look at my front yard, almost suspended in time from when I'd packed up and left just a year ago. My hydrangeas were in full bloom, lovely rounded balls of pink petals. It was still a little early for the Black-eyed Susans. It didn't look like Barbie-girl took much interest in the garden. Everything looked just the way I'd left it. No new flowers. Robert must have hired a gardener, because as far as I could see, there were no weeds, and I knew for a fact that Robert would be better at hiring a service than getting dirt under his fine-jeweler fingernails.

"C'mon, Mom." Vic waved me toward the front door.

I took a deep breath. It was amazing that Vic could be so completely clueless about how hard this was for me. But clueless he was.

I followed him onto my old front porch, my fuzzy little dog at my heels. This was new territory for Boodles. He was my divorce dog, a gift to myself after unloading the Big Cheat. The cement planters on either side of the door were filled with tacky silk roses, courtesy, no doubt, of Barbara. So she had bothered to make a few changes, after all.

As I walked through the front door, the familiar scent of thick upholstery and potpourri made me nostalgic for my old life. Boodles ran in ahead of Vic and me and started to bark at nothing in particular, which was odd. Boodles was normally a quiet little dog.

"Dad?" Vic called out as he stepped through the foyer. I could hear his footsteps on the hardwood floor. Boodles was already halfway up the staircase.

No answer.

"He's not here. Let's go." I had no desire to see any more of my house. Their house. I really didn't want to see Barbara's imprint. I realized with a gulp that a year hadn't been long enough. It still hurt.

"*Mom*." Vic stretched out the word, just as he had when he was a child. "I'm worried about Dad. What if he had a heart attack or something?"

I sighed. Vic was a good kid. He was just worried about his dad and there I was dwelling on my own pain. "All right, let's go upstairs." I held onto the banister for emotional support. *Focus! This isn't about you!*

I heard Boodles whining at the top of the stairs, out of my view. I trudged slowly up the steps, letting Vic take the lead. He passed his old bedroom, and then Heather's, and stood in the doorway of the master bedroom. Stunned. Silent.

"Don't come in here, Mom." Vic's voice was flat and urgent, like he was trying to protect me.

Suddenly, I kicked into mother-mode and left the hurt-wimp behind me. I lunged past Vic in the doorway and stood there. Shocked.

Lying on what used to be our pillow-top bed was Robert

Blumer, in just his skivvies, with what looked like several bullet holes in his abdomen. The mattress was soaking up all the blood, as there was none on the floor that I could see.

For a moment I stood there like a solid mannequin. It was hard for me to tell if I was horrified for my Victor and my Heather, or if I still had feelings for that detestable dirt bag who had been my husband and bed partner for nearly thirty years, and who was now, very clearly, dead.

CHAPTER 2

Vic pulled out his cell phone and punched in 9-1-1. Only it wasn't much of an emergency anymore. He made a few more calls to the store, to his wife Marcy, and to his sister Heather. I made a quick call to Shelley to tell her why I wouldn't be there for a while. We made our way down the stairs and out the front door.

I held Boodles on my lap, clutching his soft, curly coat. He leaned into me, like he knew I needed him. Vic sat on the front porch step beside me, head down, his fingers gripping his hair. I moved closer and put my arm over his shoulders. He looked so much like his father, but I could never hold that against him. I was crying myself and starting to wonder if all my nasty anger really just masked the fact that I was still in love with Robert Blumer. My husband. My ex.

A dead man.

Suddenly Vic sat up. "The diamonds. They were in Dad's suit jacket pocket."

Now, we'd just seen his dad, and he wasn't wearing any suit, that's for sure.

"I have to go see if the diamonds are there. Those stones were on memo. They're worth at least two-hundred-grand together. It could wipe us out."

I held onto his shoulder. "Honey, you can't go in there." I knew enough from watching *Law & Order* and *CSI* to know that Robert and the bedroom formerly-known-as-mine was, at this point in time, an official crime scene.

Vic stood. "I have to go in."

"Aren't we insured?" I asked, instantly realizing that I'd said 'we,' as if I were still a part of Blumer Fine Jewelers, which I most certainly was not.

"Oh, insurance," said Vic.

I was relieved to see that I'd stopped him from doing something stupid, just as two police cars pulled up with flashers but no siren. Then Barbara's Corvette, Heather's old VW bug, and even Myrna showed up on the front lawn. Apparently, Janine could hold down the fort after all. It was going to be a bizarre family reunion. With police.

Barbara came storming up to me, wagging her manicured finger, the redness in her face peeking out behind her facade of makeup. "You bitch! You finally did him in."

Boodles started barking again. *Good boy. Go bite her*

ankles. I bit the thought back and instead said, "Calm down, Barbara, we're all upset here."

But Barbara was in no mood to be calmed, especially by me. "Where are the cops? I'm going to tell them all about you." And with that, she flipped her lovely mane of brown curls and headed to the detective who was busy questioning Vic, while two uniformed officers entered the house.

"Excuse me," said Barbara, her voice loud and brassy. It was so obvious that Robert hadn't been after her brains. Or her voice. "I can save you a lot of trouble. I know who killed my husband."

The detective swiveled his head toward Barbara, who was pointing her French-manicured index finger at my face.

The detective, who looked mildly familiar, held onto his notepad and pencil. "Excuse me, ma'am," he said directly to Barbara. "I'll be with you shortly. I have to talk with the two witnesses who found your husband first, and I promise you'll be next after that."

"*Fine.*" Barbara folded her slim arms and assumed a practiced pout.

The detective glanced over at me, probably to size up a prime suspect, and when I saw him full in the face, I nearly gasped. How had I not immediately recognized those amazing aqua-blue eyes? The thick gray hair had thrown me off, but now I knew exactly who he was. It was Bill Krieger. I'd had a four-ton crush on him in junior high, back when it didn't matter if he was Jewish or not. And come to think of it, how much did it matter when you were fifty-four and your kids were full-grown?

Heather ran up to me and gave me a full hug. "I can't believe it's true about Daddy." She gripped my hand like she was hanging onto the side of a mountain. My daughter is a younger, slimmer, version of myself. Only she likes to paint her hair blue, green, or red, or whatever, depending on her mood or her outfit. That day, it was a pansy pink that matched her oversized handbag.

"It's going to be hard for you." Tears brimmed out the corner of her eyes.

"What do you mean?" I asked.

Her tone dropped to a whisper. Apparently, she didn't want Detective Krieger to hear. "Well, you've been mouthing off about Dad and Barbara for over a year now."

I sighed. It was true. I'm not a bad woman, but one of my less attractive features is that I tend to speak my mind. It's cathartic. Sometimes it's even fun. So I'd been telling anyone with at least one working ear that Robert Blumer was an overripe skunk and his new wife also stinks. On ice. It's what I do. And it probably wouldn't bode well for me now.

Vic walked over, his normally ruddy complexion a light shade of pale. "There were no diamonds. Dad was robbed."

I didn't have any time to ponder who on earth would go to our house and rob Robert Blumer of two large diamonds — while he was in his underwear, no less — because I was almost immediately interrupted.

"Mrs. Blumer?" Detective Krieger asked.

I felt a wave of irrational fear at the sound of his voice. I scooped up Boodles and headed toward him. So far, he showed no sign of remembering junior high. Or me.

Barbara, a Mrs. Blumer of another kind, was also on her way to the detective, who kept a steady face. But there was a minute twitch to his left eye that made me wonder if he was evaluating me as a suspect. He gave Barbara an official, cop-face look. "I'll be questioning her first, ma'am. I believe that I've already explained."

Barbara rolled her eyes and sighed, but she backed off once again.

I noticed Heather was arm-in-arm with her Grandma Myrna. Heather was no fan of Barbara's. She wasn't nearly as neutral as her brother, who was already actively consoling his father's young wife. I turned and stood at attention next to Detective Blue Eyes.

"Now tell me, as specifically as possible, what happened this afternoon." His pencil was poised just above his notepad.

I told him about the call from Vic, and how we found Robert. I left out the part about the hydrangeas and the repulsively fake silk flowers in my front door flowerpots. Even so, I felt myself tearing up.

"What was your relationship with your ex?"

"Not good." I swatted some wetness from my eyes.

"And I'm sure you can find a lot of people, not just her —"
I nodded toward Barbara " — who'll say that I badmouthed
him, because I did." I stopped to pull a tissue out of my
pocket and blow my nose. "But I didn't hurt him and never
would." I could hear my voice rising to a sob and stopped
a moment to control myself. I do not like to cry in public.
"He's the father of my children." I sucked in a deep breath,
and thankfully, the tears in my eyes did not well over.

Detective Krieger looked me straight in the eyes with a
puzzled look on his face. Was it possible he was trying to
assess if I was a murderer? Or maybe he was conjuring up
memories of junior high. Who knew?

"And where were you during the hours of 10:00 AM
and 3:00 PM?" he asked.

"I was in my boutique on Fourth, just west of Main. It's
called Bella's Baubles. I make designer jewelry."

He looked decidedly unimpressed, which was okay. Not
everyone's into one-of-a-kind, colored gemstone jewelry. "Is
there anyone who can account for your whereabouts during
that time?" He was all business, just the facts, ma'am, a
regular Dragnet kind of guy and not at all like the cute Billy
Krieger who'd flirted with me in junior high.

"Well, I worked alone in the morning and early
afternoon. Just my dog, Boodles, and me. My sister, Shelley,
showed up at two today." I gave my Boodles a little squeeze,
and he licked my fingers. I tried not to show my concern. It
didn't look like I had an alibi.

"Were there any customers?" His aqua eyes were on his notepad.

"Yes!" I was so excited that he'd discovered my alibi that I would have kissed him right then and there on the lips, but even I know when to show restraint now and then. "There were at least three customers, and one of them almost bought something." I brightened and then, on second thought, dimmed. "She's coming back, I think, but I have no record of who she was."

He folded over his notepad. "That's it for now. But keep yourself available, in case I have further questions." He handed me a card. "If you think of anything else, give me a call."

If he wasn't the detective investigating the murder of my Robert—excuse me, Barbara's Robert—I might have been intrigued at the request to stay "available," which I most certainly was.

But as I flipped my cell on to call Shelley again, I saw the increasingly furious Barbara advance across the lawn to Detective Krieger.

"It was her. I'm sure of it," she cried, with renewed energy. "She'd do anything to get back at Robert—and at me."

Well, la-dee-dah was all I could think, as I tapped on Vic's shoulder to ask for a ride back to work.

$\mathscr{C}$HAPTER 3

$\mathscr{S}$helley gave me a big, sister-sized hug as soon as I walked into Bella's. Boodles put his paws up on us to join in.

"After you called, I had one of the other moms pick up Elena," she said. Her lightweight frame leaned into me, and I could feel myself starting to sob.

Shelley pulled back and looked at me. "What gives, Bella? Are you mourning Robert? After what he did to you?"

If it had been anyone but Shelley I might have smacked them. But she has a lot of markers on her side. She'd listened to me cry through the breakup and divorce for more than a year now. I owed her.

"I really don't know how to explain it, Shel. He was my

husband for twenty-nine years. It just shakes me up, that's all."

"Are you sure that's it?"

Thank God, she wasn't asking me if I'd done it. I couldn't bear to think that Shelley would think I could actually murder anyone, even a skunk like Robert.

Just then, the store door jingled. But instead of a paying customer, it was my mother. Her hair was its usual wind-resistant blond, and she wore pearls every day, just like June Cleaver. She was as casual as she got outside her Bloomfield Hills home, in a peach pantsuit with matching one-inch heels. She paused to look me up and down a bit, as if I were ten years old and the cookie jar was cracked. "Now, you didn't do it, did you dear?"

Leave it to my mother. Sometimes I wonder how I survived childhood. Any warmth in that household came from the heating vents.

"Of course not!" I fairly shouted at her.

"Well then." She patted her armor-plated coiffure. "There is nothing to worry about. And no reason to put off meeting this fine young man I've found for you."

Great. I'm the prime suspect in my ex-husband's murder, and my mother decides it's time for me to go on a date. You have to understand that my mother can't fathom the idea of a woman living alone, which explains the fact that she's on her fifth marriage to Albert, her richest catch yet. No one ever accused my mother of being overly sensitive—at least not to anyone else's feelings.

"It's not a great time now, Mom." I kept my voice as even as humanly possible, under the circumstances. "I'm kind of taken up with Robert's murder right now."

"You've been divorced from that...that man for a year now, so I can't see why it should be any of your affair." Her hands fluttered up to pat her stiff hair again.

I steadied myself against the glass counter. "First, he's the father of my children, Mom." I could hear the irritation in my voice. "Not to mention the fact that, thanks to that Barbara bimbo, I'm probably their prime suspect."

"There's no need to be vulgar." She sniffed. What she didn't know was, if she hadn't been in the room, I would have said 'bitch.' "And there's no reason under the sun to turn down the opportunity to meet this fine young man. He's a perfect catch, and you've been alone too long."

Now, realize that anyone under sixty qualifies for "young man" status in my mother's worldview. The other thing is that my mother is about as flexible as her hairdo and more persistent than a lingering cough. And after fifty-four years of experience with her, I decided there was only one logical end to this conversation. Well, two.

First, I sighed. Out loud. Then I said, "Tell him I'll meet him at eight at Ben's coffee shop on Main. You know, on the corner of Sixth."

"Thatta girl," she said, as she and her immovable hair turned and headed out the door onto Fourth Street.

"You'll never learn." Shelley frowned. She wore a pair of clear plastic gloves, like they use to make sandwiches at Subway, and squirted down every smooth surface in my store.

I didn't answer right away. I had enough on my plate to worry about without engaging in another fight with Shelley about our mother. She stopped wiping and stood glaring at me, a wad of paper towel grasped in her tightening fist. I could tell by her white knuckles it was time to talk.

"Okay, I give. What won't I ever learn?"

Shelley resumed wiping the glass, making me wait a bit for her sage answer. "You don't know how to say no to her." She sprayed the floor tile with blue glass cleaner. "It's easy, you know. I learned how to do it in college."

"Well, I didn't go to State on a scholarship like my brilliant baby sister. I went to Wayne." Wayne State University is the local college, close to downtown Detroit. Most kids who go there live at home. It's a budget-friendly choice for poor people and nerds. I had apparently been both in my college years.

"Oh, blah, blah, blah." Shelley stood up again, giving me her full attention. "You were the one accepted into the Center for Creative Studies. You were the one who was an artist, who knew what she wanted to do with her life. Not me. So don't try to lay that old guilt trip on me."

Shelley had been a math whiz in high school and went to Michigan State on a full scholarship that was supposed to encourage girls to go into engineering or higher math. Once she got there, she pretty much majored in partying and had nothing to do with math anymore, unless you counted her husband, Mitch. She met him at Michigan State, and he's a CPA.

Truth be told, I did envy her years at State. Maybe if there had been money to send me away to college, I wouldn't have fallen for Robert Blumer.

"Okay, okay," I said. "I'll let up on the guilt, and you can stop analyzing me."

She tossed the used paper towel into the basket, along with her disposable plastic gloves. Shelley rarely holds a grudge. "Fair enough. I can analyze you later. What do you want to order in tonight?"

Before I had a chance to answer, a customer jingled through our front door. After that, it was one after another. Some had heard about Robert, others had not. It wasn't until nearly seven-thirty that Shelley and I ate our order of room temperature moo-goo-gai pan from Oriental Treasures.

Shelley scooped in a mouthful of brown rice. "You know, we're forgetting something important here."

"Hmm?" I had my own mouth full and didn't want to talk.

"Someone killed Robert." Shelley wiped the side of her mouth. "And whoever did it is still out there. Creepy!"

I actually hadn't thought about that yet. I was still too blasted by the reality of seeing Robert's dead body and worrying that I was very likely a prime suspect. I sat up straighter in my bench chair and dropped a piece of chicken to Boodles. "Think it's dangerous out there?"

"It might be dangerous in here for all I know. So when's the funeral?'

"Vic called and told me they're waiting until the autopsy's done." I speared a bigger chunk of chicken. "I don't know what the big deal is about an autopsy. It's more than obvious what killed him."

"They have to be careful. They screw up any part of the investigation, and a murderer can go free."

"You watch too much *Law & Order*." It was true. *Law & Order, CSI Miami, Murder She Wrote, Monk*. Shelly had clocked many hours in front of the tube while Elena was growing up.

"You say that now, but you'll be glad I watched, if you need my help."

That shut me up. She might have been underemployed her whole life, but Shelley was undeniably smart. And if old blue eyes started to home in on me during his investigation, Shelley could be a big help. "I'll take whatever help I can get." I raised my Styrofoam cup of Coke in the air.

She did the same with her unsweetened iced tea. "Cheers!"

"*L'Chaim.*"

"So, is it time yet for your big date?"

I looked at my diamond-set Minnie Mouse watch, a gift to myself for my fiftieth birthday. "In about five minutes. You mind closing up? If I start running right now, I'll be almost on time."

CHAPTER 4

I walked into Ben's Coffee Shop with my Calvin Klein lime leather bag on my left shoulder and Boodles in his matching Bark Avenue carrier on my right. Keep in mind that while I love designer labels, I love a bargain even more. I just about never pay full price for my clothes or accessories.

The strong smell of freshly ground coffee filled my head, giving me a vicarious caffeine rush. I looked around the fashionably chic shop. No strange-looking middle-aged losers glancing around, so maybe I'd arrived first. I sank into one of the brown and black upholstered armchairs and waited for my date. Ben, the owner and also my former-brother-in-law, peeked out from behind the cash register. I was surprised to see him there; he usually worked the daytime shift.

Now, we weren't supposed to be friends anymore, but that just wasn't the case; I divorced Robert, not Ben. He walked out from behind the counter, arms outstretched. His face drooped with sadness, and I could suddenly see a strong resemblance to his dad, my former father-in-law, Lou.

"I didn't expect you here on the late shift," I said, by way of apology for not finding him before I sat. "Especially with what happened today with Robert."

"Come," he said. "I need a hug."

I stood up and exchanged the embrace. Ben smelled of Old Spice and espresso. His hug was firm, but his chest heaved spasmodically with deep and heavy sobs.

"What did my brother do?" I could feel his warm tears soak through my yellow silk blouse.

"It's okay, Ben. It will have to be okay." There was a catch in my throat, but I was tearing up no longer. A numbness was settling in, and I was getting more accustomed to Robert's death. More quickly, I'm sure, than I would have had we been happily married.

I pulled out of the hug and took a good look at Ben. He'd never been that close to Robert. They were so different. Robert was tall, dark, and undeniably handsome, with the polished sophistication that matched his Armani suites and Manolo shoes.

Ben, however, was medium height, pudgy, and bald,

with kind blue eyes that were still brimming over with tears.

"Why aren't you with your family tonight?" I asked the obvious question.

"I'll leave it to my mother and that wife of his to make the arrangements." I could hear the bitterness in his voice.

"Oh," was all I could say.

"He never shoulda left you." Ben shook his head side to side. "If he hadn't turned his head to that bimbo, he'd still be alive. I know it."

"You think she did it? You know, she's telling the police she's sure it was me."

Ben sat on one of his upholstered stools. "Of course, she'd point the finger at you, Bella. She's guilty as sin, that one."

I sat back down in the comfy chair, stunned. I really hadn't given enough thought—okay, any thought—as to who had actually killed Robert. "But why, Ben? What would she get out of killing him?"

Ben's blue eyes flattened to a dull, steel gray. "It's usually about the money, Bella. Follow the money, and you'll find out who killed my brother."

Just then, the bell on the coffee shop door tinkled, and in walked my date. I could tell, because he glanced through the sparse crowd looking for a woman alone, which I wasn't, as I was still grasping Ben's hands.

"My date's here." I pulled away from his fleshy grip.

"A date!" Ben looked upset. Even though it had been a

year since the divorce, I think he had some kind of cockeyed belief that if I remained faithful, eventually Robert and I would get back together somehow. Well, that obviously wasn't going to happen now.

Ben wiped his hands off on the front of his apron, as if I suddenly had the cooties. "Isn't it a little early to date?"

I looked him straight in the eye. "Robert left *me*, remember? And my mother tries to fix me up just about every week, so just give me a break, all right? It wasn't my idea."

I wasn't sure if that satisfied him or not, as he abruptly turned and went back to his place by the cash register, where a twenty-something guy stood waiting to pay for an over-sized chocolate-chip cookie and a latte. I turned to look at my date, who had given up scanning the place and was now intently reading the menu up on the wall behind Ben.

He looked presentable enough, standing there in pressed dress khakis and a button-down navy shirt. He was anywhere between fifty-five and fifty-nine, hard to tell, with no stomach bulge (yay!) and a fairly thick head of salt and pepper hair, as well as a beard. The emphasis was on the "salt," but oh well.

"Are you here to meet a Bella?" I gently tapped him on the shoulder.

He startled, like I'd zapped him with a ray gun. *Oh no, skittish.* Well, of course there had to be something wrong with him. My mother hadn't set me up with a winner yet.

"Are you she?" he asked. What a pompous twit.

"If you mean, am I Bella, then yes."

He extended his hand, and we shook. Limp fish. Now how hard is it, exactly, to learn to give a normal handshake? And what is the deal with the limp fish thing anyway? What's the point?

Okay, I told myself, don't give up yet. Sometimes my shit-detector is on too high for my own good. And it's a faulty detector at that. I had married Robert Blumer, and we all know how well that turned out. So I decided to give this guy a chance.

He released the wimpy hold on my hand and smiled. "Larry Bernstein."

I took a closer look at Larry. He wasn't much taller than me, so probably about five-foot eight or so, which should be okay, but the heart wants what it wants. Still, this was just coffee. Well, in my case a cappuccino, but I was going to have to wean myself off of measuring all men to Robert. Even if he had been a weasel, Robert had been drop-dead gorgeous, no pun intended. I like that in a man.

"Bella Blumer," I said.

"What's with the dog?" He nodded at Boodles, who was ignoring him.

"This is Boodles." I tried to get some enthusiasm in my voice. But truth to tell, it just made me sound squeaky.

"But why did you bring him here?"

I didn't want to sound defensive because if this dude

didn't care for Boodles, he could take a flying leap. So I took Boodles' cue and ignored the whole subject.

"They have great desserts here, if you're hungry." I could hear the edge of annoyance in my voice.

Sensitive guy that he was, Larry never noticed.

After we ordered our coffees—I had my usual cappuccino with a dusting of cinnamon, and Larry, exciting dude that he was, had a decaf, black, and no dessert—we sat, sinking into two upholstered chairs that sidled up to a round, art deco coffee table.

Larry leaned back, spreading both arms out over the back of his chair. "So you're a person of interest."

"Excuse me?" I sat straight up in my seat and wiped some cream from my upper lip. Did this guy mean that he was interested in me? Not necessarily a good thing. Or was there something I'd missed on the news? Even worse.

"You're all over the news." He tried to conceal an amused smile. "Boy, your ex-husband's new wife is quite the number." He hesitated. "No offense."

I wasn't sure if he meant that Barbara was a "hot" number or a piece of work. Anyway, I was a lot more concerned about the "person of interest" thing. I suddenly lost interest in my cappuccino, just as my cell phone rang out the tune of Michael Jackson's "I'm Bad," an homage to my ex.

I fished through my oversized, soft leather, lime bag for my cell phone. It was Heather, my daughter, calling from our house. She was living with me in my divorce bungalow until she could afford her own place. No problem. I actually liked the company.

"What is it?" I didn't take the time for hellos, I was so worried about Larry's bad news.

Heather whispered, "The police were here, Mom. They were looking for you and asking all kinds of questions."

I grabbed Boodles and walked to the women's room, without excusing myself, so frazzled that I left my lime bag and dog carrier with Mr. Wrong.

"What did they say?" My mouth went dry, and the thought of sipping my cappuccino made me nauseous. My gut was screaming danger, and I knew right then that I was 'the one' the police were after—even though I was totally innocent.

"They wanted to know where you were, and I said that you were on a date."

"A date! Why did you tell them that?"

"It's the truth, Mom." Heather sounded suddenly as defensive as she had when she was in high school, denying she'd ever smoked pot. "Anyway," she continued, "what's the big deal? You're a divorced woman. How could it make you look bad?"

"Maybe it makes me look cold. I don't know." I held my hand to my forehead. Here I was, minding my own business, living my own life, and first my skunk of a husband leaves me for a bimbo. Then he gets himself killed—and it implicates me!

"They want to talk to you."

"Well, it will have to wait till tomorrow." I was suddenly feeling stubborn. I was an innocent person in no mood to be pushed around by the police.

"Mom, have you been watching the news?"

I looked at Boodles, innocently resting in my arms, blissfully unaware of the crisis I was in. "No, I've been avoiding the news. It's entirely too stressful."

"Well, come home now before the ten o'clock news comes on. It's all about Dad. And you. And it doesn't look good."

"I know Barbara's been mouthing off." You could bet the bank on that.

"Mom, it's more than Barbara," I could hear the panic in her voice. "There's all kinds of people on the news: your hairdresser, your customers."

"What about them?" I asked in a harsh tone, but I kind of knew what she was getting at.

"They're all quoting you and all the rotten things you said about Dad and Barbara."

"It's a free country," I said, but I could hear my voice deflating. "Everything I said about them was true."

"But there's more, Mom." Her voice broke, like she was trying to avoid crying.

"What is it?'

"They say on the news that Dad was shot four times—

and the murder weapon was a Glock 19. Isn't that the same kind of gun Dad gave you?"

I gasped. About five years ago, Robert had gotten it into his head that we should both have protection, that we were targets, being in the jewelry business. So despite my protests, we bought his and hers Glocks and took shooting lessons and obtained concealed licenses. Robert had liked it and usually carried his gun with him. But not me. I locked it up in Robert's private wall safe, in our bedroom, and promptly forgot about it. Till now. If someone had used *my* gun to kill Robert, I was looking even more guilty than ever, big mouth or not.

"So are you coming home now, Mom?"

"Right away." I nervously glanced around the coffee shop. "We really need to talk."

"Bye, Mom," she said.

We both clicked off. I walked back to the table and slipped my phone into my open bag. "Got to go," I said to Larry, grabbing my purse and carrier off the chair. "Sorry, but I have to cut this short." I looked at him, and I swear the man was almost drooling. Apparently, he was turned on by dangerous women, which I most certainly am not!

I was hoping against hope that he wouldn't garner the nerve to ask for my number, when he said, "I'll give you a call. Your mother gave my mother your number."

Thanks, Mom. That was all I needed on top of everything else — a deranged, not-so-secret admirer. I smiled weakly.

"It looks like I'll be busy, but maybe in a few weeks."

He held his fist up to his ear, like a phone, with extended pinky and thumb. Then with an added wink, he smiled. "Don't worry. I'm as patient as the rock of Gibraltar."

Hoping Larry might take a hint (fat chance) I turned on my heels and said "Bye" while I was no longer even facing him.

Out in the warm summer night, I took a deep breath and inhaled a bit of Royal Oak fumes, the essence of one of the motorcycles roaring past. It was Monday, motorcycle night. There were Hondas parked in front of Ben's and Suzuki's parked across the street. Leather-clad aging Boomers hung around the mild night air, looking like wannabe tough guys.

It was only about five or six blocks to my bungalow, so I hitched my lime bag and empty carrier onto my shoulder and started hoofing it, letting Boodles carry his own weight — and have a night walk at the same time. My feet hurt, and I started wondering if it was time to graduate to lower heels. My three-inchers were killing me.

Damn the shoes. Damn the blisters. I fast-walked home and burst through the front door.

"Heather?" I called out. I dropped my bags to the floor and fell onto my over-stuffed couch, kicking off my shoes and rubbing my tired feet. Boodles got into the act and started licking my toes. I sighed just as Heather walked into the room and slouched on the red leather high-back. "Hi, Honey. Are you okay?"

"I'm fine, Mom, but I'm really worried about you. I think the police have it in for you."

I swallowed hard. "They have to question everyone, Heath."

"I know. I know. But they mostly asked me about you — how you feel about Dad, what you say about him, stuff like that."

"They're probably listening to Barbara."

"That witch!" Heather never had warmed up to a step-mom who was just seven years her senior.

"She probably thinks I really did it. Me and my big mouth." I was really starting to regret all the nasty things I'd said about that bimbo. Even if they were true.

"Maybe *she* did it," said Heather, "and she's just trying to pin it on you!"

This stunned me into silence for a moment or two. That made two people in a row who figured it was Barbara. "But what would she have to gain by it? I don't get it."

"She thinks she's such a hot number." Heather was more into pink hair and nose rings than Barbara, who was more into the beauty queen look. "She might have been tired of Dad but wanted all the money. They signed a pre-nup, you know."

"A pre-nup?" That caught me by surprise. I didn't know Robert had been so careful about marrying his new model. Or that Heather was so good about keeping secrets.

"I'm sorry I never told you about it" Heather was a

master at reading my mind. "TMI. I figured you were already hurting enough, without getting more details."

"So what does she get if he dies?" Sue me, I was wildly curious.

"As far as I know, if he dies, she gets everything, but not so much if she left him, maybe a year's salary or something."

"That stupid ass!" I meant, of course, my Robert, who'd set himself up for murder.

"We have to prove she did it." Heather sounded so determined, but I was exhausted.

I put both hands on my cheeks. "I'm not proving anything. I'll just call the police."

"I don't think they'd buy it. With you, they have motive and opportunity."

"Barbara has motive and opportunity too." I lifted my head and looked Heather in the eye. "She lives with him. She could have used that gun easier than me! I haven't seen that thing in probably five years."

Heather paused to pet Boodles' silky curls as he'd jumped into her lap. "They don't have the gun yet."

"Well, that makes sense. Whoever shot Dad took it with them."

"They're searching the city, looking to see if it was thrown in some dumpster."

"So what did they want from you?"

"They laid it on thick, telling me all the bad stuff you've said about Dad." Heather nervously twisted her strawberry hair. "Maybe they were hoping that I'd spill my guts. You know, be mad at you for killing Dad." Her eyes were kind of puffy, and her makeup was smeared. It was obvious she'd been crying.

"Were you at Gramma's tonight?"

"Yeah, everyone was there but you and Uncle Ben. Even Aunt Stella showed up to show Gramma support."

"I guess Ben doesn't like Barbara any more than I do."

"Well, duh," said Heather.

It was a lot to take in. Robert's death. Not going to see Myrna, who I actually liked, at a time like this. The police coming to my home with questions. I sat back on the couch, head in hands, thinking I could get into the fetal position if it wouldn't totally freak out Heather.

"I need a lawyer."

"You sure do, Mom. But who?"

I dug into my mental memory bank. "Ron White was a good divorce lawyer." I'd made out good enough in my split with Robert.

"But you need a criminal lawyer, Mom. What about Quinton Tiger?"

Quinton Tiger is something of a homegrown national celebrity. He made his name defending the Hemlock Association and went on to make millions.

"No, I don't think I could stomach that." The thought of extended contact with that pompous ass made my left eye twitch. "Besides, I think he's more into things like suing the city."

I looked at the clock. It was ten-thirty. Apparently, we'd missed the news, which was just as well.

"Oh, Mom, one more thing."

"What now?"

"Dad's funeral." Heather's voice cracked just a bit. "Vic told me he heard from the police that they'll be done with Dad tomorrow. So it's probably Wednesday morning at Hoffman Schwartz."

"So soon?" Jewish funerals were always done as quickly as possible, sometimes in twenty-four hours. But I'd assumed there would be a delay because of the murder investigation. And the autopsy. I shivered at the thought of Robert on a metal table. "What about the coroner?"

"I guess Gramma asked to get it all done ASAP, and they promised her that they'd be done with the autopsy tomorrow."

It was all happening so fast. Killed on Monday, buried on Wednesday. Sounded like the old nursery rhyme.

"I'd better call Shelley and see what we'll do about the shop." I was hoping Shelley could hold it open for me.

"I already called her. She wants to close up Bella's so she can go too."

I shivered and groaned at the thought of Robert's funeral. Of course I had to go, but it was the last place on earth I wanted to be. I had no desire to be eyeball-to-eyeball with Barbara, when I was already knee-deep in doo-doo. At least I had a day to get emotionally ready.

I let Boodles out the back door for a quick whiz. "Good night, Honey." I kissed Heather on top of her strawberry-red head, knowing full well there wasn't a chance I'd sleep at all that night.

CHAPTER 5

When the alarm went off at eight on Tuesday morning, for a brief, delicious moment, I thought that I'd just been having a bad dream, that Robert was still alive, that my long-forgotten gun wasn't floating around somewhere in Royal Oak, waiting to incriminate me, that I could wake up, go back to kvetching about Robert and his bimbette, and all was well with the world. But as I trudged over to the bathroom in my pink boa slippers, I knew it was real. I knew I had to deal with it.

I made my way down the steps, holding onto the walls of the staircase, as if I had a massive hangover, which I most certainly did not. I was miserable all over again, and it was Robert's fault. Just as I was starting to get over the betrayal and the divorce, off he goes and gets himself killed in a way that points the finger of blame at me.

Heather, God bless her, must have made some coffee, as it smelled delightfully like fresh brew, and I knew if Heather made it, it was going to be strong.

I walked into the dining room that doubled for eating area in my bungalow, and there she sat, wrapped around her coffee mug, staring into the brown depths like she was commiserating with a wishing well.

I let Boodles out the back door and poured myself a cup. I sat across from Heather, who hadn't moved. "Are you okay?"

"No." A tear dropped into her coffee, which was going to be salty as well as cold by the time she got around to drinking it.

"Heather, I didn't kill Dad."

"I know, but he's still dead." Her eyes were red-rimmed and barely open.

"Did you sleep at all last night, Honey?"

"No."

"It's going to take a while to get used to all of this, of Dad being gone." I was having a hard time with my words. It's never good to lose a family member, I'm sure. But I hadn't been very charitable about the divorce, so I didn't quite know what to say about Robert's death. "He was a better father than he was a husband, I guess."

Heather sucked in a deep breath that turned into a sob. "I'm not so sure about that," she said. "But I miss him anyway."

I put my arm around her. "I loved him for a long, long time. We're in this together, you know."

"I know. And I thought it couldn't get worse, but it did."

"What are you talking about?" I didn't like to be clueless, but at the moment, I really was.

"Jason broke up with me last night, after the eleven o'clock news."

"What?" I thought of Jason, he of the nose rings and that ridiculous round thing that some people put in their earlobes to stretch them out until there's a hole in the center like a doughnut. They made me wonder what kind of surgery would be required later to get those ears back to normal. "Jason dropped you because of the news?"

"His dad wants to run for mayor next year, and he doesn't want to be associated with bad publicity."

"And Jason went along with it?" That was hard to believe. "He looks like such a rebel. Why would he care what his father thinks?"

"More like a hypocrite." Heather's voice grew a little stronger, sounding more angry than hurt. "He didn't want to give up his father's credit card."

"I thought he worked at Hair Apparent." That's where Heather went for her spiky haircuts. The odd colors she did at home. They were all washable — making it easy for her to change colors to match her moods.

"Now I'll have to find a new place for my hair." Another

tear fell into her mug of cold coffee.

I wanted to say he wasn't worth it, that he had no backbone, that he was obviously not financially independent, that she was probably better off without him, but I kept my mouth shut. If she got back together with him, she'd forever remember what I'd said, and we'd never be close again.

"There's probably ten other hairdressers in Royal Oak. You'll find someone."

Heather sat there silently, so I decided to change the subject.

"Are you going to work today, or did you call in about, you know, Dad?" I asked. Heather worked at Billy Bob's on Fourth Street, Royal Oak's only Country Western Bar and Grill. I had thought it odd when Heather got the job last fall, but apparently, they didn't mind the rainbow hair and nose ring so long as she wore her cowboy boots and bandana when she went to work.

"No, I'd really rather work to get my mind off everything. I'll go to Gramma Myrna's tonight." She moved her runny eyes in my direction. "I hope you don't mind me leaving."

"I'm fine," I said, "except for the part that the police seem to think I'm a suspect. So when are you going in to work?"

"Not till eleven to get ready for the lunch crowd." She poured her coffee into the sink and refilled her mug.

Heather had graduated from the Art program at Michigan State. But so far, there was no one willing to hire a talented acrylic painter. Since the downturn in the economy, all ad agencies were scaling back. While she still used the covered back porch as a studio, and sold paintings here and there at one of the local art galleries, she had to wait tables to make a living. Tough stuff.

I was thinking of asking her, again, if she wanted to go back to school to find a new way to make a career. But there was no point asking her now. I was barely making enough money at Bella's to keep myself afloat without putting a kid through college again. And, of course, we couldn't ask her father to help out any longer.

Heather flipped on the TV. I made myself some toast and made my way to the living room, after letting Boodles back in the house. It was time for the 9:00 AM report.

Diana Adams, an attractive, black anchor woman, sat at attention. "Good morning, Detroit. Our top story today is the Robert Blumer murder." The footage on the screen was the front of Blumer Fine Jewelers. "Royal Oak police are scouring the neighborhood to find the murder weapon, a Glock 19."

My heart sank.

"Police report that they have a person of interest but no official suspects, as yet."

The screen cut away to the front of my store, the Bella's Baubles sign, encrusted with multi-color gem-like glass crystals. "While police haven't yet named the person of interest, it is well known in Royal Oak that Robert Blumer and his former wife, Bella Blumer, had a contentious divorce that was final exactly one year to the day before his murder."

A picture of me, arm-in-arm with Robert, taken in "happier days," according to the newsreader, flickered on the screen. My shoulder-length wavy brown hair had looked great with that white silk suit. That was back when I could afford my designer favorites, some of them even full price. I couldn't help but think that we'd made such a handsome couple.

The screen cut away to Mila Kerin, my hairdresser at Mila's Majic Salon. "She did complain about him all the time," said Mila, a microphone held to her mouth by the off-screen reporter. "She took the divorce real hard." I couldn't help but notice that Mila was speaking of me in the past tense.

There was another cutaway to Barbara, her hair all big and perfect, but her brown eyes flashing anger. "That woman never gave us a moment's peace. She called me and Robert names. I wouldn't put *anything* past her!"

The screen flickered back to the anchorwoman. "Police are most likely investigating the link between this sad anniversary and Robert Blumer's demise. Mr. Blumer was an active member of the Royal Oak business community and the past president of the Royal Oak Chamber of Commerce.

"In other news . . ."

Heather flipped off the TV.

"They've all but shipped me off to prison." I shivered beneath my silk robe.

Heather shrugged. "We'll have to figure out what we can do about it, I guess."

I guess!

"So how was your date? I didn't even ask about last night." It was Heather's turn to change the subject.

I stood and headed toward my bedroom staircase. "It was another loser from Gramma Harriet."

"She doesn't give up, does she?"

I took that for a rhetorical question and went up the stairs with Boodles at my heels. The phone rang while I brushed my teeth. I checked out my nightstand phone's caller ID, white foam dripping onto my silk robe. I grabbed the cordless and headed back to the sink. I was spitting while saying, "Hi, Mom."

"You didn't call me," said my ever-sensitive bulldozer of a mother.

"I've been kind of busy." What an understatement!

"So how did your date go last night, dear?"

Talk about a one-track mind. This woman was going to marry me off again if it was the last thing she did.

"He was a dud." I rinsed my mouth and toothbrush and wiped it dry on my towel.

"Stop eating on the phone," said my mother, "and you are way too picky. He's young, he's Jewish, and he's single."

I sighed. "Mom, he's in his fifties, like me, which doesn't

qualify as young. He's probably single for a very good reason."

"His wife was a tyrant."

"Mom, you're getting his mother's point of view, and I suspect she's biased. The guy was creepy."

"Creepy! What do you mean 'creepy'?" This wasn't asked in a way that made me think my mother was curious. It was more of an indictment of my judgment in men, and anything else.

"He seemed to be turned on by the media attention. I think he actually likes the idea that I could be a murderer. I think he believes I killed Robert and that turns him on."

A silence hung between us on the phone line while I waited for my mother to respond. "Well, I don't like that." And just when I thought it was safe to go to sleep, she added, "We'll just have to find someone else."

"No, Mom, not now. I'm kind of taken up with the—"

"I'll call you later." As if she suddenly couldn't hear a word I said, she hung up.

CHAPTER 6

About a half hour later, I headed out my side door, dressed as inconspicuously as possible in my oh-so-conservative, Jones New York suit. Mixed with my lapis and gold beads, I felt business-like, even if it was squashing my usual style. I'm more into primary colors and pizzazz. I peered around the front of the house. All was clear. No cameras. No reporters.

Then I noticed a TV-7 van parked a few houses over, and I was sure that I was being filmed. It was a relatively short walk down Fourth Street from my bungalow to my shop. I could see two men with cameras slung over their shoulders like oversized, unfashionable purses, as well a young female reporter dressed in the evening gowns they wear these days instead of the business suits of the seventies and eighties.

I slipped on my sunglasses and quickly put Boodles in his carrier to speed the process of getting to my store. I realized that I should have worn walking shoes — the pavement is tough on heels when you're in a hurry. I had to watch my steps as I walked over the railroad crossing that angled across Fourth Street. By the time I reached Center Street, a full city block from my store, the paparazzi descended.

"Why did you kill your ex?" asked the evening gowned reporter.

I picked up my pace.

"Did you do it in a moment of heated passion?" This from a thirty-something Ken Doll kind of guy, dressed in a grey suit with a black T-shirt.

Of course, I said nothing as I started to run, key in hand. The whole crew followed me into the alley behind my shop. As I fumbled with my door lock, I swear there were about five microphones in my face, and the requests for confessions were loud and blurred. My normally placid Boodles started growling and snapping as I finally turned the key and ducked inside.

Ten o'clock. Opening time, and a sea of cameras, microphones, and satellite vans crowded the front of my store. It looked as if an assortment of good-looking people, who had apparently abandoned acting aspirations and settled for TV reporting instead, were camped on my section of Fourth Street.

Frazzled, I stumbled to my bench and put Boodles into his tiny sky-blue bed atop my jeweler's bench. As he settled in for a much-needed nap, I noticed that the cameras were still rolling and pointed at me! I considered banging on the windows and demanding that they all leave, but it occurred to me that would just give them great footage for the News at Noon. Instead I rifled through my lime bag and came up with Bill Krieger's business card. He picked up on the first ring.

"Detective Krieger."

"Hi. This is Bella Blumer. Is it legal for the news people to harass me in my own store? They're filming me as we speak. Isn't it an invasion of privacy?"

He chuckled. "Sorry, no. If they were filming into your house, I'd send over a squad car. But there is no expectation of privacy in a retail establishment."

"How am I supposed to do business?" I was angry. "They're going to scare away my customers!"

"Calm down, Mrs. Blumer. They're not going to be there forever. Just act natural and go about your work, and they'll go away."

"That makes sense." But still, I felt violated.

"While I have you on the phone, I just want you to know that we are going to need you to come in for questioning."

I blew out a hard breath that billowed my lips. "Is it urgent? I have to work today."

"It isn't urgent yet," he said, and I thought that 'yet' was more than a little cryptic. "But keep yourself handy."

I figured that they were waiting to find my gun—and maybe the missing diamonds—before they could get serious about their 'person of interest.' This was a good thing. Once they found the gun and the diamonds, it would point them to their real suspect.

"Call me Handy Andy," I said. Nervous. Stupid. Joking with a homicide detective when I was their major suspect was probably not smart. But too late, I already said it. "Thanks for the advice," I added.

"Goodbye," he said, and we both clicked off our cells.

I tried my best not to look at the window, to better ignore the gathering storm of bad publicity, when my phone rang once again. It was Shelley.

"Hi Shel." I put the phone on speaker so it wouldn't start frying my ear.

"So how are you holding up? Want me to come in early?" She wasn't supposed to come in until about noon, so it was nice of her to ask.

"There's not much point." I snuck a glance at the paparazzi and their cameras pointed in my direction. "The news people are out here in force, and they're scaring the customers away."

"I'm coming right over!" She sounded angry. There is no lack of backbone in my family, I can tell you that.

"It's not usually that busy in the morning." I didn't want

to put her out. "It's possible that no one would have come in yet anyway."

"I'm coming anyway." I expected she'd come with a torch. "Nothing I'm doing is more important than scaring off those vultures."

"Okay, but Detective Krieger told me that what they're doing is perfectly legal. Besides, it would only give them more juicy stuff for the noon report."

"Oh." She deflated. "Um, so how was your date last night?"

I filled her in on Larry the letch. I told her I imagined he was practically drooling at the prospect of bedding what he figured was a dangerous woman.

"Yuck! What was Mom thinking?"

"She doesn't think. She won't be happy till I have a penis back in my life."

Shelley laughed. "Bella, you are so crude, but somehow it works for you."

I chuckled for the first time since Vic and I'd found Robert, and it felt good. "Maybe it's a good idea for you to come here early after all, Shelley. I could really use the support, even if you aren't coming to scare off the vultures."

"Can you hang on till eleven?"

I looked at the clock. It was ten-fifteen. "No problem," I said, "See you soon." And we both clicked off our cells.

I did my best to keep my eyes off the front of my store. The throng of cameras and reporters could only make me feel nervous or angry. Or both. So my only choice was to do what I do best—make jewelry. I walked over to my safe, which was thankfully perpendicular to the window, so I didn't have to worry about being filmed while putting in the combination to the lock. I turned three times to the right for fifty-three, the age I was when I'd bought the safe; two times to the left for twenty-seven, the age Vic was a year ago, at the time of the end of my marriage and the beginning of Bella's Baubles, and one time right again to twenty-five, for Heather.

The lock clicked into place, and I turned the handle down and opened my tiny safe. Inside were nestled trays upon trays of loose, drilled beads, colorful natural gemstones, fourteen-karat yellow gold and sterling silver wire, fasteners, spring rings, catches, and of course, trays of jewelry already made and ready to return to the showcases after a night's stay in the safe. You can't get jewelry store insurance if you don't put it all away in your safe every night.

First, I pulled some of my pendants and bracelets and carefully placed each piece on a velvet display in my showcases. Then came the earrings and a few odd cufflinks and tiepins. If men liked jewelry as much as women do, I could have twice the business. I spritzed and wiped the countertops clean and returned to my safe for inspiration. A quick sidelong glance at the window showed a thinning crowd of paparazzi, so I continued following Krieger's advice. Apparently, my newsworthiness decreased dramatically when the paparazzi saw what I actually do each day.

I returned to my safe to start planning some new necklaces for the Sunday Art Fair and for stock in general. I was particularly taken with some multi-faceted blue topaz beads. The light from my bench lamp shimmered over the stones. I pulled some smooth, mirror-finish, silver spacer beads for contrast and set to work designing a Bella's Baubles original. There is nothing like creative contemplation to get your mind off your problems.

By the time I'd designed a teardrop lapis and blue topaz pendant to hang from the topaz beads, and added some oval lapis beads for contrast, the news orgy crowd had thinned out to just Evening-Gown-Girl. She was apparently persistent and angling to make a career move on my misery. It was nearly 11:00 AM and time for Shelley to show up.

A shadow crossed my front door, and I looked up. But it wasn't Shelley; it was my mother. I fairly ran to the door to get her away from that reporter. I opened the door in time to hear Mom say, "My daughter didn't kill anyone, young lady. So don't you dare ask me how I 'feel' about it. Now pack up your notebook and your camera man, and get out of here."

Yay, Mom!

With that, she turned her head of immovable blond hair and nearly bumped into me, trying to get into my store and away from that reporter.

"Thanks, Mom." I gave her a hug.

Mom was never openly emotional. She patted my back and pulled away. "What a ridiculous girl," she said, and that was that.

"What brings you here?" It was unusual for my mother to visit Bella's Baubles two days in a row, or even two days in a week for that matter. "Are you worried about the case the police are trying to build against me?"

She patted her lacquered hair. "I was in town to pick up some flowers and I thought I'd come here to invite you to dinner tonight. Do you have any plans?"

Gee, my 'plans' were to work until six, and then make it through the evening, and hope that if the police found my gun that it was covered with someone else's fingerprints. Or that they'd find the diamonds. Whoever took those diamonds was surely the murderer. "Just busy with work and some personal things." This would be obvious to anyone but my mother.

"Well, Albert and I are having dinner at The Club tonight, and we'd like you to be our guest."

"Thanks, Mom, but like I said, this just isn't a very good time for me."

She frowned. "I don't think you understand. I want to make it up to you for fixing you up with that Bernstein fellow. I didn't dream he would be such a cad."

"That's okay, Mom." I knew where this was going. It

wouldn't be just Mom and Albert at The Club. She was trying to fix me up again, two times in two days! That would be stressful enough, even if I weren't dealing with Robert's death and all the fallout.

"I've already made the reservations. You know you're not doing anything anyway."

"I'd really rather not." This was actually an understatement. The truth was that I'd rather have a root canal without an anesthetic, but fighting the issue with my mother was unbelievably one notch worse.

"Nonsense! Stop being a stick in the mud. Meet us at The Club at eight." She headed for the door. As it jingled open, she added. "And be sure to wear something nice. This one is a doctor. He went to U of M."

"Goodbye, Mom." I was already resigned to my fate.

"See you tonight, dear," she said, and off she went, she and her helmet of hair, both as unmovable as the Rock of Gibraltar. I noticed that Evening-Gown-Girl was gone. I couldn't blame her for being cowed by my mother. I had fifty-four years of experience with her, and I still couldn't hold my own.

I sat at my bench and spoke to Boodles, who'd jumped on my lap. "There's no saying no to Gramma Harriet. So what's another free dinner?"

Boodles answered by licking my forearm.

"I agree; it feels like I'm kissing up. But what choice do I have...?"

The door jingled open while I was in mid-sentence.

"What choice do you have about what?" It was Shelley, ready for the day and dressed for work in her very best dark blue jeans with a new black polo shirt, probably both from Target. Or Wal-Mart. When God handed out fashion sense, he'd only given it to Mom and me. Our dad had been as rumpled and fashion backward as Shelley. But you had to love them anyway. Fashion isn't everything.

"Oh, it's about Mom. I'm going to dinner tonight with her and Albert."

"And who else?" Her hands were on her hips. It drove her to distraction when I was a wimp.

"It's just dinner," I said weakly. "And she didn't say."

"After what she put you through with this Bernstein twerp?" Shelley narrowed her eyes.

"This is Mom's way of making it up to me."

"More like it's Mom's way of getting her way." Shelley snorted as she put some jewelry from the safe into the front window display.

"I have more important things to worry about than Mom and her manipulations." I heaved a big sigh that I swear came right down from my toes. "I'm a murder suspect. Unless I can come up with some money for a private investigator, I think I need to do some investigating myself."

Shelley pulled her chair up to my bench, clearly intrigued. "Like what? Where would we start?"

I grabbed her arm. "Does this mean you'll help?"

She gave me a big hug. "Of course I'll help you! What do you think, I'll sit around while the police put you away for something you didn't do?"

I bit my lower lip, tasting my freshly applied lipstick. "How about we do a search on Barbara? Find out all we can on Google."

"I'm a whiz at Google." Shelley pivoted back to her desk and fired up her laptop. "You have to pay for some of the background searches, but it would be money well spent."

While I sketched a few possible designs and played with a few loose, fluted jasper stones, Shelley worked feverishly on her search.

Finally she looked up. "Well, it looks like our young Mrs. Blumer was married before." She paused. "And to an older man."

I put down my tools, jumped up from my bench, and wiped my hands on my jewelers' apron. "Who was her husband? You have a picture?"

Shelley gestured at her laptop screen, and there, posing for the camera, as annoyingly beautiful as always, was Barbara Dennison, hanging on to an attractive, but much older man.

"Is that her bridegroom or her father?" I stuck my nose up close to the screen to get a better look.

"Wait a second, let me enlarge it." Shelley played with a couple of the computer keys, and I had a close-up of Barbie and her first—well at least I thought it was her first, as far as I knew — hubby.

"Let me look up the divorce record in the State files. It's public record, you know." Shelley feverishly clicked on the keys, and I waited by her side to see what would turn up.

After a considerable wait — don't things always seem to go in slow-motion when you're in a hurry? — she opened the divorce record of Barbara Wilkins and Richard Dennison, age twenty-eight and forty-two, respectively. It seemed that our young Mrs. Blumer was an experienced heart breaker.

"We should call him up and see what he thinks the ex Mrs. Dennison," said Shelley.

"Can you find out where he works? Maybe one of us could stop by for a visit."

Shelley smiled. "We could give him a call. Maybe give some advice to the lovelorn."

"I like the way you think. Can you find his phone number?"

Shelley did her search magic on the keyboard. "There's a Richard Dennison, forty-five, who is a podiatrist in Roseville."

"That sounds about right." I mentally calculated his age if he'd been divorced from Ms. Barbara the Beautiful for all of three years.

"You think we could get him on the phone?" I nervously twisted the edge of my denim jewelers' apron.

"There's no guarantee we'd get to see the doctor unless we made an appointment. Why don't we give it a try?"

Shelley picked up her cell and punched in his number. She put the phone on speaker.

"Dr. Dennison's office," said one of the most annoyingly perky voices I've had the misfortune to hear.

"Could I speak to Dr. Dennison?" Shelley's voice was no-nonsense and all business compared to the perky one.

"Can I ask what it's in regard to?"

"It's a personal matter, and urgent."

I crossed my fingers hoping that Shelley's gambit would pay off.

"I'm sorry, but he's with a patient right now. Can I take your name and number?" She pronounced 'number' with enough energy to power the city.

Shelley reluctantly gave her cell phone number and just her first name. "Tell him that it's very important."

Apparently the doctor wasn't suspicious by nature because within the hour he returned Shelley's call. Unfortunately, she was at the counter and I had to take the call.

"Is this Shelley?"

What could I do? I had to lie. "Yes, this is."

"So what's the urgent matter? Who are you?"

Geez, I don't know what idea Shelley had up her sleeve, but this wasn't working out for me. I didn't know whether she planned to play it straight or not. Without a plan, I had no choice but to go with the truth. Well, the truth as if I really were Shelley.

"I have to be honest with you, Dr. Dennison. My sister is in trouble. Your ex-wife, Barbara, married her ex-husband, and now I'm sure you've seen in the news that he's been murdered." I spoke in low tones, so as not to be overheard by my customer.

"Oh, my God, has Barbara been charged with murder?"

I quickly made my way into our tiny bathroom, turned on the faucet, and shut the door. I felt like I was living in a spy novel.

"No, I'm sorry if I didn't make myself clear. The police think that my sister killed her ex-husband, but I know she didn't do it."

I could hear him heave a huge sigh of relief. Apparently, he still had feelings for Barbara.

"So what can I do for you?" The pleasantness of his voice went down a notch.

"I really don't want to be nosy, but I'm wondering if you could tell me the nature of your divorce? You see, Barbara remarried, not so long after your divorce, once again to an older, more established man." I was proud that I figured out a way to say 'a man with money' without sounding crass.

"That's a personal matter. What do you want to know?"

"Did she get a big settlement in the divorce? Do you feel that she was out for money?" There. I had to say it and I did.

He paused. "She did okay. Lucky for me, my practice took off after the divorce, so I got off easy that way."

"Did you feel that she took advantage of you?" I knew I

was getting into pretty touchy territory, but what the heck? He was going to be mad at Shelley, not me. I smiled. If this wasn't so important, it might even be fun.

He took a deep breath. "So you're asking if my ex-wife married me for the money?" There was more than an edge to his voice; he was angry.

"I'm just looking out for my sister." I kept my voice even, as if I hadn't noticed his anger.

"Are you trying to implicate Barbara in murder?" His voice revved up a notch. I was glad I wasn't the next person in line to have my toenails trimmed. It sounded like he might rip them out.

"Do you think she's capable of murder?" How I managed to keep my voice so sweet, I don't know. Maybe I should have been an actress.

"You have a lot of nerve calling me. First, you ask if my ex married me for money, and now you're saying that she killed someone. I have to get back to work. Don't ever call me again!" With that, he hung up, and I was left with an annoying dial tone.

Just on cue, Shelley knocked on the bathroom door. "What's going on in there? Who are you talking to? On my phone?"

I handed her cell over. "That was Dr. Dennison."

"So what's the scoop? Did he spill on Barbara?" Shelley put her phone atop her desk and dropped into her chair. I returned to my workbench.

"He was pretty defensive of Barbara, doesn't feel that she married him for the money, and doesn't think she's capable of murder."

"Oh, my God." Shelley's eyes opened so wide she looked like she'd just sat on a pin. "I can't believe you asked him that!"

I smiled and pointed to her phone. "Better yet, *you* asked him." And despite all the pressure, or maybe because of it, we both burst into laughter just as the bell jingled and our shop door opened.

"What's so funny?" said a matronly-looking Royal Oak woman clutching a bag of cupcakes from the Double-D Cup Bakery.

"It's hard to repeat." Shelley walked up to the counter. "How can I help you today?"

By the looks of this obviously faux redhead, she was likely to eat the Double-D dozen all by herself before she made it to lunchtime. Ms. Redhead looked me over from head to toe. Either she was a not-well-closeted gay woman, or more likely, she'd been watching the news and was trying to size me up for herself.

While Shelley waited on the not-so-subtle redhead, the door jingled again, and we were both fairly busy till about one-thirty, when we slumped in our seats. Boodles jumped into my lap, and I scratched behind his tiny ears.

"So our talk with Dr. Dennison didn't prove anything." Shelley rested her elbow on her desk, and her chin in her hand.

I smiled. "If getting married multiple times was a felony, we'd have to visit Mom in jail."

"Well, at least we tried. So what do you say to Middle-Eastern today?" That's Shelley's favorite food. Probably mine, too. Metro Detroit is the home to the largest Arab population in the country. This means we have the most wonderful selection of Middle Eastern restaurants outside of the Middle East. This is a good thing if you like amazingly delicious homemade food.

"I could go for a hummus and lamb shawarma." My stomach grumbled reminding me that it was time to eat. There is nothing like work to get your mind off your troubles — and your appetite.

Shelley faxed in an order to the Beirut Bistro, one of three Middle-Eastern restaurants on Main, not far from our store. Almost as soon as she walked out to pick up the order, Vic walked in. His eyes were red, probably from crying, and he looked uncharacteristically disheveled, like he'd just rolled out of bed.

CHAPTER 7

I walked over to the door, arms outstretched. Unlike my mother, I'm a hugger. It's good for the soul.

Vic returned my hug. He bent his six-foot frame over and rested his head on my shoulder, as he had as a child. I could feel his tears bleed through my blouse, and his chest was heaving. He had been very close to Robert. It was obviously very hard for him.

"Let's sit down," I said, as he stood straight from our hug. "You want a Coke?"

He nodded, and I went to the tiny refrigerator just outside the bathroom door and turned and handed it to him.

Vic opened the can and took a slug of dark bubbles. "It's

just not the same there without Dad." Tears welled up at the corners of his eyes. "It's so weird there. Quiet." He wiped his mouth with his sleeve. Once again, out of character for my buttoned-up Robert Blumer clone. My heart ached for him.

"Has the press been bothering you?" I asked, thinking of Evening-Gown-Girl and her entourage.

"The press *and* the police. Questions, questions, and more questions."

"Oh," I said, wondering why the police hadn't contacted me yet. Krieger had said to keep myself handy. I guess they were saving me for the kill.

"They've questioned me, Gramma Myrna, and Janine." He took another sip and gave a quiet burp. "They spent a long time with Barbara."

"What did she say?"

"Oh, they didn't question us out in the open. They took us one at a time into the diamond room." The diamond room is a private office at Blumer's with glass walls. That's where serious diamond customers get a private viewing when they're contemplating a big purchase. You can't hear what they're saying, but they're quite visible.

"So what did it look like when they were questioning Barbara?" This wasn't idle curiosity. That bimbo had it out for me, and I figured the more I knew the better.

"Oh, she looked pretty agitated, waved her arms around. Sometimes I could even hear her voice, so I know she was shouting." Vic held the cold can up to his forehead.

"You have a headache? Want an aspirin?"

He nodded.

While I pulled out my pillbox from my lime bag, I had to ask, "Did you hear what she was saying?"

"No, Mom." He popped two aspirins in his mouth and washed them down with the last of the Coke. "It was mostly muffled. But I think I did hear your name now and then."

I groaned.

"Sorry, Mom. I know she has it out for you."

I didn't know if he was apologizing for the fact that he was always cordial to Barbara or if he was apologizing on behalf of Barbara, but I really couldn't blame him even if it *was* annoying. She was his father's second wife, and he worked with her.

"It's okay, Vic." I gave him another hug.

"I've pulled all of Dad's Motown things out of his office, and I'm putting it up on the main sales floor. It's kind of like a memorial to him." His voice cracked.

I could feel my eyes tearing up despite myself. I knew exactly what he was talking about, and that was a perfect tribute to Robert, who had been enamored of everything Motown. I think he owned every record pumped out by Berry Gordy in the '60s and '70s. He had framed, signed black and whites of Diana Ross, Marvin Gaye, Smokey Robinson, and the big cheese himself, Berry Gordy. But the biggest prize of all was the photo of Robert shaking hands with Stevie Wonder. Robert had been quite the groupie in his younger years.

"I think that's a wonderful idea. Dad would really like it."

Vic shook his head and looked down at the floor. "I've been talking to the police; to that Detective Krieger."

"And?"

"Well, you know about the funeral, right?"

I tensed at the thought. "Yeah, Heather told me, but she didn't say the exact time."

Vic cleared his throat and crooked a finger to wipe the side of his eye. "Hoffman is going to call later today, but I'm pretty sure it's going to be at ten tomorrow. Heather, Barbara, Gramma, and I are going there today to make all the arrangements."

I could tell he was still numb with grief, and I was really sorry I couldn't help him. I obviously couldn't go with him to Hoffman's to plan the funeral. That was Barbara's job.

"What about Marcy? Will she go with you?" Vic's wife is a doll. I got lucky in the daughter-in-law business.

"She'll be there."

"Then you'll be okay." I gave him yet another squeeze. "You married a good girl."

"Thanks, Mom." He stood up and handed me his empty Coke can. "I'd better get back to work. It's getting kind of testy there. Barbara and Janine don't get along anymore."

I thought of flamboyant, beauty queen Barbara and

the somewhat zaftig Janine. Zaftig is the Yiddish word for fluffy, or plump. I wondered what they would be fighting about. "They're both under a lot of stress," I said. "I'm sure it will pass."

"Hope so." Vic gave me a peck on the cheek and headed out the door, almost bumping into Shelley, who was on the way back from her run to the Beirut Bistro. They exchanged quick hugs, and the door jingled itself shut as Shelley put our lunch order up on the counter.

"Vic doesn't look so good." She handed me my lamb and hummus on pita and went to the bathroom to scrub up before lunch. If she hadn't been such an underachiever, she could have been a nurse. Or a health inspector. Put that obsessive-compulsive nature to work. That way her hands would be dry and raw for good reason.

"He isn't doing so well," I said. "The funeral's tomorrow."

THE REST of the afternoon was uneventful. Shelley was interrupted from her lunch a few times, to wait on customers at the counter. After another lull, I asked Shelley if she minded if I took a break.

I took Boodles with me so he could empty his tiny bladder on some of the trees that line Fourth Street. When we reached the corner of Fourth and Center, I stopped to window shop at Noir Negligee. It was a shop originally opened to cater to the large gay clientele that lived in and frequented downtown Royal Oak. But it turned out that heterosexuals liked all the kinky garb and paraphernalia as much as gay people. So, my open-minded business neighbor, Chaz Cunningham, magnanimously sold to anyone with a buck.

I eyed the fishnet stockings and ten-inch heels; I kid you not. I looked at the thigh-high boots and the provocative whip. This was definitely not a place for normal people of any sexual persuasion.

"Shopping for something?"

I was startled by a male voice coming from behind me. I turned to look. It was none other than Larry Bernstein, he of the dangerous-woman fetish. Considering his leanings, this was not where I wished to be standing with him.

"Just taking a break," I said, in as curt a voice as possible. "Don't you have to work?" It occurred to me that I had no idea what he did for a living, or if he worked at all.

"I have time off right now." His eyes rested not on my face, but a good twelve inches lower.

I would have asked him what that meant, but I didn't want to give him the impression that I had any interest in his work, or in him. Instead, I told him that I had to get back to work myself.

"But you just walked out your door," he said, his voice smarmy and suggestive.

"What, are you stalking me or something?" This guy was really creeping me out.

"Stalking is a pretty harsh word, don't you think?"

Larry was the kind of guy that my Bubbie Sophie would have said, 'if you spit in his face, he'd say it was raining.' So why waste the spit? Just for the record, "Bubbie" is a common Yiddish name for grandmother.

"I've got to go. Please don't walk with me. I need to be alone." With that, I scooped up Boodles and walked as fast as I could in my heels while maintaining my dignity. I barreled through my door at Bella's.

"What's the matter with you?" Shelley looked up from her laptop.

"I was accosted by that Bernstein creep." I told Shelley all about our not-so-chance encounter.

"Let's call the police." Shelley grabbed her cell.

I held up one hand. "Wait, Shelley. I really don't want any more contact with the police than is necessary. I'm already on their shit list." I paused as another reason occurred to me. "And this would definitely get me front and center in the news."

"Like you're not already there." Shelley put down her phone.

"I don't think he's dangerous." I hoped it was true. "I'll take care of him myself."

That was apparently good enough for Shelley. She tapped on her laptop keyboard and started in on some

paperwork. I put on my CD and started listening to Barry
Manilow sing the '70s. Sue me; I love the guy. "The Way We
Were" was probably not the best choice, considering my
current circumstances, so I flipped it over to "Bridge Over
Troubled Water," because it was perfect for the occasion.

By the time I'd heard Barry belt out the rest of the '70s,
as well as half the funky '80s, I was nearly done with my
newest piece. The lapis and silver gleamed in my bench
light, and I'd wrapped silver wire around the drop mother-
of-pearl and wired seed-sized lapis beads around its
perimeter. It was lovely. I put it around my neck to see how
it looked 'live.'

Shelley was at the counter with a customer when in
walked Candy Cooper. I had gone to high school with
Candy, but time hadn't been as kind to her as it was to some
people. She had several chins, even though she really wasn't
much heavier than me. Her hair was an unnatural blond —
but whose isn't at our age? If I were Candy, I'd have those
chins removed, but so far, she hadn't asked for my opinion.

"What's that you just put on?" Candy reached over and
fingered my newly-made treasure.

"I just made it." I carefully unclasped the lapis necklace
and held it up for her to see. "Why don't you try it on?"

She hesitated. "Actually, I came in to have my beads
restrung." She put an opera-length strand of freshwater
pearls on the counter.

"Come on, you know you want to." I flashed her my

devil-may-care smile. "It doesn't cost anything to try it on."

"Well, all right then." She turned so I could put the pendant over her head and fasten it behind her.

She peered into the mirror on the showcase. I have to say the beads did a good job of distracting from at least a few of Candy's chins.

"It looks gorgeous on you," said Shelley, who had finished up with her last customer.

"How much?" Candy smiled at her image in the mirror.

This is why I appreciated a math-whiz partner like Shelley. Whenever I made a new piece, I wrote down a list of all the parts I used — the gems, the spacers, the findings — and the hours of labor, and Shelley would tally it up and figure out the exact cost, as well as the retail markup.

Candy's eyebrows shot up to the ceiling. My designs do not come cheap. But I offered to throw in a free restringing for her pearls, something I could do myself, and the deal was done.

Shelley ducked into the bathroom just as I finished writing up the order. It surprised me when Candy piped up with a comment about Robert. I'd been hoping to have a normal sale without having to get into the nitty gritty of my personal life.

"So how does it feel?" she asked.

I pretended not to understand what she was talking about.

"About Robert being gone. I mean, is it a relief, or do

you miss him?"

Candy had lost her first husband to cancer and her second to divorce, so it didn't seem to be as nosy a question as it might have been from someone else.

"It's hard to know how I feel about him," I answered honestly. "I've been too busy dealing with the fallout, especially because he was murdered."

"I wouldn't blame you if you did it," said Candy. She must have seen the look on my face, because she added, "Not that I'm saying you did it. But I understand the hurt of a cheating man." Candy's second husband had been a looker — and a serial philanderer.

"Yes, life would have been very different if we hadn't hired that...." I hesitated, "Barbara." I had been about to start to speak my mind again, and I decided against it. My venting had obviously gotten me into a lot of trouble and it was time for a change. I could hear the toilet flush and the water rush from Shelley washing her hands.

Candy narrowed her eyes. "You don't seriously think that Barbara was his first?"

I was truly taken aback. What she said made logical sense, but I'd never considered it. I'd always believed that while our marriage wasn't perfect, Barbara was the first and only reason it had been destroyed. Of course, I didn't say that to Candy. "I don't think so!" I said, trying to suppress the anger in my voice.

"I'm sorry." She patted my forearm. "You're going

through a tough time, and I shouldn't have said that."

I noticed she didn't say she was wrong, just that she shouldn't have said it, but I let it go. She was, after all, a paying customer.

But long after she walked out the door, I sat at my bench deep in thought. Robert had cheated on me, with Barbara, during lunch, doing 'nooners' in our bedroom. I was sure of that. But as I thought about it, he'd always gone off for long lunches, for years, always without me. What if he'd been cheating on me forever?

I swallowed hard. That would mean my marriage had been a lie pretty much forever. The only difference was that, once he met Barbara, he'd decided she was worth dumping me. As bad as things were going, this actually made me feel even worse.

"What's wrong?" Shelley slid into her chair, her eyes on my face.

"Just a little depressed." I felt like I was really telling her the truth, just not the whole truth.

Shelley looked at her watch. "It's four-thirty. You don't look so good. Why don't you go home and take it easy for a little bit before you go out to dinner with Mom and Albert tonight?"

I groaned out loud. Shelley was being nice by not rubbing it in that I was going on Mom's mission to set me up with Mr. Right.

"Thanks, Shelley." I gave her a big hug and peeked over

her shoulder. No reporters had reappeared. It looked like I could safely walk home with Boodles and collapse, which is exactly what I did.

By the time I woke up from a nap on my overstuffed living room couch, it was seven-fifteen. This gave me exactly fifteen minutes to get ready for dinner, or I'd be late. I let Boodles out back and made a quick change into a knee-length red and white Yves St. Lauren evening gown I'd bought at the resale shop, matched with my signature Bella's Baubles ivory and onyx beads. I added my diamond drop earrings, a gift from Robert on our twentieth anniversary and I saw my eyes cloud over in the mirror. Had he been cheating on me then?

I shook my head, just like Boodles would after I'd take off his leash. *No wallowing!* I told myself. Whether Robert had been cheating on me or not, I had to get back to the business at hand. I had to keep my eyes, ears — and mind — open to anything and everything that could prove my innocence. I'd have to deal with anything else later.

CHAPTER 8

I slipped on my red patent Jimmy Choos and let Boodles back in the house. I gave him a big smooch on the lips; Shelley would just die from the germs. I threw a few tiny treats in his bed — the one with the crown embroidered in it. (Don't judge me. You would spoil him too, if you had the chance.)

It wasn't until I was on the entrance ramp of I-696 that it occurred to me that this was the first time since the cataclysm that I'd be at The Club. I'd been a member there with Robert for all the years of our marriage. It's a good-old boys club for Jewish clientele. It wasn't announced on the marquise or on the front awning, but a good sixty-percent or more of the members were Jewish. And the others? They must have had their reasons.

I hadn't minded the place when I was married, but I dreaded going there under the newest circumstances, with my name on the news and in the paper. My mother was apparently oblivious, and I'd not considered this myself until I'd kissed Boodles goodbye and slid into my Escalade.

No reporters lurked outside my house. The mayor of Detroit had been caught bare-assed in yet one more extra-marital dalliance that afternoon, and the reporters had apparently swarmed like killer bees to the Manoogian Mansion to harass His Honor and wife. I felt sorry for his wife.

I adjusted my mirror, and my thoughts turned to Barbara. Was she capable of murder? If she'd planned it all along, she was actually doing a bang-up job of murdering Robert and framing me at the same time. If she knew that my gun was in Robert's wall safe — and that's an *if* — then meeting him at home in the morning (with the ready alibi of her standing date with Loozie), shooting him with *my* gun, and then pitching it and going to her alibi coffee date, would be the greatest of ploys.

It was the work of a mastermind, even if I didn't think Barbara Baby was that smart — or cold-blooded. In my gut I was sure she'd done it, just not yet clear on the details. It was the perfect murder. Somehow, I would have to pull it together and expose her. She was obviously pure evil. After this night, this "date," I would have to get my mother off my back so I could work on saving my sorry butt.

I shuddered as the narrow canyon-like walls of I-696 in Southfield gave way to the open road in Farmington Hills. As annoyed as I was with my mother and her matchmaking, I fervently wished that she was my biggest problem.

I took the Orchard Lake exit and headed north, past all the trendy strip malls and big box stores, past Temple Shalom and the new Sephardic Synagogue, till finally I found the discreet, understated "WBCC" sign at the side of what looked like a single-lane wooded driveway. I turned, wended my way through the woods, and came to stop beneath the front entryway, also understated by the West Bloomfield standard of style.

"Hello, Mrs. Blumer." It was Mike, the attendant. He was on the wrong side of thirty-five and had been parking cars at The Club for the past fifteen years.

"Hello, Mike." I handed him my single car key that I kept in my purse for just this purpose. "Take care of my Baby." I was trying to keep it light, like there wasn't a cloud of notoriety hanging over my head.

He put two hands in the air in mock horror, my key dangling from his forefinger. "Don't shoot, Mrs. B., I promise to be good."

I gave him a weak smile and headed into The Club. Another attendant, who was blissfully quiet, held the large oak door open. I slipped inside without a word.

It was darker inside than out, as it was only eight o'clock in July, in Michigan. My eyes adjusted to the change. "I'm here to meet Albert and Harriet Kurtz in the dining room," I told the attendant, who was obviously new.

He pointed the way. The empty hall was dark green and hushed in the way air-conditioning can render a room during the heat of summer. The main dining room sat at the far end, overlooking the golf course. Massive mint green drapes topped the two-story windows, floor to ceiling. They were open wide to show the gently sloping greens. A mother swan and her chicks were gliding silently in a distant pond. The only thing missing was a rainbow, and you might think you made a wrong turn and made it to heaven.

My mother discreetly waved her hand. "Bella, dear, come and meet this nice new young man."

I took a look at the man sitting next to my mother. You could hardly call him "new." Let's say that this guy looked previously owned, like a Cadillac. When he stood to greet me, I could see he was about my height, five-foot-six or so, and rotund, something like the fat guy in Oliver and Hardy. Strike one. He was bald in the old-fashioned way. Rather than shaving his head like the young bucks do, he had a pathetic comb-over that would shame even Donald Trump. Strike two.

"Christopher Bluestein." He shook my hand. At least it wasn't like Larry Bernstein's limp fish.

"Nice to meet you." I settled into the upholstered dining room chair.

"So how does my mother know you?" I asked.

Bluestein hesitated, so my mother jumped in to save him. "He's my hairdresser's brother-in-law."

I tried not to look at Bluestein's horrific comb over, which might qualify for three strikes all by itself.

"Chris was divorced last year. He has three children," my mother said.

I decided to be polite and conversational, maybe give the guy a chance. "Oh, and how old are they?"

"Twelve, ten, and three." He shifted nervously in his seat. Maybe the topic of his children made him uncomfortable. I could have waited for him to ask a question himself, so that it would seem less like an interrogation and more like a normal conversation. But there were no questions forthcoming. Either he was overwhelmed by my recent notoriety, or he was a social dud who had no clue about making small talk. Either way, not a good thing. So I decided to break the silence.

"So what kind of doctor are you?" I was guessing a pathologist, someone who didn't have to talk to patients.

"I'm a gynecologist."

"Oh," I said. *Strike three! Strike three!* This guy was over and out. Even if he were handsome and had personality, that would be an issue. "*So how was your day at the office, dear?*' Obviously, most male gynecologists were married, so I might be alone in this. But this was a deal breaker. Over and out.

I sat back in my comfortable chair, confident that when this dinner was over, I would never see Dr. Bluestein again.

After the waiter took our orders, Albert piped up with a question to break the increasing moments of silence. "So how did a nice Jewish boy like you get a first name like Christopher?"

"Good question," said the doc, "and one I'm asked a lot." He reached for a sourdough roll and buttered it. "My mother isn't Jewish, and she sort of stuck to her guns when it came time to name me."

"But you were raised Jewish," rushed in my mother, who was still hopeful she'd made a match.

"I went to Hebrew school and had a Bar Mitzvah."

That didn't qualify to me. A lot of people forget they're Jewish once they've had their Bar Mitzvah. That is, until they get married and want to raise *their* kids Jewish. And so goes the cycle. Not that it mattered to me. I'm not the greatest Jew on earth. Robert hadn't been either. He'd been more faithful to The Club than he was to Temple Shalom. Or me.

"I see you in the news a lot, lately," said Bluestein.

I wondered if he knew he was entering dangerous territory. A heavy silence hung over the table, as neither my mom nor Albert said a word, and I kept my mouth sealed shut.

"Oh, bad topic," he said. "Small world, though."

"What do you mean, dear?" asked my mother.

"Barbara Blumer is my niece—on my mother's side, of course." How do you like that? This loser turns out to be Barbie-girl's uncle.

Well, that sealed the deal. Both my mother and Albert were distant, but polite, for the rest of the meal. After Albert signed the bill and we headed for the front door valet, my mother gave me a rare hug and whispered an even rarer apology. "I'm sorry about this one, dear. I'll make it up to you."

"No need, Mom," I said, but it was too late. She was already shaking Bluestein's hand goodbye. I would really rather that she not make it up and leave me alone. But my mother has the tendency to hear only herself speaking; at least when she's speaking to me.

Later that night as I slipped into bed, Boodles snuggled down on the pillow next to me. It was nice to have him around, especially when I anticipated a night of insomnia before Robert's funeral. But I knew I would really rather have a male human next to me in bed instead of a sweet dog. (Sorry Boodles, but that's the truth.) Of course, I'd never ever admit that to my mother, or she'd have men lined up outside my shop door, with not a one of them even close to being Mr. Right.

CHAPTER 9

offman-Schwartz is one of only three Jewish funeral homes in metropolitan Detroit, down on Nine Mile near the Lodge Expressway. This is the place for Reform and secular Jews, and perhaps a few Jewish atheists to bid their families and friends adieux. And it was the perfect setting for Robert's final farewell, despite his mother's more Conservative Jewish leanings.

It was Wednesday morning. I held Heather's hand as we walked from the parking lot toward the massive front glass doors. Heather wore a lovely black jersey dress that flowed daintily around her army boots. I wore a crisp, light blue blazer over my filmy white skirt and three-inch, strappy, blue Jimmy Choos. It all worked perfectly with my Bella Blumer blue-topaz pendant and matching topaz-and-lapis drop earrings.

Heather planned to ride in the processional to the cemetery in the limo, along with Vic and Marcy, and Gramma Myrna. Oh, and with Barbara. I thought it was maybe better if I didn't go to the cemetery.

The cemetery. The thought of Robert in a cemetery suddenly made me panic. "How can I go in there? Where am I supposed to stand?" I squeezed Heather's hand, thinking of the room in the rear of the chapel, which was reserved for the immediate family, which I was not.

"I want you to stand next to me." Heather had a firm set to her deep purple lips that somehow looked right with her pansy-pink hair and lavender nose ring.

"But, Barbara . . ."

"Screw Barbara," said Heather, with a little more anger than I expected. "You're my mother, and I want you there."

"She'll be mighty pissed."

"So what! Since when do you care about what that bimbo wants?"

Heather was using my very words. But things were different now. Robert was dead and I was a suspect.

"I'm not going in the limo with her! I don't think I can even handle going to the cemetery." It was true. The thought of enduring a graveside visit with all the attending drama made me sick to my stomach.

Heather broke her stride and turned to face me. "Okay. That's fair." What a reasonable daughter I raised!

"So it's a deal?"

"Deal." Heather gave my hand an extra squeeze as we walked through the double glass doors.

The entry hall had the gloomy hush of a funeral home and smelled of fresh flowers with a faint scent of mothballs. We made our way to the family greeting room in front of the sanctuary, to the right of the lectern where the service would be held. Large stained-glass windows filtered in multi-colored light. The air conditioning was cranked up so high that I felt I was in a refrigerator. I shivered, thinking of Robert, who had likely been in a refrigerator all night long.

A murmur of voices filled the family reception room. I squeezed Heather's hand yet again, and we walked in together. Vic and Marcy held hands and stood by a table stocked with fresh Kleenex. Vic was pale, and his eyes were bloated and red-rimmed. I hugged him with all the love I could muster and pulled Marcy into the embrace. "I'm so sorry," I whispered to Vic. I know how much you loved him." Vic pulled a tissue from his pocket and dabbed his eyes.

Myrna sat just beyond Vic, against the back wall, her face buried in a bouquet of wet tissue. I tapped her on the shoulder and gave her a hug. She hugged me back but was uncharacteristically quiet. I couldn't blame her; she'd just lost one of her two sons.

I took her hand. "I'm really sorry, Myrna. I loved him for twenty-nine years. It wasn't my choice." I could feel the tears brimming over and sliding down my cheeks.

She squeezed my hands, her face also wet. "I know, Bella. You're a good girl." Kind words, indeed, for the number one suspect in her beloved son's death.

Barbara's best friend, Loozie, a tall blond thing, stood next to the evil queen herself, who looked resplendent in a skintight, black pinstripe suit with a gold lamé clutch and matching spikes. What a floozy! What a mid-life crisis trophy wife! I tried not to look, but it was like an eclipse. They tell you that you'll go blind, but you look anyway. This was a widow? You had to be kidding me!

Heather tried to pull me back to the other side of Vic and Marcy, when she struck.

"What are *you* doing here?" Barbara fairly shouted, hands on her hips, still clutching that wildly inappropriate dress bag.

What a skank! I mustered all the strength and dignity I could find. "I'm here because the father of my children is dead and I want to comfort and support them."

She practically lunged at me. I was in a state of shock.

"He wouldn't be dead if it weren't for you, you bitch!" she shouted.

The buzz of conversation in the room went totally silent.

I tried to keep my voice still and calm, but I could hear a waver when I talked. "I've had nothing to do with him—or you—for the whole year, so just back off!" I was proud that I hadn't added the word, "bitch."

But apparently my restraint did not have a calming effect.

"You complained about us every day!" The words came out in a whine, and I could see her nostrils flair. I had the fleeting thought that Barbara wasn't nearly as glamorous without the mask of makeup. She stared daggers at me through her false eyelashes. "We were in love."

Was I actually supposed to feel *sorry* for her? "You slept with him when he was *my* husband. I don't owe you a thing." I knew I was shouting, but I didn't care.

"The police know you did it." Now she was fairly hissing, thinking that she 'got' me. "They know he was killed with your gun."

That was it. "Listen, bitch. It might have been my gun at one time, but it was in *your* house, and I'm thinking *you* did him in!"

Barbara raised a hand as if to smack me one in the face, but Vic caught her arm. For a split second, I thought I saw a flash of light.

"Stop it! Both of you." He pulled Barbara to the other side of Loozie. "My mother is staying," he said to her. He turned to me. "And you, Mom, would you please stand at the other side of Heather?"

My heart was pounding out of my chest, and I think that I was in too much shock to actually speak. So I silently made my way back to Heather.

"*I* want to stand there." Barbara obviously had a better

constitution for wild fighting. "I'm the wife, and *I* should be the first one people see when they walk in."

So we all shifted places and Barbara got her coveted spot at the entry to the reception room. Our little histrionics ended just in time, as Ben and his wife, Stella, arrived. The general buzz of conversation started again as an admiring throng of family, friends, and customers lined up outside the door, coming to pay their last respect to Robert and his dysfunctional family.

After a perfunctory handshake for Barbara and a chest-squeezing bear hug for me, Ben and Stella quickly sat on either side of Myrna, and the visitation began. My lime bag started to cut into my shoulder, so I put it against the back wall, under Ben's chair, close to Myrna.

As I turned to face the crowd, I was suddenly enveloped in another full-frontal hug. It was Janine. She's not a petite thing, that Janine. She's somewhere around five-foot-nine, and her once-svelte figure was long gone, making her look like a well dressed, red-headed Pillsbury dough girl. She was sobbing, and I was surprised. Janine had never shown much emotion in all the years I'd worked at Blumer's.

"I'm going to miss him. He's been part of my life for over ten years."

"So you're not going to blame me for killing him? Like Barbara over there?" I tipped my head in the general direction of Barbara, afraid to upset the temporary détente with eye contact.

"Oh her," said Janine. "After the way they carried on, I wouldn't blame you if you killed the both of them."

"I didn't kill anyone and don't want to." I released her fleshy palms. This was getting serious. Everyone figured it was *me*.

My tone must have been a little harsh, because she left me without another word and took Ben's seat next to Myrna.

Before I could turn and face front, I was surrounded by a trio of cackling women, the Schultz sisters, all avid customers of Blumer Fine Jewelers. Not a one had yet made it to Bella's Baubles.

"We can't believe you're actually here," said the first Schultz sister, Golda, "with what they're saying about you in the news."

They all murmured in agreement with each other.

"This is supposed to be a condolence call." I could feel my face turn red. In an effort to ignore them, I turned to see who was next in line.

"Ollie," I called out. "Excuse me, please," I said to the Schultz sisters, my tone not at all as polite as my words.

Ollie Gleason released Barbara and reluctantly made his way over to me. Ollie, the Royal Oak Cadillac-Chevy dealer, was Robert's best friend and golfing buddy. They were in the Rotary together, and Temple Brotherhood. The only thing they didn't have in common was looks. In addition to wearing an obvious toupee, Ollie was overweight and misshapen, like his top half didn't match his bottom. And

Ollie had the good sense to still be married to Glenda, his wife of thirty-two years. He held out one hand to me. No hug.

"What? Robert's gone, and you want to shake my hand?" I took a good look at him. He was taking in short breaths, like he was ready to pass out.

"Ollie, are you okay? And where's Glenda?" I couldn't imagine why Ollie's wife wouldn't make it to the funeral of her husband's best friend.

"Oh, I'm fine." His eyes darted around the room, looking at everyone and everything but me. "Glenda is under the weather, couldn't make it."

"I'm sorry. Give her my best." I decided to be gracious, even if he was acting like a jerk.

"Sure." He looked over my shoulder at either the window or the ceiling, I couldn't tell. How awkward could this get?

Move on, I thought, willing him to leave.

"Bella!" I heard Shelley's voice and heaved a sigh of relief when she gave me a hug. Her husband, Mitch, hugged me as well. And Ollie, thankfully, disappeared from view.

"You don't look so good." Shelley released me just in time for her only daughter, Elena, to give me another good hug.

"Everyone thinks I did it, and it's making me crazy!"

"Everyone thinks you did what?" It was my mother, her blond hair in a perfectly starched updo, her arm still linked with husband Albert Kurtz, he of the most ridiculous black toupee on earth, next to Ollie's anyway, and a wad of cash he happily lavished on my mother.

"They all think she killed Robert." Shelley put her arm around my shoulders for support.

"Why, that's rubbish." My mother wouldn't swear if her life depended on it. I'd picked up my salty language in college, a great relief from my prim and proper upbringing.

"Did you see the paparazzi out there?" Shelley fluffed up her pin-straight auburn hair. "This place is loaded with photographers."

I gasped. Photographers. I hadn't anticipated that. They hadn't been there when Heather and I had arrived.

"Don't worry," said Shelley, "I asked Myron Hoffman if they were allowed in the sanctuary and he said, no, they weren't even allowed in the building. They're hovering around outside though, waiting to make footage for the evening news."

I felt myself starting to shake. "This can't be happening." Just when I'd thought Robert couldn't hurt me anymore, here it was. I looked directly at Shelley. "What am I going to do?"

Shelly gave my shoulders an extra squeeze. "Well, we'll have to prove them wrong."

"But how?" I admired her bravado, but come on! I was a struggling retail jewelry designer and Shelley was a retired bookkeeper and a mom. No Mrs. Marple in sight.

"I've been talking about it with Heather," said Shelley. "And we agreed that we have to meet tonight and figure out who really killed Robert. We really need to formulate a plan."

Shelley would usually refer to Robert as "that skunk" in deference to my feelings, but I could see that she was toning things down for the skunk's funeral. Very tasteful of her.

"And Mitch has a lawyer for you," said Shelley.

Mitch took me by the elbow and whispered in my ear. "I hope you don't mind, but I've already called an old college friend, Rich McIntyre. He's a top-notch criminal defense attorney."

I felt myself start to tear up. "Thank you, Mitch." I gave him a hug. "I didn't know where to look for a lawyer."

I heard my mother's high-pitched tone. "Can I help?" she asked, clutching her orange Versace handbag and looking even more earnest than she had while planning my last date.

I sighed, my mind turning to ugly thoughts of Larry Bernstein.

"We can all meet tonight," said Shelley.

"Let's make it at my house." If the cameras were going to be rolling, I'd rather be secure in my own home.

As I gave my mother and Shelley an extra big hug, I noticed a classically tall, dark, and handsome man walk in and give the same to Barbara. He looked vaguely familiar.

"Who is that guy?" I asked no one in particular.

"That is Dan Eckles," said Marcy, who'd appeared by my side. "Barbara's ex."

"That's awfully cozy. I wonder what he's doing here!"

"Some men like dangerous women," said Marcy, making me think of the Bernstein twerp.

"How do you know him?"

Marcy laughed. "I clean half the teeth in Royal Oak. I have the inside scoop on a lot of things."

"That's great," said Shelley, "then you can help us figure out who really killed Robert. You in?"

"You mean, do I think my mother-in-law killed my father-in-law?" Marcy smiled. "Of course not. That's ridiculous. Count me in. I'll help any way I can. But it can't start until at least eight-thirty. We have the Shiva house to think about."

Rather than visitation in funeral homes, Jews console the bereaved by visitation at a designated home after the funeral — either the home of the deceased or at a close family member or friend's house. In this case, it would be held at Myrna's, apparently because Robert's house was still a crime scene, or maybe Myrna just wanted it that way. Shiva means "seven" in Hebrew, as traditionally Jews mourned in their homes for seven days. But most contemporary Jews hold this visitation open for three to five days. Myrna had planned it for three. I didn't plan to attend at all. The less Barbara, the better, if you know what I mean.

I glanced over Marcy's shoulder, looking for Vic, and

noticed Janine, still sitting next to Myrna, her head back against the wall, eyes closed. She sure seemed to be taking this hard. Then I saw Vic, in an animated conversation with his Uncle Ben and his two cousins, Adam and Ethan.

One of the Hoffman-Schwartz employees announced that it was time for the service. All visitors left the reception room to sit in the sanctuary. I remained in the room with my fractured and dysfunctional family. I grabbed a seat on the other side of Myrna and sat with my eyes closed as I listened to my son Vic, the rabbi, and Barbara, one by one extol the virtues of Robert Blumer. I was too numb to really feel the experience.

When the service was over, I thought of the paparazzi, who most certainly wanted a picture of me. I spotted my lime bag behind Myrna and fished around for my lipstick. Properly fortified with Chanel's latest shade of rouge mystery, I hugged Vic and Heather goodbye. The pallbearers were Ben's sons, Adam and Ethan, Ollie Gleason, and three of Robert's friends from way back. As they made their way down the center aisle of the sanctuary, I planned my escape. I wanted to slip out among the crowd, so as to avoid the paparazzi who, I figured, would be looking for me over at the cars parked for the processional. I was proud of myself. It was a good plan, and it would have worked out perfectly.

If I hadn't run smack into Detective Krieger.

CHAPTER 10

"Excuse me." I tried to dart around him and mingle with the crowd.

"I need to talk to you." He held onto my arm, giving my body mixed signals. I found him terribly attractive, much more so than the perverted Larry Bernstein. But the reason he was holding onto my arm wasn't social. It was all business. He was latching onto his prime suspect, and I knew it.

I stood in place with him, and the crowd walked around us. "Listen," I said, "This is a bad time. There are cameras out there waiting to take a shot at me, and I want to slip out with the crowd."

"They're going to find you at the cemetery," he said.

"That's the point. I'm not going to the cemetery."

"Why not?" I could see him dying to pull out his pad of paper and take notes.

"I promised my kids I'd come to the funeral service, but it's just too painful to go out to the cemetery."

"What do you mean, *painful*?" Could he be that dense?

"Are you married?"

"Divorced." A pained look flashed across his face. "Twice."

"Would you want to go to your ex's funeral, with her new boy-toy there, out gunning for you?" Oops. Bad choice of words. I could see his jaw tense. Didn't want him thinking I was into guns. "That's just an expression," I added. *Damn, now I've drawn attention to it.*

The sanctuary was now almost half empty.

"Look, I really have to go." Over the exit doors, I could see Ethan and Adam hoisting Robert's coffin into the hearse. The cameras were rolling and flashing. Off to the side of the hearse was Larry Bernstein, all eyes on me with the cop.

I swallowed hard. "How about I meet you later? I promise to answer anything you want." I spoke in a rush, hoping he'd let move on and get out of there.

"How about now?" This cop was relentless. "I'll help you get to your car unnoticed, and you can meet me at the station.

"On Fourth and Lafayette?"

"That's the place."

"Let's go." I tried to blend in, once again, with the now-dwindling crowd.

"Grab my arm," he said. "They're not expecting you to be a couple."

So grab I did, and I couldn't help but notice the ripple of electricity I felt at his touch. But I chose to ignore it for the time being. I put my head down as we walked at the pace of the crowd, all the better to not be noticed.

"Bella!" I heard a voice call out. I kept my head down and glanced to the right, moving only my eyes. It was Larry. Damn! What a numbskull pain-in-the-ass schlemiel.

"Bella, it's me," he called out, once more, and I could see him cutting through the crowd, making his way to Detective Hottie and me.

"Go away," I fairly hissed by the time he reached my side.

That was it. The cameras started flashing, and a microphone was thrust in my face.

"Why did you kill your ex-husband?" asked Alecia Stelleretto, she of Fox Channel Two, her sharp voice cutting through the chatter of the crowd.

"Out of the way," said Detective Krieger, expertly parting the crowd. I felt like I was being pulled through rough waves at the beach by a strong arm.

"Are you her bodyguard?" Alecia asked, as she pointed a microphone at his face.

He reached into his vest pocket with the hand that wasn't holding onto me and pulled out his badge. "You're interfering with an investigation," he said, his cop voice deep and emotionless.

"Is Ms. Blumer under arrest, sir?" asked a male voice brandishing a Channel Four microphone.

"There will be no comments," he said, as we walked so fast that it might as well have been running. The cameras and microphones followed.

"Which one's your car?" he asked.

"The white Escalade," I said, and we jogged the rest of the way to it, which is no small feat in three-inch heels, let me tell you.

When I noticed that we were no longer being followed, I unlocked the car with my remote and flew inside in one fluid motion.

"Go straight to the station," said Detective Krieger.

"Yes sir!" I was trying not to be annoyed with how he was ordering me around. I wasn't a criminal and didn't care to be treated like one.

As I drove out of the Hoffman-Schwartz parking lot, I could see why the local paparazzi had stopped their chase. Surrounded by cameras and with all the microphones in his face, Larry Bernstein stood, telling his story. What that story would be, I had absolutely no idea. I'd just met the man two days ago. I felt my stomach do a complete somersault.

Further in the distance, I could see my son and daughter climb into the limousine with their Gramma Myrna. And Barbara.

The car directly behind the limo was a brand new, silver-white Cadillac. I wondered if it was Ben's, although I thought he was more of a Camry kind of guy and not a Detroit-booster. Then over to the Cadillac walked Janine, who slipped into the driver's seat.

That was odd. Either it was a borrowed car or a rental. Or her husband, Tom, a mechanic, was making more bucks that I thought he did.

But there was no time to dwell. Detective Krieger's car lit out of the parking lot onto the service drive, and I could see that the Larry Bernstein interview was coming to a close, as some of the microphones were no longer in his face. Then some of the cameramen started walking in my direction.

I turned the key in the ignition, and my trusty Escalade roared to life. I expertly backed out of my spot and headed out in the opposite direction of the cameras. I maneuvered the car quickly through the lot and headed toward the exit, blessedly unmolested by the press. But as I turned onto the service drive and took a quick peek back at Hoffman-Schwartz's lot and the funeral procession lineup, I could see all the TV cameras rolling. And pointed at me.

THE ROYAL Oak Police Station was built in the 1950s, a fairly nondescript utilitarian building. I'd parked right in front and optimistically put a quarter in the meter for a half hour of service. I checked my Minnie Mouse watch. It was eleven-thirty, and Boodles wasn't used to being left home alone this long. But it hadn't seemed right to take him to the funeral.

When I opened the plate glass door, there was an ominous buzz and a sign telling me to sign in immediately. Uh, oh. Very official, this police stuff. So sign in I did. The cop behind the glass looked at my signature and then at my face, sizing me up, I suppose, to see if I looked like a murderer to him.

He gestured without a smile. "Go through the doors to your left. Detective Krieger is waiting for you."

I felt an involuntary shiver, and it had nothing to do with the air conditioning. I took a deep breath as I was buzzed into the back. *No smart mouth!* I sternly told myself. *Answer questions as briefly as possible. Show no emotion.* I hitched my lime bag up on my shoulder. Who was I kidding? It would take every ounce of strength I owned to behave that way.

I was buzzed through the door. Another stern-faced guy led me back to a classic interview room. I was struck by lack of any semblance of color. The room was beige on gray with perhaps a touch of grime. I followed, resolving to stick to my vow of silence.

"Have a seat." Krieger gestured toward a gray plastic chair on the opposite side of the table. What? No naked light bulb? No rubber hose? What *do* they do with rubber hoses? I decided I'd rather not know.

I could hear the hum of a loose, fluorescent bulb. I sat, back straight, perched on the edge of my chair.

"Want some coffee?" he asked.

I imagined the brown glop that would pass for coffee in a place like this, mentally comparing it to my treasured cappuccinos. "No thanks."

Detective number two walked in and sat in another plastic chair. Oh, good cop, bad cop. I definitely watched too much TV.

"This is Detective Riley," said Krieger.

"Nice to meet you, I think." I could have smacked myself. I'd had no intention of saying anything that was even remotely sarcastic, and there I'd done it before we even started.

Riley smiled. He looked to be in his early thirties, a young George Clooney. "Guess you're not too glad to be here."

Well, duh. I decided not to answer that one.

Krieger opened a file on his desk. Oh my, they already had a file on me. The shiver I'd felt when walking in melted into a cold sweat. I could feel droplets trickling down my centerline and stopping at my bra. It occurred to me that my hair was probably in humidity meltdown. Not pretty. I had to pull myself together. Fast.

"We have a lot of witnesses who say that you've been pretty vocal about your ex." Krieger pulled a piece of paper to the top of the file. From what I could see, he was trying to lead me into talking. But where I grew up, that wasn't a question. My mouth stayed shut.

"One of your acquaintances said you called Robert Blumer a skunk."

Of course I did. He *was* a skunk. But my mouth stayed shut. Yay me.

"Five of your acquaintances quote you as calling Barbara Blumer a 'bimbo'." His voice was monotone cop, but was there a twitch of amusement at the corner of his mouth?

"Four separate people quote you as saying that Robert Blumer deserted his family and destroyed your life."

It was working. It was getting impossible to keep my mouth shut. I felt like a whale with a plugged blowhole.

"Seven of your acquaintances quote you as calling Robert Blumer a 'lying cheating scumbag'."

Who were all these people so ready to stab me in the back? My concentration on sealed lips broke. "Look." I sat rigid on the edge of my seat, my lime bag on my lap. "Robert Blumer *was* a lying, cheating, dirt bag. And a skunk." I was on a roll now, ill advised or not. "And Barbara *is* a bimbo." I put my purse down on the tiled floor and my hands on the edge of the chipped Formica table. "But all I did was vent. I was upset, and I probably complained too much. Everyone has a vice." I leaned back in my chair. "But I wouldn't actually hurt him." I was thinking that was true. Part of me still loved the skunk, though I didn't like to admit it, even to myself.

"We don't have the murder weapon yet, but bullets retrieved from the scene match a gun registered to you." No twitch of amusement here. Krieger's face was all cop. Riley's too. So glad I'd had the heads up on that from Heather. It suddenly occurred to me that I hadn't yet called a lawyer.

"I don't have that gun. I left it with Robert when I moved out last year."

"Can you prove that?" asked Riley.

I frowned. "How can you prove you didn't take a gun?"

"Why didn't you take your gun with you?" This time it was Krieger, still looking stern. It was terrifying.

"It was Robert's idea to learn how to shoot. I took the lessons, and we both were licensed, but I don't like guns."

"Where was the gun kept?" Now it was Riley's turn. They were coming at me like machine guns, ra-ta-tat-ta-tat.

"It was in a wall safe in our bedroom. I haven't seen it in years."

"It wasn't in the safe," said Krieger. "Where did Robert keep it?"

"How would I know?" I could hear the pitch in my voice getting higher. These two were serious.

"You have a gun registered to your name, and you don't know where it's kept?" This time it was Riley. What did these two do? Rehearse? I was getting increasingly stressed out.

"Don't I have the right to a lawyer?"

Krieger leaned back in his chair, Mr. Comfortable

watching me squirm. "You're not under arrest."

"Yeah, right," I said, "but you're talking about a gun and motives and you think it's me — and even though you're wrong, I think I should get a lawyer."

I stood up to leave. I had to call Mitch as soon as I left this place and get the number of that lawyer guy he'd told me about. Just thinking that I needed a lawyer — a criminal lawyer for God's sake — made my head start to spin.

"Why don't you sit down," said Krieger. "You don't look so good."

"I have nothing more to say." I held my lime bag cross-armed against my chest and turned awkwardly to leave.

"Riley, why don't you get her a glass of water?"

Riley dutifully jumped out of his seat and left the room. So nice to have a toady working with you, I thought, but thankfully kept my mouth shut.

"Sit down, Bella," said Krieger. "You haven't looked so bad since you forgot your lines at the seventh grade forensics competition."

He *did* remember me! His frown lines had softened, and he once more looked mildly amused.

"Here, have some sugarless gum." He offered me a stick from his desk drawer.

I wrinkled my nose. "No thanks." The fact is that I don't believe in fake sugar. The real stuff is all I eat. Why fight Mother Nature?

Riley returned with a standard-issue plastic cup, filled

with filtered office water.

Just then, my cell phone rang with my unfortunate selection of Michael Jackson's "I'm bad, I'm bad." I dove into my lime bag but couldn't find the phone. Frantic for that stupid song to stop, I dumped the contents on the tabletop. I picked up the phone amid the purse debris and, of course, it was none other than Larry Bernstein. That cretin! I pushed the ignore button and threw the phone back into my purse. As I scooped up my wallet and the rest of the mess from Krieger's desk, I came across two folded papers I knew didn't belong in my purse.

A smarter person would have ignored them till she got home. Maybe I was already on stress overload, or maybe I'm just plain stupid. To be kinder to myself, I knew that I was innocent, so I quite unfortunately let my curiosity get the better of me. I picked up the folded papers and squeezed. I could feel two hard something's inside. I opened the first surprise package in my purse and gasped.

In my hands, inside the folded diamond paper, was one three-carat diamond — without a doubt, the first of the two gems missing from the Robert Blumer crime scene. The second was obviously in the other diamond paper. I wasn't the only one who was shocked.

"Put down the stones." Krieger's all-business voice was back. "Both of them."

My hand trembled when I put the diamond papers on the interrogation table. "Someone put them there. I had no idea..."

Riley interrupted me. "When did you take them, Bella, before or after you shot your ex-husband?"

I couldn't help it. I'm not made of stone. I burst into tears and sat on that hideous plastic chair, my head dropping into my lap. One of them, probably Riley, left the room. I couldn't tell because I was too busy bawling my eyes out.

When he returned, Riley unkindly jerked me up from my chair and put my hands behind my back. You see it all the time on the news and on TV shows, but it's not the same when it's you. I could feel the cold metal against my wrists, and I was all at once out of control of my life. Riley held my upper arm with a tight grip and led me into the bowels of the building. No one had yet read me my rights, so I didn't think I was under arrest. Apparently, I was being held for questioning. I tried not to imagine how I'd be treated if I were actually being arrested. Through the fog of panic, I could only think of Boodles and how long it was going to take before I could get home. I think they call that denial.

CHAPTER 11

After they confiscated my lime bag and all its contents, I was booked, traumatized by having my police mug shot, and manhandled by a butch policewoman who appeared to enjoy it. I was then allowed a phone call. I tried calling Bella's Baubles, but apparently Shelley was still at the cemetery, as she didn't answer her home phone or her cell either. The matron in charge of me looked to be about thirty-five, and my best guess was that she was probably good at PE in high school. Let's just say, not someone I'd take out for lunch and shoe shopping at Somerset. Still, she didn't seem to mind that I made one unsuccessful call after another. I punched in 411.

"I'd like the number of Richard McIntyre, a lawyer. I nervously chewed on my cuticles, playing havoc with my

French manicure. "I think he's in Birmingham or Bloomfield Hills."

"It's Bloomfield," said the operator. "Would you like me to dial direct?"

"Yes, please." I worried that my matron's patience could run out.

"McIntyre and Associates," said a female voice nasal enough to rival Fran Fine, the Nanny. Who would want a voice like that representing their firm? Never mind. Just so long as he was a good lawyer.

"This is an emergency," I said to the nasal one. "My name is Bella Blumer, and I'm at the Royal Oak jail, being held on suspicion of murder." I took a deep breath, proud that my voice hadn't yet cracked. "I need to speak to Mr. McIntyre right away."

The nasal one informed me that Mr. McIntyre was out — probably to lunch, I'd think — and would get to the jail as soon as possible.

I wanted to tell her to blow her nose, but instead I just sighed. I reminded her that I was referred by my brother-in-law Mitch Moss and said, "Thanks, and please tell him to hurry!"

The Royal Oak holding cell was, shall we say, a little more "basic" than the questioning room. It had a concrete floor, a rickety cot, and a black plastic chair. All the comforts of home, if you were from a third-world country.

There wasn't much to do. Being me, my first impulse

was to imagine redecorating the place, starting with some of those hardwood flooring planks I'd seen at Lowe's. A little paint, a few pictures, maybe a throw rug or two, and the place wouldn't be half bad. It occurred to me what I should do for charitable work! Redecorate the Royal Oak holding cell. Or the third world.

After a while, I realized that if I didn't concentrate on the problem at hand that I might spend a lot of years in a "basic" place like this, and that I'd better get to work on proving my innocence.

Obviously, someone had planted those diamonds in my purse, probably at the funeral home. But who? Myrna? I'd put my bag next to her. I hit my forehead with my open palm. What an idiot I was, always leaving my lime bag open. I'd left it there, in the back of the room where anyone who had the inclination could plant them on me. Everyone knew I was a prime suspect. Whoever had done it was hoping the police would check my purse, but they didn't have to! I'd done it for them.

Just as I started to make a mental list of all the possible suspects at Robert's funeral, another matron appeared and told me that my lawyer had arrived. I looked at the clock. Two hours since I'd called. Not too bad, even if it felt like I'd been there for days.

I followed the matron through a maze of hallways and doors until we came to a conference room, similar to the "interview" room, complete with windowless walls, the standard Formica tables, and the ever-present plastic chairs. This time, they were a pale scuffed blue.

"Hello, Bella." Richard McIntyre extended a fleshy hand. He looked more like a Southern good-old boy than a Midwestern lawyer, but oh well. "Have a seat, have a seat," he said, his voice as charming as it would have been at a social gathering.

"Is it really private here?" I worried that the police were listening in.

"Everything we say here is privileged information, and it is totally illegal for the police to listen in on any of it."

I heaved a sigh of relief.

"Now, they have a lot on you." McIntyre licked his lips, reminding me of a large dog licking his chops in anticipation of a big bone. "Witnesses to your motive, crime scene bullets match a murder weapon registered in your name. Not to mention the diamonds stolen from your ex-husband, later found in your possession."

"I know it sounds bad, but I'm not guilty. Someone set me up!"

"That's what they all say." He gave a slow smile. "I'm not here to judge, just to give you the best defense possible."

I stared hard at the man, and the light in the room seemed to dim. "I don't care what 'they' all say, Mr. McIntyre, I didn't kill anybody, and if you don't believe me, I'll find a lawyer who does."

"About me being your lawyer…" He scratched the light

brown hair on the side of his head. "We do have to talk retainer here. Your brother-in-law was kind enough to refer me, but I'm afraid I can't work for free."

First this loser implies that I killed Robert and then he's asking for money! "Get out!"

"Pardon me?" He truly looked confused.

"You heard me, get out!"

"I'm afraid I don't understand."

"Well, let me clue you in, Mr. McIntyre. I need a lawyer who believes in my innocence, and you are not that person."

His good-old-boy face hardened into a sneer. "Well, good luck finding any sane person who doesn't think you're guilty as sin. And my visit here isn't free. I'll send you a bill."

I stood up. "Goodbye, Mr. McIntyre."

He gathered up his papers. "You're making a big mistake. I'm one of the best lawyers in Oakland County."

"I'm not the one making a mistake here." I could feel my teeth grit in determination.

Shortly after he left, a matron returned and led me back to my cell. I laid down on the lumpy cot and waited for the tears, but I was too numb to cry. Where was my family anyway? Wasn't anyone home from that funeral yet? And I was going to give Mitch an earful about that lawyer. What a jerk!

THE POWERS that be scheduled my arraignment for the next morning, Thursday, at 8:00 AM sharp. The recently-built, stately Royal Oak Courthouse looked older than its years. I could still smell the varnish and new-building smell. The high ceiling and polished cherry paneling looked rich and expensive. I was impressed. The structure presented was infinitely more impressive than the police station. I'd never been there before, because apparently you had to be accused of murder to get invited. So all the same, I wished I'd never seen it.

My mother and Albert sat behind me in the empty gallery. Next to me sat my court-appointed attorney, who was the best I could get on such short notice. Looking about twelve years old, he wore dark, round glasses that made him look like his name should be Poindexter. Or Harry Potter. I was formally charged with the murder of Robert Blumer, after which Poindexter informed me that I would be bussed, courtesy of the Oakland County Correctional Facility, to Pontiac, the County Seat, for further processing and a bail hearing.

My mother stood stiffly while Albert reached over to give me a supportive hug. The bailiff none-so-gently shooed him away.

"Where's Shelley?" I croaked.

"She's minding the store," said Albert. "She really

wanted to be here for you."

I stood there, handcuffed in my bright orange prison suit, tears falling freely down my cheeks, dripping onto the floor.

"We'll be there for you in Pontiac," said Albert, his voice both reassuring and gentle. It only made me cry at his kindness.

The wheels of justice moved fairly swiftly for me, no doubt due to the influence of Albert, who always seemed to know and be loved by everyone—especially the well-connected.

After a scenic drive and a long tour of our county corrections system, my bail was set at one hundred thousand dollars. Presumably, even though I looked guilty as hell, the judge determined that I was not a flight risk. I guess it pays to have adult children, an elderly mother, an ongoing local business, and a stepfather named Albert.

If I'd gone to a bail bondsman, it would have cost me a non-refundable ten grand in order to borrow the whole one hundred thousand dollar bail. That's how they make their money. I really could not afford a non-refundable ten grand. The entire bond amount gets returned if you show up to court at the appointed time. So, I was greatly relieved and uncharacteristically willing to have Mom's generous Albert Kurtz post the entire wad of cash on my behalf. It pays to have friends in high places—or at least a stepfather with more money than God.

My mother and Albert offered to drive me home from
Pontiac, as my Escalade had been impounded for evidence.
I was lucky enough to get my lime bag back—after God
knows *who* had been pawing through it.

It drizzled as I climbed into the back of his full-sized,
silver Cadillac sedan, happy to be once again wearing my
very stale funeral outfit. Albert handed me a copy of the
Royal Oak Times. I gasped. The Robert Blumer story took
over the entire front page. There was a picture of Robert, a
business portrait he'd taken about two years ago, looking
handsome and chic. I could see the collar pin beneath his tie
and his rakish, yet business-like smile.

There was a picture of me looking into the camera from
my Escalade at the funeral home. It made me look guilty, as
if I was eluding the police. The cherry on top of this front-
page calamity was a photo of Larry Bernstein, along with an
article, apparently the result of an interview with the creep.
The worst photo was of Vic holding Barbara back from
smacking me one at Robert's funeral. The caption read,
"Blumer Funeral Sparks Catfight."

"It was even worse on the news, dear," said my mother.
"I don't know how I'm going to show my face at bridge club
this week."

*Gee, sorry, Mom. Good to know that you're more worried
about your embarrassment than about me.* I kept that thought
to myself; I already owed her a fortune, so it seemed wise to
keep my mouth shut.

"Just tell them I'm innocent."

"I know that, dear." She patted her helmet of hair. "But I don't think even one of them is going to believe me."

"Don't worry." Albert's voice was slightly muted by the 'swish-swish' of the Cadillac's wipers. "I believe you one-hundred-percent, or I wouldn't have paid that bail."

Enough said. How could I argue with that? My mother had good taste in men, starting with my father, who died when I was only seventeen, back when I was more than a handful. Aside from my dad, there were two more deaths and one divorce, proving that while she might be exacting and picky, my mother doesn't believe in living alone.

"I wonder who took that picture of me and Barbara at the funeral."

"I can't imagine," said my mother. "I didn't see anyone with a camera."

She had a point. I remembered Shelley telling me that no press was allowed in the funeral home. "It must have been a cell phone!" I said.

"But who would do that, dear?" asked my mother.

"I think I remember a flash, so that must have been it." Of course, it would have been helpful to know exactly who took the picture, because it was likely someone who wanted to make me look bad. That thought made the hair stand back on my neck. Was it someone involved in the murder? Had the murderer been at Robert's funeral? A wave of fear started in my heart and radiated through my arms and legs.

I shut my eyes and focused on Boodles. I would get to hold him in just a few minutes, and everything would be all right.

As we came closer to my bungalow on Fourth, I heaved a sigh of relief to see Heather through the front window. I was certain she'd taken care of Boodles overnight. But my relief faded when I saw two uniformed officers, one male, one female, removing my computer and laptop with latex-gloved hands. There were news vans parked on the other side of Fourth, filming my life for the six o'clock news.

"Oh my!" My mother sounded truly upset. Whether it was for me or her reputation I could only guess.

"Just drop me off," I said while opening the car door. "I'll take care of it."

"You sure we can't help?" My mother narrowed her eyes at the police.

"I'll be fine." I put my hand on Albert's shoulder. "I appreciate it more than you know, and I promise you'll get every penny back."

Albert patted my hand in answer. "I'm in no hurry."

I slammed the door shut and ran to face my extremely harried daughter. Just as Albert and my mom drove off, my heel caught in the groove between the grass and the sidewalk, and in my rush forward, it broke off, twisting my ankle. I ignored the pain that shot up my shin, as well as the steady drizzle that was most certainly destroying my hair. I limped through the front doorway. "Heather?"

As I hobbled closer, I could see she was crying.

"They had a warrant. I had to let them in."

Leaping off the couch, Boodles raced over and danced around with joy at the sight of me, paws up against the same outfit I'd worn to Robert's funeral. I scooped him up and put my other arm around Heather. "Don't cry, Honey, you didn't do anything wrong."

Heather pushed my arm aside. Her face was blotched with anger. "I know that. It's just such an invasion of privacy." She sucked in a long sob. "They've gone through all my... things."

"I'm so sorry, Heath," I said. "It's all because they think I killed Dad."

"I know." She sat on the leather armchair, head in hands. Thankfully, there were no police in the living area. "And it's not your fault either. But everything is just so messed up." She swiped at her face, all dirty with mascara smears. "And now it's all right here."

"And you miss Dad," I said, realizing that it wasn't just about me.

Heather put her arms around my neck, her chest heaving with each sob.

"Believe it or not, I miss him, too," I said, not surprised anymore that I meant it. How do you stop loving someone after nearly thirty years of marriage, even an apparently unhappy one? I pushed her pansy-pink hair back from her face. "Why don't you go wash up and go to work?"

She wiped her stained cheeks with the back of her hand.

"I was supposed to be there a half hour ago, but I didn't want to leave Boodles, and I can't take a dog to work."

I put my arm across her shoulder and gave it a squeeze. "Well, I'm here now, so go ahead and wash up."

"They won't let me in there. They think I'll screw up their investigation."

"I'm so sorry, Honey. Well, then, go to work and wash up there instead." It occurred to me that I wasn't going to be able to wash up or change either. And here I was in yesterday's funeral outfit, now damp from the rain, bottomed off with broken Jimmy Choos.

"I'm sorry I pushed you away before. I was just upset." Her eyes stared off in the distance, as if she was studying our neighbor's lawn.

"I understand." But part of me wondered if Heather didn't blame me, at least a little bit, for not being strong enough, or good enough, or *something* enough to have held onto her father. I couldn't help but wonder if she was right.

AFTER HEATHER left for work, I asked the female officer how much longer they would be.

"At least another hour." She made no eye contact with the common criminal she believed me to be.

I sighed. No spunky comment sprang to my lips, nothing that I had to hold back. They had my car, they had my computers, and for at least for the next hour, they had my house.

"Can I change my clothes?" I could hear the annoyance in my voice; I resented having to ask permission from an unfriendly stranger for the use of my house.

"Sorry, ma'am," she said, her voice not in the least bit sorry. "We need you out of our way until we're through with our investigation."

I'd already endured a totally unnecessary pat-down at the Royal Oak jail, and now this.

I was just about to reach for my cell when it started to ring "I'm bad, I'm bad." The two officers carried out my business files. Good grief—what did that have to do with the price of tea in China? What did they do? Send over some rookies?

I looked at the phone. It was Larry Bernstein. I instantly hit the "ignore" button and hoped he knew exactly what I was doing. I sat on my overstuffed couch, Boodles on my lap, and dialed up Shelley.

"Bella's Baubles." Her voice was brisk and businesslike.

"Shelley, it's me."

"Bella?"

"Yes, it's Bella, and I need a favor."

"Name it." Her voice sounded distracted.

"I'm stranded at my house, no car—the police took it, and they're ransacking my house, as we speak, for clues." I didn't even mention the rain, which was pouring down in rivulets at this time as I looked out my front window.

"Oh my God! What do you want me to do?"

"Thanks, Shel." I could pick up the faint scent of wet dog, which was oddly reassuring. At least one thing in my life was normal.

"If it wasn't raining, and my heel hadn't broken, I'd walk over to the store for God's sake." I peered over Boodles to take a look at my broken shoe. "Could you lock the door and come here and get me, and oh...bring me some of your clothes?" The moment I said it, I knew it was a ridiculous request. All Shelley wore were jeans and button-down shirts, or possibly a fitted T-shirt or polo. She added style to her look with my jewelry and maybe lip-gloss on a good day. But for the most part, our looks were diametrically opposite. However, under the circumstances, without access to my house, I was willing to make do. We were roughly the same size and I was desperate.

"No can do," said Shelley.

"What do you mean?" Her abruptness upset me.

Her voice took on a whisper. "It's absolutely swamped here. The publicity about—you know, Robert—has been great for business."

"Are they buying?"

"Oh, yeah." Her voice was almost lusty. Shelley has the business head, and I'm the designer. Nothing excites her more than a big fat bottom line.

"Okay, then I'll have to think of something else then. Or

wait."

Just then an unmarked cop car pulled up to the curb and out walked Krieger himself. Despite the circumstance, I couldn't help but find him attractive. Too bad he hadn't executed that pat down last night instead of the overweight butch-looking policewoman, who probably got a thrill. Yuck!

The squad car door opened.

"Something's come up," I said to Shelley. "Gotta go."

"Get here as soon as you can." Her voice was no longer a whisper. "I need help!"

We both hung up, and Boodles jumped out of my arms. Krieger walked in like he owned the place. After a few obligatory growls, Boodles started to seriously sniff his pant legs.

"Are my pants safe?" Krieger smiled. Now that was a loaded question.

"Well, he's not a humper, if that's what you mean." I didn't return his smile. We'd see how friendly he'd be if I had a cadre of jewelers inspecting *his* house after a night in the slammer.

I noticed his crisply ironed khakis and a light blue button down shirt. Apparently, *he'd* had a chance to shower and change. "Can I ask you a question?"

"What is it?" His voice was all business.

I felt a thrill go up my spine. What was it with me and the bad boys? That was obviously the appeal of Robert

"The Skunk" Blumer, and then here came Krieger, who had ignored me at best and treated me as a criminal at worst—and there went my hormones on high. I flashed on Larry Bernstein, wondering if I shouldn't give the jerk a chance. At least he was interested.

"The question?" repeated Krieger, snapping me back to the present.

"Oh," I said, giving myself time to think. "If I were guilty, like you think; if, and I do mean *if* I killed Robert Blumer and made off with those diamonds, why on earth would I have dumped the guts out of my purse and opened the diamond paper right in front of you?"

He paused. "People make mistakes." His mouth moved, but the rest of his face was a rock.

"Trust me, I'm not that stupid."

"Look," he said, "You're better off talking to your lawyer than to me. Why don't you get on with your day?"

"I'd love to, but after my lovely overnight stay at the Royal Oak jail and my all-expenses-paid trip to Pontiac, I've been denied access to my house." I could feel myself frowning. "Not only that, but my sister says it's swamped at my store and there's no way to get there." I held up my broken shoe as Exhibit A. "And my car is still impounded."

"I'll drive you to work," he said.

Was that a hint of a smile curving at the corner of his mouth? Boy, I was so pathetic. By now, the rain had let up, but my entire body felt damp, and not in a good way.

I couldn't see my hair, but experience told me that I likely resembled Bride of Frankenstein, she of the graying Marge Simpson 'do,' without the gray.

"Can I at least get some shoes? They won't let me in there to change." *And shower*, I added, just to myself.

"I'll get some for you." Krieger headed up my bedroom stairs without asking. Had he been up there before? How did this man know his way around my house? I shook off a shiver.

"Make them match my outfit," I called out to him, but he didn't break stride, and I doubted that he'd heard me.

About five minutes later, my doubts were confirmed. He handed me my red and black plaid high tops. I'd bought them as a joke for Halloween about five years earlier and had forgotten to give them to the Salvation Army resale shop. Apparently, I made a face.

"Beggars can't be choosers." He dropped them to the floor.

The sun started to poke through the clouds. Boodles nuzzled against my shin as I removed my heels and put on my high tops. It was surely a hideous match to yesterday's designer outfit, but what a relief! I stood up and was able to put weight on both feet. (Sometimes, I think dress heels are a conspiracy against women. If only they didn't make me look so sexy.) I glanced at my feet. I sure wasn't looking sexy now.

"Let's go." Krieger took my arm as Boodles and I settled

into his very utilitarian, unmarked Mercury Marquise. He put the car in gear and headed west on Fourth Street toward Bella's Baubles.

I noticed the cameras following our every move and felt uneasy about leaving my house to the police. "Will they lock up my house when they're done?"

Krieger rolled his eyes. "We're cops. Of course we'll secure the premises when we're done."

"When do I get my car back? And my stuff?" I mentally reviewed the contents of my hard drive, trying to think if there was anything embarrassing on it.

"Your car, unless they find incriminating evidence, by the end of the week, Monday at the latest." He slowed to a stop at the light on Main Street. "Your computers will take longer. Our tech guys will go through it all."

I sighed. What an invasion of privacy. "You have the wrong person." I pulled Boodles closer to my chest. "I was framed."

"That's what they all say." His voice didn't have a hint of emotion.

"You're all persecuting me, and in the meantime, there's a real murderer out there."

Krieger signaled right and double-parked across the street from my store. "Then I suggest you go out and find him."

Was he serious? Was that sarcasm? What was it with these cop types? I opened the door. Boodles scooted out, and I held onto his retractable lead. "Thanks for the lift," I said, ever polite, as I turned to shut the door.

Krieger gave me a two-fingered salute as he went back in gear and headed off on Fourth.

Sunlight leaked out from behind some low clouds, and the humidity was back with a vengeance. I headed into my shop with Boodles, grateful for the blast of air conditioning that hit my face — and for the fact that no one would see my high tops on the other side of the counter.

CHAPTER 12

s soon as Boodles and I entered my shop, I could see what Shelley was talking about. There were at least ten people jammed into my tiny store, and all eyes were on me. I felt like a celebrity — but not in a good way.

"Good for you, Bella," said a semi-familiar woman in a blond pageboy.

Did I know this person? And why was she cheering me on?

"I wish I had your nerve, girl!" This, from a plump, matronly-looking, well-dyed brunette, somewhere in her mid-sixties.

"He got what he deserved." It was a little-girl voice that didn't match a fifty-something body.

"What's with the shoes?" That was Shelley, who darn it all, brought all talk to a standstill as every eye in the store focused on my plaid high-tops.

"It's a long story." I quickly ducked behind the counter with Boodles, putting my very comfortable, and equally ugly, high-tops out of view. Business had been okay in my shop, but it had never been this busy. The current crowd practically took my breath away.

"What kind of necklace is that?" The blond pageboy woman pointed to my blue topaz and lapis pendant. I knew the drill. I put my hands behind my neck, removed the pendant, and carefully placed it on a velvet pad on the countertop.

A series of ooh's and ah's filled my store the moment the necklace hit the pad.

"Did you wear it in jail last night?" This was from the little-girl voice no less.

Now that was embarrassing. I felt my face flush. "As a matter of fact, yes."

"I'll take it," said a woman in the back who I hadn't noticed before.

"I saw it first," said the blonde.

"No problem," said Shelley, switching into saleswoman mode. "You know Bella wears each of her creations for at least a full day, to make certain that it's as comfortable as it is beautiful."

Shelley quickly pulled a second blue topaz necklace;

this one accented with lapis and tourmaline, and put it next to the original necklace on the black velvet pad.

"I'll take that one," said the brunette.

I tell you it was crazy like that for the rest of the day. No one asked a price; all they cared about was getting a piece of jewelry created and worn by the notorious local murderess. It was pathetic and profitable, all at the same time. Not until six o'clock did the store clear out of customers for a well-deserved lull.

"I'm exhausted." I slouched at my bench. "And if this keeps up, we're going to run out of merchandise."

"Who said crime doesn't pay?" Shelley chuckled.

"I didn't sleep at all in that disgusting lockup, and I still haven't showered. I don't have a car, and they might still be ransacking my house."

Shelley gasped. "It's a good thing I do the books for Bella's at my house, or we'd be in the soup."

"Soup sounds good," I said. "I'm starving. We both missed lunch."

Just like it was on cue, the door to Bella's opened with a jingle, and in walked my mother with a bag of steaming hot bagels from Ben's. She put it down on the counter, and the unbearably enticing aroma wafted over.

"You two are a mess," she said. "And you'd better clean up, Bella. I have another date for you tonight."

"I stood up to my full five-foot-six frame, totally unembarrassed at this moment by my high tops. "No more dates, Mom. I've had it!"

"I know that Bernstein fellow didn't work out, but..."

"Didn't work out? He's a pervert and a stalker. I don't care if his mother goes to your beauty shop. And no more Christopher Bluestein!" It must have been the night in jail, the lack of sleep or a shower, an overload of stress, or all of the above, but I had developed a backbone. I opened the bag and grabbed a bagel.

"Is that the way to talk to your mother?" Her voice actually did sound hurt.

"Sorry, Mom," I said, my mouth full of too much bagel to swallow. I chewed a moment more, but my words were still garbled by my mouthful. "I know you mean well, but no more dates."

"But this one's a winner," she started.

I swallowed a huge wad of bagel. "How would you know? You thought Larry Bernstein was a nice guy. And after that, you brought me Barbara's uncle."

"What?" Shelley gasped.

I'd forgotten that I hadn't had a chance to fill in Shelley about the Christopher Bluestein fiasco.

Just then, my phone started up with "I'm bad, I'm bad." I looked at the readout. The guy must have had mental telepathy. It was Larry Bernstein. I hit ignore with maybe more oomph than I needed.

"Who was that?" Shelley had a bagel in each hand.

"The pervert himself."

"You don't have to call him that, dear," said my mother, ever polite.

"He's turned on by the fact that he thinks I killed Robert! He likes dangerous women! I am *not* a dangerous woman!" I gestured with my bagel as I talked with my hands, my mouth half full.

"You know, you could thank me for getting you out of jail." My mother's voice sounded one hundred-percent hurt.

My anger went poof. You have to admit it; she's good. She can turn me from angry to feeling about two inches tall with just one sentence. I think they teach that in Advanced Jewish Mother 303, but I'd obviously missed the class.

I dropped the bagel on the counter and gave my mother a good hug. She's about a half-head shorter than me and smells of Estee Lauder and hairspray. "I'm sorry, Mom," I said, and I really meant it. "I'm just going through a lot right now."

She hugged me back. "I'll tell you what," she said, now clearly in the advantage and making good use of it. "First, we'll clear your name, and then you'll meet him — Dr. Daniel Bienstock. He's a podiatrist."

I looked down at my high tops with resignation and shrugged. "We'll talk."

"Atta girl," said my mother.

I could feel Shelley glaring at my back. She *never* gives in to my mom. Apparently, I just don't have the backbone gene. More likely, I still feel residual guilt from the way my dad died of a heart attack the same night he blew a gasket when I'd been out late. Fair or not, it's the unspoken reason my mom holds sway over me.

"If we're going to clear Bella's name, we have to get to work." Shelley frowned in concentration. "Think, Bella! Who else was with Myrna in the back of Hoffman-Schwartz?"

"There was Ben and Stella and, of course, the rest of the family, Adam and Ethan." I paused for another bite of my bagel. "Then there was Janine, and Barbara! Did Barbara visit with Myrna?"

"Everyone did," said Shelley. "I don't think Myrna moved from that chair the whole time she was there."

"So that means anyone could have done it." I hit my forehead with my bagel, genuinely angry with myself yet again. "What an idiot I am, leaving my purse out in the open!"

"Who knew someone would plant evidence in there?" Shelley was trying to console me for my stupidity, but it wasn't working.

"It was careless of me. I shouldn't have done that."

Even my mother tried to comfort me. "It's not your fault an evil person is trying to make you look guilty, dear."

Shelley grabbed a raisin bagel and bit into it. "We have to fight back. We need a plan. How about we meet tonight?" Her voice was muddled by the bagel.

We set the time for eight-thirty, the same time as the

appointment I'd missed the night before, for my stay in the lovely downtown Royal Oak jailhouse. I texted Heather, Vic, and Marcy. They all texted back, saying they'd get there as close to eight-thirty as possible, as they were obviously going to be at the Shiva house at Gramma Myrna's. Shelley said Mitch had to be at a function for Elena, and I happily gave my mother and Albert dispensation, as they'd already done so much for me. That, and they had season tickets that night for the Fisher Theatre in downtown Detroit. So, all told, there would be five of us.

Five rank amateurs trying to save my hide. The bagel started feeling heavy in my stomach, and it occurred to me I'd better find a good lawyer. Fast.

AFTER SHELLEY packed up all our jewelry into the safe and left Bella's Baubles for the day, I sat at her desk with my fingers on her laptop keyboard, in no rush to get home. I was pretty sure the police still had both of my computers. In the old days, I would have slid my manicured finger down the yellow pages to find an attorney, seeing that Mitch's referral was such a dud. But instead, I found myself in the midst of a Google search, feeling more pathetic by the minute.

I typed in "royal oak mi criminal attorney" and I was frankly shocked to find so many results. I couldn't remember the last time there was a murder in the city. But as I clicked through the links, I could see most of the lawyers didn't practice criminal law. Instead, I saw divorce, bankruptcy, employment law, and personal injury, until finally, almost at the bottom of the first page was Fosner and McGriff. A Jew and a crime dog, go figure.

As Boodles did his bullet jump and landed on my lap, I clicked on each of their photos and read the descriptions. Roy McGriff looked like a tough guy, someone you wouldn't want to mess with in a bar. Fosner was a different kind of animal. Mild-featured, he looked more like a pleasant schoolteacher, complete with wire-rimmed glasses and a benevolent smile. Both had been assistant prosecuting attorneys until they'd switched sides and gone into criminal defense in the early to late '80s. Best yet, they were located on Main Street, within walking distance of my store. It was already six-thirty, but I took a chance and called. After the fourth ring, I was ready to hang up.

"Fosner and McGriff," said a male voice.

"Oh, you're still there," I said, feeling more nervous than relieved. I was still digesting the fact that I needed a criminal attorney.

"It's actually after hours, and that's why I'm the one answering the phone," said the voice. "I'm Max Fosner. Is this *the* Bella Blumer?"

"Caller ID?" I asked.

"Yep, I have to say that I'm intrigued. Are you looking for representation?

"Well, that depends." My mind flashed on Richard McIntyre. "I need to know what you think about my, um, situation, and of course, I need to know what you charge."

"All I know is what I've seen in the news," he said, "and I know enough to not believe everything I read."

I felt my chest tighten with fear. I'd been purposely not watching the news, listening to the radio, or even looking at the paper.

"According to the press, for the time being, you are public enemy number one."

I sucked in my breath and let out an audible sigh. "At least it's good for business."

"That's good," he chuckled, "because I charge three-hundred fifty an hour."

I grasped Boodles' curls so tightly he squeaked and jumped off my lap. "I'm not a rich woman. I don't think I had the best divorce attorney."

Fosner laughed, and the deep hearty sound of it soothed my nerves. "I'm recovering from my own divorce, too," he said. "It's been nearly eight months. That's why I moved into the Lofts on Main."

"Isn't that just above your office?"

"That's right."

Boodles sniffed at my ankles, probably wondering whether it was safe to jump on my lap, or if he'd get his fur pulled out again, poor dog. I absent-mindedly pulled him back on my lap. "I can't have an attorney who thinks I'm guilty." There. I put it right out there.

"Even guilty people deserve a good defense. That's how our system works."

"But I am *not* guilty. I did not kill Robert Blumer."

There was a silence on the line. "Listen, Bella; let's say that I have an open mind. You sound sincere, but what you have going against you is that murders are seldom random. We tend to murder the people we know. From what I read, there is pretty hefty circumstantial evidence against you."

"It doesn't matter," I said, "because I didn't do it. Someone else did, and if we concentrate our efforts on that, that circumstantial evidence won't mean squat."

There was a short silence. "Okay, Bella, I'll bite. I'm looking at my calendar, and I'm totally booked tomorrow. I'd say this is pretty much an emergency. Why don't we meet tonight and we'll decide if we can work together?"

"How much does it cost if I decide no?" This made me nervous; I already had a bill on the way from Richard McIntyre.

"We'll make the first meeting on me," he said, "whether you sign on or not."

Now that was an offer I couldn't refuse. "My family is coming over to my house at eight-thirty tonight to try and figure out who really killed my Rob...I mean...him."

Max laughed. "You can save a bundle on investigational costs. But you have to be careful not to mess up the case."

"At least they believe that I'm innocent."

"Bella, it's nearly seven. Why don't you come here right now, and I'll order in dinner. You like Middle Eastern food?"

Did I like Middle Eastern food? I practically lived on the stuff.

"Surprise me. You mind if I bring my dog?"

"The more the merrier."

As I clicked off the phone, I had the creepy feeling someone was watching me. I looked out the front window of my shop, and standing there, looking right back at me, was none other than Larry Bernstein.

CHAPTER 13

arry knocked on the door to my shop. This made me wish I had one of those old-fashioned window shades retailers used to put on their front doors and windows, so I could just pull it down right in his face.

I walked up to the door. "Go away," I said, in a voice that meant it.

"Bella, please open the door. I have to talk to you."

I turned and looked at him. "You are a nutcase! I barely know you. We shared about fifteen minutes together on a blind date. You know nothing about me or my life, and you talk to the media like you're an expert. You are a nuisance and a headache. Go away!"

His face crumpled, and I almost felt sorry for him.

Almost. No one likes their delusions shattered, I guess.

"I'm sorry, Bella," he shouted through the glass door. "I was just trying to help."

"Stop helping! You're not doing me any good."

"Let me buy you dinner."

I couldn't believe the chutzpah of this guy. Or the insanity. I had a strong suspicion he'd be quite over me by now had I not been involved in the Robert Blumer murder case.

"Sorry, I have plans." Truth was, I'd 'have plans' whether I had plans or not, but he didn't need to know that.

"Can I walk you home?"

Oh my. Did I have to call the police on this guy? Would they think I was credible?

"Go away, or I'll call my lawyer." I reached over to grab my cell phone from my bench.

"All right, all right, I'm leaving. But you haven't heard the last of me." He finally turned and walked away.

I watched from my display window until he rounded the corner on Washington and, thankfully, disappeared from sight. I quickly put Boodles in his Bark Avenue carrier and slipped out the back door, locking it behind me. I jogged up Fourth Street to Main Street and swung around the corner. I looked left, right, and behind me and heaved a sigh of relief. No Bernstein in sight.

There was zero time to go home and change. I felt unwashed and stale, as I'd been in the same outfit, underwear included, for two days. I still wore my high-tops, courtesy of Detective Krieger, beneath my long white skirt. While it was infinitely more comfortable than my heels, it was definitely not my style. Thankfully, the style in Royal Oak is a little funkier than mine. While I would normally not be caught dead in these ugly shoes, at least I didn't stick out like a hammered thumb. I decided not to make mention of it to Max Fosner, even if I did find them embarrassing.

I ducked into the Double D Cupcake Company. Their oversized cupcakes with the signature maraschino cherry on top were the current rage. Not to mention their deep dark coffees, espressos, and cappuccinos. I generally split my coffee time between Ben's and Double Ds.

"Three Double Ds and a cappuccino," I said to the girl behind the counter. She was a younger version of Heather, probably still in Royal Oak High School, decked out in unnaturally black hair and an oddly attractive spider nose ring.

"What flavor?" She shifted her weight to one side, sort of striking a pose.

I checked out all the Double Ds: dark chocolate, milk chocolate, caramel, and vanilla. That seemed to cover the basics. Beyond that were cherry frosted, chocolate chip, and something that looked like bumpy cake. I sighed out loud and sucked in the rich, fragrant chocolate aroma. It was a good thing I wear flowing chiffon skirts most of the time. They make it easier to indulge now and then, without cramping my style.

"I'll take a dark chocolate, a lemon torte, and a vanilla, please." The vanilla was for Boodles. Fosner could have the second choice.

She handed me my change and the bag of cupcakes. I curled the top of the white bag into a handle and looked up and down the street, watching out for Larry Bernstein. When the coast appeared to be clear, I made certain that Boodles was snug in his blue felt carrier, and we high-tailed it out of there.

It was nearly seven-twenty and the sun was dazzling off the sidewalk in front of the offices of Fosner & McGriff. I tried the door, but it was locked. Then I noticed a buzzer to the left.

"Bella, is that you?" A male voice spoke through the intercom.

"Yes, just me and Boodles."

I opened the door to a buzzing sound and walked into a lavishly appointed waiting room. I sat in an Ethan Allen leather wingback chair with the Boodles bag on my lap, and my lime purse and crinkled Double D bag on the floor.

A door beyond the reception area opened, and in walked Max. He wasn't exactly what I expected, even after seeing the photo on his website. And why did I have to measure everyone up to Robert Blumer? For one thing, Max Fosner was just about my height, maybe an inch or three taller, but he made up for it with his stocky build, not to mention a little bit of extra heft on the front and sides. My guess was that Max Fosner might be able to finish off all three Double Ds as an appetizer before we ever got to dinner.

He grasped my right hand in a firm and extended handshake.

"Welcome, Bella," he said. "Now come into my office. We have a lot of work to do." He glanced at my high tops.

"Long story," I said. "I just got out of jail this morning."

"Judging by the rest of you, I wouldn't think those would be your style." Max Fosner made me smile.

With one short comment, I felt understood.

Boodles peered over the top of his carrier, with nary a peep. Apparently, Max Fosner passed the friend or foe test. I followed Max through a short corridor, past some enormous copy machines, and into his office that had a window onto Main. This was high-end real estate, with the fees to match. A large, blond, curly dog unfurled himself from his spot on the floor and bumped his nose directly toward my crotch.

"Oh, excuse my manners." Max chuckled. "This is my dog, Chester. I won custody in the divorce."

"Nice to meet you, Chester." I patted his head. "The little guy in the carrier is Boodles."

Chester sniffed the bottom of Boodles' carrier. At the sound of his name, Boodles' tail went into high gear. He sniffed right back at Chester, and then all five pounds of him leapt into the air and out of his carrier. He landed on the floor, and the two dogs went right into the sniffing game.

"Looks like our little guys get along." Max opened a brown paper bag. I could smell garlicky hummus and falafel as I settled into a comfy, brown suede armchair across from his desk. Boodles jumped up on my lap, his snout in the air. I always figure that if I can smell something, it must be driving Boodles crazy with desire.

"Do you mind if he's loose in your office?"

"Is he likely to anoint anything?" So Max had a sense of humor. I liked that.

"Only if he hates you, and so far, so good."

Max chuckled. "I'll keep that in mind. Falafel?"

"Thanks." I reached over and filled my Styrofoam plate with falafel, hummus, pita, and the most amazing dark green salad. From my lime bag I opened a bag of kibble and sprinkled it onto a paper plate for Boodles. Max threw Chester a full order of pita.

"That doesn't seem fair." Max laughed.

"Don't worry, Boodles gets to lick the hummus and dressing off my plate when I'm done. It's a deal we've worked out."

"How much does he weigh?"

"About five pounds wet." It doesn't take much to fill up Boodles.

Max pulled a bowl from his bottom drawer and filled it with bottled water for the two dogs. I was impressed. Love me, love my dog. That's my motto, and considering that I'd never had a dog till the year Robert left me, it was a new one, but no less true.

After our quick dinner, Max and I crumpled our used napkins into the Beirut Bistro bag, and Boodles efficiently licked my plate while Chester stretched out in front of the leather couch. I pulled out the Double D cupcakes, and once I explained that Boodles and Chester would have to split the vanilla, Max chose the lemon torte. "For professional reasons," he quipped.

"Speaking of professional, I have to tell you that it will be hard for me to afford you at $350 an hour."

"Don't worry, dinner and our time so far is on the house."

I looked at my cell phone. "It's nearly seven-thirty now, and my family is coming to my house at eight-thirty."

He frowned. "Where do you live?"

"On Fourth, about five blocks east of Main."

He smiled. "That's practically around the block. No problem. So let's get started."

As Boodles climbed onto my lap and started to lick his face and his paws like a cat, I started to tell my tale, starting with my divorce from Robert one year ago. I told Max everything bad I'd ever said about Robert and Barbara, and everyone I'd said it too. I told him about Vic's call on Monday, about finding Robert dead, about the pre-nup between Barbara and Robert that, in my opinion, set Robert up for murder. I was surprised to find myself crying at this point, like I was in a psychologist's office. Max handed me a ready box of tissues. Maybe criminals cry a lot; he was prepared. I even told him about my family and my mother and Larry Bernstein. Max sat and nodded, listening intently.

"So do you think I have a chance?"

"It doesn't look good for you, but there's always a chance."

"That doesn't sound good enough," I said, clutching poor Boodles to my chest. He squirmed away and hopped into his safe carrier.

"They have you on motive, you don't have an alibi, and the spent shell casings point to a gun registered in your name." He leaned back in his chair, his face grim. "Not to mention the two diamonds found in your possession—at the police station, no less." He made a sound that was half laugh, half groan.

My head fell into my hands, my elbows on my knees. "I know it sounds terrible, what they have on me, but I really didn't do it." I stared at the nubby texture of his carpet. "If they lock me up, someone else is going to get away with murder."

There was a silence in the room so thick you could cut it with a knife. Boodles looked up at me, and I was ready, once again, to move on to another attorney, if I only could find one who didn't think I was guilty.

Then he said it. "I believe you, Bella."

I turned my face up in my hands, resting my chin on my open palms. "You do?"

"It looks like someone's framed you well, and it's going to be our job to figure out who."

I could have jumped up and kissed him. Instead, I whispered a "thank you," and I blinked back tears in an effort not to look pathetic.

"Here, have another tissue." Fosner handed me his box of Kleenex.

I grabbed a few and dabbed under my mascara. I probably looked like a wreck by now, between my face and those terrible shoes. I blew my nose. "What time is it?"

"It's eight-twenty. Want me to drop you off at your house?"

I hesitated. Fosner was nice and helpful, but at $350 an hour, I wasn't sure I could afford the friendship.

"Off the clock," he said, reading my mind, just like Heather.

Boodles hopped into his carrier, and Max turned off all the lights and punched a code in the alarm pad at the front door.

"Can't be too careful," he said. "I usually work with criminals, you know."

I let Boodles out of his carrier, so he could water the carefully manicured boxwoods outside Max's office door. Chester did the same.

Boodles hopped back into his carrier just before I slid into the passenger seat of Max's late-model Lexus. Chester jumped into the back seat and sat calmly looking out the window, as if he was quite used to having company in the car. Max expertly drove us to Eleven Mile, and then took Lafayette to Fourth Street. My red brick bungalow was on the right, two blocks past Washington.

"That's my house, the one with the old VW bug in the front."

"Your car?"

"No, that's my daughter's. My Escalade is being held hostage with the Royal Oak Police."

"Good thing it's an Escalade," Max said, as he put the Lexus into park. "Or I was going to suggest we sue your divorce attorney for malpractice."

I gathered up my lime bag and Boodles' carrying case. Just then, Marcy and Vic drove up in Marcy's Escort, and Shelley pulled up in her gray Prius.

"Thanks for taking my case," I said, and I really meant it. It was a monumental relief to have a lawyer who believed I was innocent. Of murder, no less.

"Want me to join in your posse?"

I paused. Nice as he was, who could afford this guy?

"Off the clock."

This guy could really read my face. Maybe that's how he knew I was telling him the truth.

I bent over and talked through his open window. "Are you sure you want to donate so much time to me, I mean, my case?"

He smiled. "Not sure why, but yes, I really want to."

Was that a sparkle in his eye? Was Max Fosner interested in more than a case? Or was he just a lonely guy getting used to his divorce? All I knew was that I was glad for the help—and I wasn't going to worry about anything beyond that just yet.

CHAPTER 14

"Mom? Are you coming?" It was Heather, standing at the front door of my bungalow.

I turned to Max. "Come on in. I need all the help I can get."

Heather had set the table with five bottles of spring water and a stack of legal pads and pens for note taking.

"We left the Shiva at Gramma Myrna's as early as we could," said Marcy, pulling the hair off the back of her neck to cool herself from the heat outside. "I think Gramma Myrna might have been upset."

"Well, this is kind of important," I said.

I looked around my house. Everything looked to be in place, with the exception of my computer, which no longer sat on a desk in my living room. I stifled a sigh.

Heather brought out some cookies from the kitchen as we sat around my dining room table. It was very quiet until I realized why.

"Everyone, this is Max Fosner, my new lawyer." I then went around the table and introduced him to Marcy, Vic, Shelley, and Heather. I'd already given Mitch my opinion of Richard McIntyre, and he'd apologized profusely, even though it obviously wasn't his fault. But Mitch couldn't be there that night because he was busy with one of Elena's activities.

"I'll be a fly on the wall," said Max, "and I'll try not to interfere unless there's a legal issue."

Vic, never one to mince words, ignored Max and looked me straight in the eye. "Can we trust him, Mom?"

I nodded. "He's the only one outside the family who believes I'm innocent."

"The only thing your mother is guilty of is a big mouth," said Max.

The room erupted in nervous laughter, so I assumed he spoke the truth. I pushed off the bad feeling; I had bigger fish to fry.

"So what's your plan of action?" asked Max.

So much for the 'fly on the wall' thing. One big mouth knows another.

"We all think it was Barbara, my dad's wife," said Heather. "I don't trust her at all."

"But would she commit murder?" asked Vic, ever even-handed in the treatment of his father's second wife, even after his father's death.

There was a still silence after Vic's question.

Then Max broke in. "This isn't exactly legal, but I can tell you from experience that there isn't a special look for a murderer. Anyone in the right circumstances is a potential criminal. So what is the circumstance? What motive would Barbara have to murder your dad?"

"Follow the money." Heather nervously ran her fingers through her pansy-pink hair.

"You mean the pre-nup?" asked Max.

Heather glanced at me, aware now that I'd already told Max everything.

"That's right," she said. "If she divorced Dad, or he divorced her, she wouldn't get more than a year's salary. What does she make? Forty-thousand? Fifty? But if he died, she gets it all."

"Not exactly," said Vic. "Dad has a will he's hinted about. I don't think he would have mentioned it to me if I wasn't getting something."

"Plus their house, his car, any personal accounts. Sweet deal," said Heather, her tone both sarcastic and bitter.

"You think she married him for his money?" asked Max.

This time, Marcy spoke up. "My father-in-law was a charming man, and I'm sure Barbara found him attractive, but there's more to it."

"What do you mean?," asked Max.

"I clean teeth at Saperstein's, and I get a good idea of what's going on in town. It's amazing how much people can say at a place where there's a hand in their mouth half the time." She smiled.

"So what's the word on the street?" asked Max. "Or should I say the word in the chair?"

"Barbara was practically engaged to Dan Eckles when she first started her job at Blumer's. Then she got involved with Vic's dad, and married him in a hurry, like she was pregnant or something. Only she wasn't."

Vic sat up straighter at the table, like he was starting to believe in the possibility that Barbara murdered his dad. "But if she did it, why would she murder him now?" he asked.

It occurred to me in a flash. "Because she wanted to frame *me*! She knew very well it was the anniversary of our divorce. And killing him that day — with my gun, no less — would absolutely point the finger at me!"

"Getting away with murder," agreed Heather.

"Did Barbara have an opportunity to slip the diamonds in your purse?" asked Max.

Now that was a good question. "I don't know. She never sat with Myrna at the funeral as far as I can remember." I paused. "You see, that's where I left my purse — on the floor next to Robert's mother. I'd love to say yes to that, but I can't."

"Maybe someone else is in on it with her," said Heather.

"Maybe Dan Eckles," said Marcy. "He was at the funeral, and he spent a lot of time consoling Barbara."

"But Barbara was with Loozie when Dad was killed." Leave it to Vic to come to Barbara's defense.

"Well, maybe I'll have to talk with Ms. Loozie tomorrow. When does Barbara meet her?" I asked.

"When they meet, it's usually at Double Ds at about 11:00 AM for coffee." Vic coughed out a wry chuckle. "And then they sometimes stay long enough to take an early lunch."

Shelley leaned forward in her chair. "I'll be at Bella's in time for you to go to Double Ds tomorrow morning." Her hair fell shapelessly to the side of her face, and she wore zero makeup to accent her jeans and light blue sweater. I don't think God ever made a better sister, even if he forgot to give her even a touch of fashion sense.

"Thanks, Shell, I'll take you up on that." I noticed that Vic was massaging his forehead and both temples.

"Please don't worry, Vic," I said, even though I was out of my mind with worry myself.

"It's not just that." Vic frowned.

"What is it, Honey?" In truth, I was now worried for Vic as much as for myself.

He dropped his hands from his forehead. "Remember I told you we're having problems with the business bank account?"

Now I felt guilty. I'd been so wrapped up in my own catastrophe, I'd totally forgotten. "Yes, of course I remember." It was a fib, but a minor one. It's not like I didn't care. I did.

"What's going on?" Shelley sat up at attention. Bookkeeping was her strong suit, and she loves my children as her own—as I love her sweet Elena.

Vic explained how for the past year the Blumer Fine Jewelers bank account, once plump and ever liquid, had become increasingly lean, even to the point of Robert recently borrowing money from the bank to make payroll.

"That's exactly as long as Barbara's been involved," said Shelley.

"That may be," said Vic, "but Barbara's always been in sales; she has nothing to do with our bank account, or with payroll, for that matter."

"Then who does your books?" asked Shelley.

"Janine's done it forever," said Vic.

I thought back on how Janine had changed through the years. When she first came to Blumer's, she'd been in her mid-thirties, a red-hot redhead, married to a hunky car mechanic, Tom Jenkins. Now, ten years later, she was more than plump and very worn out. She'd lost her sense of style and wore neutral-beige matronly clothes. Even her crowning glory of shiny hair had lost its luster and was turning a mousy brown. "She's been with Blumer's for the past ten years," I said.

"Yeah," said Vic, "and she's always done the books, and they've always been fine till now."

"I'm sure Barbara's doing it somehow." Heather absent-mindedly twisted her paper napkin.

"Who's your CPA?" asked Shelley. Even though Mitch was a CPA, Robert had always preferred to use a firm outside the family.

"Wreight and Buxbaum," said Vic. "But they only look at our books once a year. Janine sends in the reports, and they put it all together at year end."

Shelley was at the edge of her seat. "So you're telling me that Janine has always done the monthly reconciliation?"

"Janine would always do month end, and Dad would okay it," said Vic.

"Did he read it over well?" asked Shelley.

"I don't think he had to. Janine is practically family at Blumer's." Vic sat back in his chair. "Say, you don't think Janine would steal from us, do you?"

Shelley didn't answer. "Let's find out," she said. "Do you use QuickBooks? Are you the administrator?"

"Yes and no," said Vic. "Janine is the Admin, but I have all the passwords."

"Well, good," said Shelley. "I want you to get a four gig flash drive and make a backup copy of all your QuickBook records. Do that and either give me your last six months of bank statements or your online codes so I can check your statements online. I'll see if I can figure out what's going on."

Now I knew this was not a plan Robert would have approved of. He'd never wanted to share our company financial information with anyone outside the immediate family unless, of course, you counted Janine and our CPA. But it was becoming painfully clear that Robert wasn't here anymore, and his approval no longer mattered. I felt a deep sadness and an unaccountable sense of loss. Robert's grip on earth was fading.

"No problem, Aunt Shelley," said Vic, making notes to himself on his cell phone. "I'll get it to you tomorrow."

The room went silent, and it started to feel late. I really wanted to wrap things up and go to bed, my bed. The image of living in a penitentiary, complete with cold cinderblock walls and a urine-stained cot, had started to creep into my psyche, and I was doing everything in my power to push that image out. "Any other thoughts?" I asked no one in particular.

"Well, there is one more thing," said Vic. He paused.

Well, spill it, I wanted to say, but instead I just said, "Go ahead, Honey." I could raise my voice to Heather and throw an occasional plate or two, but always had to be careful with Vic. I had to give Marcy credit. She was probably a saint.

"I didn't tell the police yet, but I looked through Dad's personal files, and I know who the two diamonds were for," he said. "I mean, he only intended to buy one, but Dad was going to show him both so he could make a choice."

We all sat in stunned silence until I finally blurted, "Well, who?"

Vic spoke under his breath, as if he were embarrassed. It sounded like, "Dolly Beezus."

"Who?" I repeated.

"Ollie Gleason," Vic said out loud, and I couldn't help but notice him blush. What was the big deal anyway?

"Well, that's wonderful!" I said. "Glenda will be thrilled."

Vic hung his head. "It wasn't for Mrs. Gleason. That's why Dad kept it hush-hush."

I felt the blood rush to my head, which apparently makes my internal censor shut down. "So, Ollie took a cue from your dad and has a bimbette on the side." It was more of a declaration than a question. For some reason it stung, as if I'd been betrayed all over again. "What a scumbag," I said, apparently unable to contain my thoughts when dealing with low-life cheaters, even if they weren't my ex-husband.

"You have to tell the police." Max shifted uncomfortably in his seat. "Unless they ask, you don't have to offer the information that the diamonds were not for his wife."

"Can't Vic wait until I've had a chance to talk to dear old Ollie?" I asked, relishing the chance to ambush the randy old jerk.

Max put both hands up in the air, palms forward. "Of course, if Vic is real busy tomorrow and he calls the police by...say... two o'clock in the afternoon that would be reasonable." He looked in my direction. "And it's very clear that Vic's mother is an adult and he has no control over who she might talk with in a given day."

All that, and he didn't even wink. You had to love the guy.

I looked at the clock. It was nearly eleven. "That's it for tonight," I said. "I think we have a plan for tomorrow. I'll check out Loozie at the Double D and see if I can blow Barbara's alibi."

Vic pushed back in his chair. "Well, I don't think it has anything to do with helping you, Mom, but I'll get the info to Aunt Shelley."

Shelley stood up. "Just to be careful; don't tell Janine what we're doing. She's probably innocent, but in case she's not, let's not clue her in. She could start playing with the books — if she hasn't already."

Max pushed back in his chair, and Boodles hopped onto his lap. "Looks like I made a friend tonight."

Chester pulled himself up from his nap and started licking both Max and Boodles.

Everyone stood, and Heather and I saw everyone to the front door with much hugging and kissing. As I shut the door on Max Fosner and my family, it occurred to me that Boodles might pick 'em better than I do.

CHAPTER 15

hardly slept at all that night, despite the warm and fuzzy goodbyes. It was as if my brain was on speed. I couldn't stop thinking about Ollie Gleason and Barbara. Was Barbara literally pointing the finger at me because she truly believed I murdered Robert? Or was it a way to deflect the blame from herself?

And then there was Janine. It was getting evident that she was probably a liar and a thief. But there's a long jump from that to suspecting that she was a murderer. I couldn't make heads or tails out of Ollie. He and Robert had been best friends! Robert kept Ollie's secrets and, most likely, vice versa.

I tried to force my mind to happy thoughts. I focused on Boodles. And Chester. But that made me think of Max and my case. Then my thoughts would swirl and always come back to Barbara, the home wrecker that was still ruining my life. My gut told me it was her. But I couldn't be sure if my gut was being accurate or vindictive. The thought of Barbie Baby in jail was just so satisfying.

Despite my truly serious problems, I also worried about Max in a personal way. I had the impression that he was interested in me — and not just because of my case. While I really enjoyed his company, the heart wants what it wants. It's been that way for me since high school. And I couldn't help but feel that all the extra attention and unpaid hours showed more than a friendly interest.

When I finally fell asleep, I had fitful dreams of Barbara walking off with Heather and Vic, laughing as she waved goodbye. I'd startle awake and fall asleep, only to be ripped from sleep again and again with the jarring images. It's not a good way to sleep. Or live.

Of course, when the clock rang at six on Friday morning, I was a complete wreck. I reset it for seven, at which time I grudgingly pulled myself out of bed.

"Morning, Mom," said Heather, as I staggered down the steps and into the kitchen.

I let Boodles out the back door and poured myself a cup of Heather's strong coffee.

"You don't look so good," she said.

"Flattery will get you everything." I slid into the dining room chair across from her.

"Sorry," she said. "But it's true. You feel okay?"

"I'm not so good. It's tough stuff being public enemy number one."

Heather didn't answer, just looked down into her coffee.

"How are you doing, Honey?" My thoughts flitted over to Jason Rosen, he of the spineless behavior.

Heather pursed her lips. "I haven't heard from him in over twenty-four hours. If he wants to make up with me, he's the one who has to call."

Having kids is a double-edged sword. They bring such joy from the moment you feel the first kick. But when they're in pain, you feel it as your own.

"I'm so sorry." If I'd only kept my mouth shut this past year, rather than venting to every working ear in the Royal Oak area, Heather might not be so unhappy right now. But rather than address that worry, I said, "I know there's no Shiva tonight, because it's Friday. But are you going to be at Gramma's?" Friday night is the official beginning of the Jewish Sabbath, so people don't sit Shiva then.

Heather frowned. "There's no Shiva anymore, but Gramma still expects the immediate family over for dinner. I don't think I can take any more of it. This will be three nights straight with Barbara."

"So is this the last night?

"I think this is it. Good thing. I think Uncle Ben will explode if he sees Barbara for even one more minute."

I thought of my conversation with Ben at his coffee shop.

"I think he can deal with one more night, but probably not much more."

I scooped up a quarter cup of kibble for Boodles and let him in the back door, where he'd been standing in silent anticipation of breakfast.

Heather sat up taller in her seat. "So where are you going first?"

I watched Boodles daintily chow down on his kibble. "I guess it makes sense for me to see Ollie first, so I can get to Double Ds in time to check out Barbara's alibi and still not miss so much work." I crinkled my nose at the thought of checking up on Barbara.

"Okay, that makes sense."

We finished our second cups of coffee in companionable silence, and then I went upstairs to do my hair and get dressed. After days of fear, of wanting to blend in and hide, I decided to be myself. I put on my long, pink gauzy skirt and topped it with a matching cotton shell, then accented with my apple green designer jacket. I added one of my green peridot and pink quartz creations to make it all work. Fortified with a relatively comfortable pair of matching green espadrilles, I was ready to face the day.

I fluffed my hair from medium to big, invited Boodles into his Bark Avenue carrier, and we marched out the door together. I felt as formidable as a pit bull, even if my sidekick was a miniature Bichon. Fearsome is as fearsome does.

MY FIRST stop of the day was an early-morning pick-up of my trusty Escalade. The police had called to let me know it was mine once more. I had to assume they found nothing incriminating in it. But of course, they told me nothing. This made me a little uneasy.

It felt wonderful to climb back up into my very own driver's seat with my lovable dog on my lap. I happily adjusted my seat and mirrors. My cell phone rang out its "I'm bad, I'm bad" before I had a chance to pull out of the police parking structure.

It was Vic. "Hi, Mom, just want to give you a head's up."

"Oh? What is it?" I made a left turn out of the police parking structure and into the land of the free. The paperwork had taken so long that it was nearly ten o'clock.

"The police were here this morning, Detectives Krieger and Riley."

"Oh. What did you tell them?" I worried that I'd lost the element of surprise when confronting Ollie.

"I told them that the diamonds were for Mr. Gleason, but they didn't ask if it was for Mrs. Gleason, so I didn't say." He paused. "I didn't like it. It felt like I was lying."

"They'll find out soon enough," I said.

"That may be, but watch out for them. I think they were planning to question Mr. Gleason today."

The Gleason Cadillac-Chevy dealership is on Main Street, a little further north of Eleven Mile than Max's office. I made a right into the parking lot and scouted for a spot over a sea of cars. If Ollie wasn't selling cars, at least the service business appeared to be enough to keep him in a better class of toupee.

With no Krieger or Riley in sight, I pulled Boodles and my lime bag out of the car and walked past the service bays, heading toward the main showroom and Ollie's office.

"Is that you, Bella?

I was started by a male voice. It was Tom Jenkins, Janine's husband. I knew him well from old Blumer Fine Jewelers office parties in years past, when I was still the boss's wife.

"Hi, Tom. How's it going?" It felt awkward seeing him while I was on an investigative mission.

He gave me a nervous smile. Tom had always been such a nice guy. "I'm thinking it must be tough going for you lately." Now that was an understatement. "I'm sorry I didn't make it to Robert's funeral."

"You don't have to apologize to me." I was no longer the boss's wife and hadn't been for some time now.

"Well, I would have come, but I've taken up all my personal days this year already."

"Oh, have you been ill?" I wondered exactly why Tom had used up all his days by mid-July.

He blushed and stammered. "I'm part-time, and they're

not too flexible when it's my day to work."

I thought it was odd that Tom would be a part-timer after all his years at Gleason's, but I didn't ask about it. But it did bring a spontaneous — and nosy — thought to mind.

"That was some car Janine drove to the funeral, this year's Cadillac sedan."

He glanced at his watch, and his mouth twisted into an irritated frown. "Uh, I'd better get back to work."

I thought he was a little short with me, but I decided to make nothing of it. Either he was nervous to be around someone he thought had committed murder, or he was just worried about his job. Either way, it really didn't much matter. We said quick goodbyes with well wishes and headed our separate ways in the July heat. I could practically see the steam rising off the parking lot blacktop as Boodles and I made our way to the showroom.

I headed straight for Ollie's office, bypassing the receptionist's desk. Not only had Ollie been Robert's best friend, but also I'd bought my Escalade and every car before it at this very dealership, since my marriage to Robert.

Ollie's office door was ajar, so I knocked and burst in at the same time. "Hi Ollie." I pasted a cheery smile on my face.

Ollie was bent over a file cabinet. He pivoted so fast his toupee looked slightly askew as he faced me. "What are you doing here?"

His unfriendly tone made me wince. "Relax, Ollie, I've

just come to ask you a few questions."

He bunched his lips together. "The police just left. I told them everything I know."

"Did you tell them that the diamonds were not for Glenda?" Geez, my voice sounded harsh, like he was cheating on me, not his wife.

His thick lips pursed into a giant frown. "Now where would you hear something like that?"

"I have my sources."

"I was buying them for Glenda." His jowls shook slightly, and his voice wavered.

"Then why all the cloak and dagger stuff, Ollie? Why didn't you just come into the store with Glenda and pick them out?"

Ollie put his hand over his mouth, and then straightened his toupee. "Uh, oh, it was supposed to be a surprise, that's why."

What a lousy liar.

"You could have come to the store alone." I could hear my voice rise in anger. "Come on, Ollie, it wasn't for Glenda, was it?"

Now it was Ollie's turn to get angry. "So what's it to you? What difference does it make? Why don't you mind your own business and get off my back!"

I put my hands on Ollie's desk. "The difference is that I need to know the truth. I need facts. I have to understand what happened that day because I'm the one in trouble here — and I didn't kill Robert!"

Ollie grabbed onto his desk, and pulled up to a standing position. "Are you saying I killed him, Bella? What are you getting at?"

I was momentarily stunned. I hadn't thought of Ollie as a suspect up to this point. "No, I'm not saying that at all. I just want to know what your plans were on Monday. When were you supposed to meet Robert and look at the diamonds?"

Ollie sat back in his chair, obviously relieved. "Rob was supposed to come here at eleven to show me the diamonds." He stared at his hands. "After that, we were going to head out to an early lunch at George's." He looked up. "But he never showed."

I wanted to tell Ollie how much pain he was causing by choosing to buy a diamond for someone new, when he was still married to Glenda, his wife of thirty-two years. But I didn't want to spoil the Hallmark moment.

"Thanks, Ollie. I'd better be leaving now."

"That's a good idea." His eyes were back on his hands.

Neither one of us said goodbye as I grabbed Boodles and left. I opened two car doors to let the heat out of my Escalade. It was nearly ten forty-five, and it was already a hot one. I called Vic on his cell.

"Vic speaking."

"Did you figure out a way to keep Barbara in the store?"

"Just a moment please." Vic put me on hold and picked

up about a nanosecond later. "Hi, Mom. I'm in my office with the door shut, so now I can speak openly."

"So what's the deal? Should I go to Double Ds?"

"Yes, go right now. Barbara always meets Loozie there at eleven, and it's about ten to eleven right now."

"What did you say to Barbara to keep her in the store?

"Marcy had one of her friends call about five minutes ago to make an appointment to shop for an engagement ring—but only with Barbara."

"But what if Barbara calls Loozie?"

"I've got it covered. I told Barbara to start setting up for the client in the diamond room, and told her that I would call Loozie. But, of course, I won't. I'll claim I just got too busy and forgot."

"What about her cell phone?"

Vic sounded nervous. "It's Blumer store policy not to take your cell into the diamond room. Distractions can destroy the sales process. You know that."

"What if Barbara calls Loozie on the store line?"

"She won't, or hasn't," said Vic. "I've been watching her every move. Oh, a customer's at the counter. Gotta go!" And he clicked off.

At this moment, I'd already parked my Escalade back in my garage where it belonged and I was fairly sprinting to Double Ds in my green espadrilles, my hair and Boodles' ears flying in the humid breeze.

I stopped at the corner of Fourth and Main to catch my

breath but picked right back up after a second or two. I reached the door of Double Ds at exactly nine minutes after eleven. Who needs a gym when you have a life like this?

Coffee drinkers filled more than half the walnut seats at Double Ds. People on laptops and tablets enjoyed the free Wi-Fi, and a long line of customers waited to place their orders. You could practically inhale the caffeine from the thick aroma of fresh-brewed coffee. I took a moment to catch my breath while frantically searching the crowd, looking for Loozie, who appeared to be a no-show.

I sat at a vacant table and took out my cell to call Vic.

"This is Vic," he said, after the third ring.

"Loozie's not here," I whispered into the phone. "Did Barbara have a chance to call her?"

"Negative. She's in the diamond room now."

"So, if you didn't call her, and Barbara didn't call her, where is she?"

"Beats me." His voice was clipped, his mind more on business than his mother's investigation. "Someone's at the counter. Got to go." And he clicked off.

As I slipped my cell phone in my purse, I noticed an attractive younger man sitting in the far corner, his eyes soulfully gazing at the front door. It was none other than Barbara's former fiancé, Dan Eckles. My antennae went up. Could he be waiting for Barbara?

CHAPTER 16

This was no time to be shy. My life was on the line, after all. So I pulled a doggy treat out of my purse and gave it to Boodles, who'd been getting restless from all his time in the carrier.

Then I walked over to Eckles.

He was very handsome in a classic sort of way. His dark black hair was perfectly combed back, with one stray spot where it fell at a measured angle on his forehead. He wore a dark gray business suit, and he wore it well.

My motor was on high. "Waiting for someone?"

He startled at my words; that's how intently he'd been staring at the door.

"No."

I could tell he was lying. This guy had it bad for Barbie-girl. But bad enough to do Robert in? I figured I'd have to look into that, too.

"Then why are you staring at the door?" I hitched my lime bag up on my shoulder and put Boodles and his carrier down on the upholstered seat that Eckles evidently was saving for his date.

"What's it to you?" He said it in a tone that meant 'mind your own business.' To further prove to me that he was the perfect match for Barbara, he added, "Would you mind moving that mutt off my chair?"

Boodles growled under his breath. Sometimes I swear the dog knows more English than he lets on.

"Are you meeting Barbara?" I have to admit; sometimes I have more chutzpah than brains.

"That is none of your business." This time he said it out loud.

Boodles, bless his miniature heart, responded with a full-out growl. I distracted him with a biscuit, (Sorry, Dog Whisperer, but it works) and we headed out the door.

Out in the glaring July sunshine and hairdo-destroying humidity, I put Boodles on his leash to walk back to my shop. He needed to release some energy and liquid, and frankly, my shoulder needed a break. Five pounds isn't a lot unless it's been on your shoulder all morning.

By the time I opened the door to Bella's and enjoyed the blast of refrigerated air, it was just about eleven-thirty. Boodles made a beeline for the water dish under my bench, took his fill, and then hopped from my chair to my bench drawer, then onto my bench top, where he casually rotated himself into nap position.

Shelley looked up from her laptop. "So, what's the scoop?"

"I think I discovered a lot." I dropped my purse and Boodles' carrier on the floor and started pacing. "First I went to Ollie's, and he admitted shopping for a three-carat diamond, but he tried lying and saying it was for Glenda. When I pushed him on it, he got agitated, and wondered if I was accusing him of murdering Robert."

"Wow." Shelley frowned. "That's a weird response." She stood from her desk and started pacing with me. There's not enough room for even one person to pace in my store, but somehow we managed to make room for the two of us. We basically circled around between my bench and Shelley's desk, trying not to bump into each other.

Shelley stopped in her tracks, and I actually did bump into her, getting a face full of pin-straight Shelley hair. It smelled like herbal shampoo, but still, I brushed my face off with my fingers.

"Why don't you talk to Glenda and get her take on this?"

"I can do that. Maybe she'll tell me more than Ollie will let on." I took in a deep breath. "But..."

"But what?" asked Shelley.

"That's a pretty tricky topic for Glenda. I don't want to be the one to let her know that Ollie is, you know..." I hesitated. "A skunk."

Shelley pressed her lips tightly together and shook her head. "I don't see that you have a choice, Bella. Your neck is on the line. We have to follow every lead on this or you could spend your life in jail. If *you* won't go, *I'll* go check in on Glenda."

"You don't even know her, Shelley."

"Well, it's that important."

I rubbed my face with my hands, still careful not to smudge my makeup. "Okay, I'll go. But I'm not happy about it."

"I don't think we have a choice." Shelley flipped her hair over her shoulder. "And what did you find out at Double Ds? Was Loozie there?"

"No." I plopped down on my bench chair. "Marcy was right on target. Dan Eckles sat there, waiting for Barbara. Loozie was nowhere in sight."

"Oh my," said Shelley. "Talk about motive. Barbara, or Dan, offs Robert, they get all his money, and get to be together as a couple, maybe even in your old house."

I felt the blood rush to my head. It had been right there in front of me, but once Shelley said it out loud, it became crystal clear. That viper had come into our store—well, what used to be my store—seduced my husband, only to marry him with the intention of killing him for the money. It made perfect sense.

I picked up my lime bag and hoisted it on my shoulder.

"I'm going to Blumer's. Watch Boodles for me."

"Bella, you think that's a good idea?" Shelley's eyebrows twisted into a knot.

But it was too late; I wasn't about to listen to Shelley or anyone else. I imagine my face was beet red. I rushed out the door, my espadrilles stomping the pavement in anticipation of my confrontation with Barbara.

I don't remember much of anything till I burst through the door at Blumer Fine Jewelers. Vic sat in the diamond room with a client. Myrna and Janine were each at their desks behind the counter. Myrna looked up to say hello, but it wasn't the time for the two of us to talk. I was out for blood.

"Where's Barbara?" I peered through the showroom and the back offices; she was nowhere in sight.

Myrna glanced around, looking for her.

"She's in the john." Janine looked up from a stack of papers on her desk. "What's going on?"

"None of your business." I remembered what she'd said to me at Robert's funeral and how certain she was, like everyone else, that I'd murdered Robert.

Just then, Barbara appeared, all slim arms and perfect brown hair.

"You!" My shout took her by surprise. There were no customers in the store, except those in the diamond room with Vic, and I was hoping they wouldn't hear what I had to say.

"What?" Barbara was startled. I'd caught little Miss Mouth off guard, and it was *my* turn to be on the attack.

"I'll tell you what! You've been pointing the finger at me, mouthing off to the police and to the press. But all the time it's been you!"

Barbara glided to her desk in an effort to ignore me. I followed her.

"You've been telling Vic and everyone else that you're off meeting Loozie, when all this time you've been meeting Dan Eckles. You destroyed my marriage, and you were probably cheating on Robert the whole time!" I was livid.

"That's a lie!" Barbara finally found her voice. "I've been meeting Loozie."

"There was no Loozie there today." I held onto the old familiar Blumer's counter for support. "Only Dan Eckles, mooning at the front door waiting for you. What, did you kill Robert for the money?"

Barbara put her long red fingernails on her chest. "That's ridiculous. That doesn't prove anything." Her voice was loud, but her eyes darted left and right, like a guilty person looking for a lie.

It occurred to me that she was talking about proof, not fact, like she was living Bart Simpson's "I didn't do it. Nobody saw me do it. You can't prove anything." I think she realized it didn't look good, and she was scared. Score one for the Bella!

Just then the door to the diamond room opened, and out

walked Vic, shutting the door behind him. "What's going on out here? Why are you here, Mom?"

I looked at Vic, who was frowning, then at Myrna and Janine. Myrna looked horrified. I couldn't read Janine. Was she upset or trying to hide amusement? But then, Janine hated Barbara as much as I did, so that explained that.

"I was just leaving." I turned and walked out of Blumer Fine Jewelers without another word.

"YOU'RE KIDDING! She looked scared?" Shelley had on her disposable gloves and was wiping down the counter. She put down the spray bottle and rag. "Either she's scared because she did it—or she's scared that her affair with Eckles makes it look like she did."

"Well, I think she did it, and she's trying very hard to pin it on me!"

Shelley peeled off her plastic gloves. "You might be right, but I think we need more proof before we go to the police."

I paused, a little frustrated, because I really, really wanted to go to the police and point the finger at Barbara. Then I sighed. "You're probably right. So what do we do next?" Not only did Shelley watch more than her fair share of TV detective mysteries, but she's smart. So I listened to her.

Shelley held a finger to her chin, pondering. I was Pinky and she was The Brain. "I think we keep investigating and find out as much as we can about everybody."

I rolled some malachite beads around on my bench. "So who do I go to next?"

Then we both said together, "Glenda!"

I DECIDED to go for the element of surprise, take a chance and go directly to the Gleason's home. Glenda Gleason had been a full time housewife and mom. After their kids flew the coop, she volunteered at Temple Shalom and the very chauvinistically named Royal Oak Junior League.

The Gleason's lived on "The Hill" in Royal Oak, not too far from my former home. Theirs was a huge, English Tudor with brown brick and a beige chalet motif. I figured that despite all the volunteer hours she kept, there was a good chance I'd find Glenda at home, and it turned out I was right. The doorbell rang just once, and she appeared at the rounded front door, all five feet of her. She was short of height, but very rotund, a perfect match to Ollie. I wondered what his new model looked like.

"Hi Glenda." I felt sad about causing a bad day for Glenda Gleason, but I tried to not let it show in my voice.

"Hi, Bella, why don't you come in?" She opened the door wide and ushered me in, not at all wary of me, like her husband. She gestured toward their perfectly appointed living room, now done in all white-on-white as a testament, I'm sure, to the fact that their boys were grown and gone.

As I sat down, she said, "I've been meaning to call you. I'm so sorry I didn't make it to Robert's funeral."

"I understand. Ollie said you were under the weather."

"Hmm," she said, "well that was a good excuse, but the truth is we've been going through a tough patch in our marriage. I just couldn't handle going with him. Anywhere."

I hesitated. If I brought up the diamonds and she didn't know about them, I could be single-handedly ruining their marriage. On the other hand, if Ollie had been helpful, I wouldn't have had to be there. With the image of the Royal Oak jail in my head, I plunged in.

"Glenda, are you aware of the fact that Ollie was the one who was looking to buy a three-carat diamond, and his choice of two were stolen from Robert?"

"Omigod!" Glenda stood up, and her face turned bright red. "That bastard! He was looking to buy Loozie a diamond like that?"

Now it was my turn. "Omigod! Ollie's girlfriend is Loozie?"

Glenda gripped the back of a white wingback chair. "I don't mean to be rude, Bella, but you have to go now."

"I'm really sorry, Glenda," I said, and I meant it. More than most people, I could really understand what she was going through. "I'll let myself out."

Glenda still gripped the chair, motionless, biting both her lips, when I closed the door behind me.

I have to tell you, I felt more like a PI than a jeweler that day, even if I felt like a skunk as well. It's really not fun to crush people's lives. I left Glenda Gleason's, and slowly drove back toward downtown. I didn't rush. I didn't call Shelley. I felt too frazzled to talk. Loozie and Ollie? What, was Loozie planning a murder too?

I could see a thirty-something having interest in Robert. He was trim, handsome, and had a certain panache. But Ollie? He was prematurely old, misshapen, and there was that ridiculous toupee. Loozie was a knockout. So it was hard — correction, it was impossible — to believe that it was love, at least on Loozie's part.

I STOPPED off at George's Coney Island and brought back some Coney dogs, cheese fries and Cokes. Boodles jumped up on my skirt, partly with joy for my presence, but more so with excitement at the smell of the Coney dogs.

Shelley looked up from her desk. "So?"

"Ollie's been cheating with Loozie," I said breathlessly, as I dropped the Coney bag on the counter.

"Ollie? Loozie? That doesn't make sense." Shelley took a peek into the George's bag.

"That's what Glenda told me, and I guess she would

know."

"But how? How does she know?" Shelley looked upset. Every time an unexpected man is caught cheating, it kind of rocks your world, and not in a good way.

"I didn't ask Glenda how she knew. After the topic came up, she got real upset and asked me to leave."

"Think you could talk to her again?" Shelley reached in to the George's bag and pulled out the wrapped hot dogs and fries. Boodles' ears perked up and his nose twitched.

"Only if I have to. It was pretty painful."

"We might have to." She took a huge bite.

Just then, the door jingled open and in walked Max Fosner, not looking at all like a criminal defense attorney. He wore crisply ironed khaki pants and an equally well-pressed dark blue, short-sleeved shirt. But unlike Dan Eckles or Robert Blumer, he didn't wear it well. The collar rested unevenly on his fleshy shoulders, and his pants lay crookedly on his hips, over which protruded a sizeable belly. I had to admit though; he did have a thousand-watt smile.

"Hi, gals," he said to Shelley and me, and then he faced me directly. "I didn't hear from you, Bella, and I'm dying to know what you found out."

I could feel myself frown. I'd planned to call Max after work to fill him in and still keep my bill as low as possible. This murder charge was going to cost me a fortune.

"Stop with the face." He leaned across the counter,

touching my arm.

I didn't get a tingle or a rush at his touch, but it did feel good. Reassuring even.

"I was in the neighborhood. It's off the clock."

Geez, could everyone read my mind? Was I that transparent?

"But you work right down Main," I said, in very mild protest. "You're always in the neighborhood. I don't want you to go broke on my case."

Max laughed, and his hand hadn't left my arm. "Don't worry about my bill. I won't charge for drop-ins like this, and I'll keep the cost down as much as I can." He smiled. "Thank God, I have other clients." He released my arm. "So, Bella, tell me what you found out today."

I told him all about my trip to Ollie's dealership, how Ollie tried to deny that the diamonds were for him (and for another woman no less) and how defensive he got, worried that I was implicating him in Robert's murder.

"Interesting," said Max, "and do you mind if I take a bite of your Coney dog?"

"Go ahead." I figured Shelley might die — or at least not eat — if she had to share her lunch with a stranger biting into her sandwich.

Max took a big bite and grabbed a napkin from the George's bag to wipe the corner of his mouth. "So go on, what else did you find?" he asked, his mouth full.

"Well, I don't know that it has anything to do with

Robert, but I did find out that Tom Jenkins, Janine's husband, has only been working part-time for the past six months."

"Now that's interesting. Gives the woman more motive to skim from the till, so to speak." Max took a sip of my Coke.

Shelley visibly cringed at the sight.

"Bingo," I said. "And there was that Cadillac she was driving at the funeral procession."

"A Cadillac?" said Shelley.

"Yeah, I asked Tom about it and, come to think of it, he clammed right up."

Shelley sucked air at the bottom of her Coke. "I guess we'll see what I come up with when I go over all the Blumer bank statements." She stuffed all her lunch debris into her empty Coke cup. "You really think she had anything to do with the murder?"

"People kill for money," said Max.

I thought of Janine. She'd been a pretty put-together thirty-something when she first came to Blumer's about ten years ago. But she grew, quite literally, to a matronly-looking thing with two school-age kids. The oldest was thirteen, I think. Other than the fact that she assumed I had murdered Robert, I never really had anything against her. I really couldn't imagine her stealing from the business — and I certainly could not imagine that she'd kill Robert. That was ridiculous.

"I don't think so. She's not the type," I said.

"No one's the type," said Max. "Take it from me."

"Still, I don't think she's our number one suspect. Barbara holds that honor."

Shelley pulled the top off her drink and crunched on the ice cubes. "First, let's see what I find in the books."

"How could I forget?' Max hit his forehead with the palm of his hand.

"What?" Now he had me curious.

"I think we have another prime suspect possibility." Max grabbed one of my cheese fries.

"Don't chew! Tell me first! Who are you talking about?"

Max ignored me and took a small bite. "That creep who's been stalking you — Larry Bernstein."

I was stunned. "What does Larry have to do with anything? The only reason I know him is because my mother, bless her annoying matchmaker heart, fixed me up with him."

Max chuckled. "Can't wait to meet your mom. She sounds like a doozie."

"She's a doozie all right, but what about Larry?"

Max cleared his throat. "I didn't tell you this before, but I went to Southfield High with Robert — and with Larry Bernstein."

"You went to Southfield?" Southfield is a large suburb just a few miles west of Royal Oak.

"I graduated in the same class as Robert."

"Did you know him?" I asked, feeling slightly wistful

for my previous life, despite myself. It used to be so uncomplicated.

"No, not real well. I knew who he was, but we were never friends. Remember, there were over a thousand in our graduating class that year. We came from different junior highs, so I barely knew him."

"But what does that have to do with Larry?"

Max snuck in an extra cheese fry. "Well, Robert was always such a ladies' man." He glanced sideways to see if I was upset, I guess.

"Go on," I said. That was old news.

"Robert and Larry were on the varsity tennis team. Larry was one of the top players, even though he was a junior when Robert and I were seniors."

"And?"

"Yeah, get to the point," said Shelley. "You never know when a customer's going to come in, and I want to hear this."

"I had a friend on the team, that's how I know about this. Both Robert and Larry were vying to be captain, and the coach gave it to Robert because he was a senior, even though Larry was the better player."

I sighed. What was he talking about? "Here, have another cheese fry." I handed the bag to Max. "Come on, that's ancient history, and nowhere near a murder motive."

"There's more." Max threw three cheese fries in his mouth and chewed for a moment.

"What?" Off the clock or not, Max was taking too long to tell this story.

Max wiped his fingers on a brown napkin. "Larry was wildly in love with Fran Berger. They'd been going together for a year." He paused for emphasis. "And Robert stole her away."

Shelley looked up from her desk. "But that was high school. He's in his fifties now, for God's sake."

"Fifty-five," said Max. "But Larry was devastated. Worse yet, Robert dated her for a month, and then dumped her, and she never went back to Larry."

"But didn't he marry? Have kids?" Shelley was in full detective mode.

I was feeling a little tingle in the back of my head, and then a flush came over my face.

"What is it?" said Max.

"What?" I said, hoping that for once I could keep a poker face.

"Spill it," said Shelley. "He's your attorney, for God's sake; let's get it all out in the open, Bella."

"There's another reason it could be Larry," I said.

"What?" Max gripped the edge of my counter.

"Well, he actually had an opportunity to drop the diamonds into my purse."

CHAPTER 17

"What do you mean?" asked Shelley. "When could that have happened? He didn't go back to where your purse was near Myrna. He wasn't even in that part of the funeral home."

I took a deep breath, upset with myself. "On my date with him at Ben's, when I left the table to talk to Heather on my cell, I took Boodles, but not my purse. It's too hard to carry two things and talk on the phone. I wasn't looking at him at all when I was on the phone. He could have slipped them right in there."

Just then the door jingled open and, thank God, in walked a bona fide customer. Even at reduced hours, I was going to owe Max a fortune. Not to mention the fact that

I had rent, utilities, and taxes on the business end, and a home mortgage payment with all the trimmings. It was quite a nut to crack.

Shelley, Ms. Bottom Line, God bless her, hopped right to the counter. For a change, it was a businessman, early fifties, in a suit. I figured he was from one of the law firms on Washington.

"Meet my partner, Marty McGriff." Max gestured toward the suit.

Shelley shook his hand.

"He needs an anniversary gift for his wife, so I told him to buy it here."

McGriff smiled. "He wants you to be able to pay his bill. Nice to meet you."

"Yeah, so don't be cheap," said Max.

After we exchanged all the pleasantries, Max went back to the Larry thing. "Yeah, he's married, has one kid, I think. But it was never a happy marriage. She divorced him right after the baby was born. He's been alone most of his adult life."

"And you think he blames Robert for all that?"

"It's possible."

"But my mother introduced us. It doesn't make any sense."

Max touched my arm again. "Bella, why don't you ask your mother whose idea it was to fix you up—hers or Larry's mother's?"

"Oh." I was getting his point. Maybe Larry had orchestrated our fix-up. And this whole thing could really explain his seemingly instant infatuation with me. It could also explain why he was eager to talk to the press and implicate me.

"Geez, it's going to take me forever to figure out who killed Robert."

The door jingled open, and in walked a more typical customer, an aging, tall blond Lonnie Anderson lookalike, probably in her early forties.

"I have to go," I whispered to Max, as Shelley was still waiting on McGriff, who was checking out some of my diamond-set pendants.

"Let's meet for dinner and we can go over what to do next."

I hesitated, for many reasons, not the least of which was Max's bill.

"Off the clock and my treat." Max turned on that high wattage smile.

McGriff looked over his shoulder. "You're going to bankrupt us on this one," he said, gesturing toward me.

I smiled. "Tell you what, dinner's on me. How about Billy Bob's on Fourth? Let's meet at seven-fifteen."

Max extended his hand. I offered mine in return. Instead of a shaking, he covered my hand with the two of his and whispered in my ear, "It's going to be okay. I promise."

LATER, WHEN the store cleared out of the tall blond Lonnie lookalike and McGriff, and a few other customers who had stopped by in between, Shelley slouched at her desk. It was three o'clock. I fell into my bench chair, exhausted. Boodles hopped onto my lap and licked my fingers, making me think of food.

"I need a pick-me-up. How about some Double Ds?"

"We should be a lot fatter than we are," said Shelley.

Actually, I am ever so slightly zaftig. Shelley, bless her heart, is a perfect size six, no matter what she eats. This annoys me, even though I know she exercises every day. I, on the other hand, am allergic to exercise. Exercise merely brings on the urge to nap. Or eat.

"Good genes," was my response.

"Thanks, Mom," said Shelley. Our mother still cut quite a trim figure at seventy-eight. Truth is, Shelley takes after Mom and I take after our dad, who always carried a few extra pounds — that might have contributed to his sudden heart attack when Shelley and I were in our teens.

"You know, Bella?"

"What, Shelley?"

"I think you have another problem."

"What do you mean, 'problem'?" I could guess what she was talking about, but I feigned innocence in case we weren't talking about the same thing.

"It's about Max."

Bingo!

"You think he has a personal interest in me, right?"

Shelley laughed. "The man is hot to trot."

"And I haven't trotted for some time now." I was joking, but I wasn't smiling.

"Bella, if you're not interested, you should let him know." She is my terminally honest sister, not to mention that she's my only sibling.

"But I don't know if I'm interested." This was true; I didn't.

"Then you should tell him that." Shelley sounded matter of fact. She sees things in black and white, especially when it's someone else's problem.

"I like being with him. He makes me feel safe."

"Is 'safe' what you want?" Shelley had never approved of my attraction for bad boys — Robert Blumer included.

I thought about it for a second or two. "It never was before. But I'm going through so much right now, I can't tell if I like being with him, or if I just like the fact that he's helping me get through all of this crap."

"Crap it is," said Shelley, just as the door jingled open. The Double Ds had to wait, because she and I were at the counter nonstop until it was time to close the door at six o'clock.

Shelley and I closed up shop, putting all the most expensive Bella Blumer creations into my safe and adding a few inexpensive items in the front showcase for the evening window shoppers. I then rushed out the door and hurried down Fourth Street, stopping now and then to let Boodles make his mark on Royal Oak. The sidewalks were crowded with aging Yuppies (we might all have been urban professionals, but none of us could any longer be accused of being young) either heading home or making their way to one of the trendy restaurants on Fourth Street or Washington.

When Boodles started to tire, mostly from the July heat, I lifted him into his carrier. By the time we reached my bungalow, a welcome cold blast from the central air hit my face. It was one of the many improvements I lavished on my Craftsman home with the spoils from my divorce from Robert.

I ran upstairs, stripped off my outfit, and put on a simple Oscar de la Renta silk tank top and matching silk capris, and bottomed it off with a pair of black Manolo knock-off slides. I added a pair of onyx and pink cloisonné earrings, my own creation, telling myself that I would have coordinated this outfit, even had I been eating alone tonight, which was sort of true. I'm not much for jeans. I'd dressed up a bit for Max, but I told myself that I would have done the same if I were meeting a girlfriend. And I almost believed that, too.

At seven twenty-one, I walked into Billy Bob's, feeling light without Boodles. Royal Oak is small. Unless you use valet service, which is not available at Billy Bob's, chances are you might have to park nearly as far as my house. So I'd walked, assuring my hair a humidity meltdown.

Max waved from a booth near the bar. Billy Bob's, a creation of a Texas transplant, was filled with saddles, spurs, and chaps on the walls, and even a few Stetsons dangling from the ceiling. Country music twanged over hidden speakers, someone whining about a cheating "wahf." A mechanical bull sat on the dance floor, but there were no takers at such an early hour, before anyone had a chance to down the requisite number of tequilas or beers. A few brave souls wore cowboy boots and even a hat, but mostly it was the help, who had no choice.

Heather, her hair a bright green beneath her tan Stetson, came over and gave me a hug.

"I thought you'd be at Gramma Myrna's tonight," I said, slipping into my seat.

Heather shrugged. "I've been there every night. I told her I have to work, and I do. Friday's a great night for tips."

"Do you have our table?" asked Max.

Heather shook her green head. "No, but I'll see if I can switch."

"That would be great," I said.

"What did you find out today, Mom?"

Obviously, Billy Bob's did not provide the greatest opportunity for a private conversation. Everyone practically shouted because of the music and loud conversation, but if you concentrated, you could overhear the people in the next booth.

I leaned into Heather's ear and loudly whispered, "I learned a lot. Barbara's been cheating on Dad with Dan Eckles, and Ollie's been cheating on Glenda with Loozie!"

"Omigod!" Heather slid down into the booth next to me. "So now we know for sure that Barbara just led Dad on to get his money?"

I looked over my shoulder. A young mom and her baby sat in the booth behind me with her middle-aged parents across from her. "The walls have ears, Heather." I could feel my lips tighten into a frown. "We'll talk about this when you get home."

"And Ollie? And Loozie? Come on!" Heather stared at the table as if it were a crystal ball. "It's too much!"

I put my arm around her. "Heather, I'm sorry. I should have waited till your shift was over to tell you."

Max reached across the table and touched one of Heather's hands. So he *was* a touchy feely guy. Maybe it wasn't really about me. "Are you all right? Are you going to be able to get back to work?"

"Sure." She slipped her hand out from under his and stood. "I'll be back in a few minutes for your order." With that, she evaporated into the hubbub of Billy Bob's.

"Oh boy, I forget sometimes how emotional she can get."

Max reached over and put his hand on mine. "She'll be okay. Maybe her work will distract her."

I looked up toward the bar, and my heart sank even lower. My hand slipped from Max to my chest. "Oh no!"

Max swiveled his head to look in the same direction. "What now?"

"It's Jason, Heather's ex, with a new girlfriend."

"The curly-headed guy with the blonde?"

A voice from behind me squealed, "Are you *the* Bella Blumer, the one who's been in the news?"

So much for privacy. All eyes turned toward our table.

Max stood. "Let's go. We can order out." He grabbed my arm, and we high-tailed it out of Billy Bob's and into the Royal Oak sunshine. The heat hadn't let up yet. It still felt like it was about ninety degrees, probably because of the soupy humidity.

We walked east toward Main. I suggested that we pick up some shawarma pita wraps and a couple of Double Ds. "We can eat at my house."

"Sounds like a plan," said Max.

BY THE time we reached my bungalow, it was about eight-fifteen, and I was ravenous. Boodles jumped on me, and then did his little dance of joy, running in cute little circles around my ankles.

"That was rough," I said, when we were finally eating our shawarmas.

"I know." Max wiped some grease off his face with his napkin. "The only worse thing than an unhappy child is knowing that you had a hand in it."

I put the shawarma down and sighed, a big, chest-aching release. "I don't know how much more of this I can take."

"Bella, let's concentrate on what we *can* do. Once we find out who really killed your ex, a lot of these other problems will clear right up."

I let out a deep breath. "So what do we have?"

Max was more than halfway done with his sandwich. He finished chewing and wiped his face. "You tell me. Who does your gut say did it? Who would kill Robert and stand aside while you take the blame?"

I didn't have to ponder. "Barbara," I blurted. "She has everything to gain. She stole my life, my house, and all our assets."

"Wait a minute," said Max. "What about the pre-nup?"

I sighed. "I just found out about it this week myself."

"I don't suppose you can get me a copy."

"I have no idea where Robert would have kept it. And I don't have access to his things. So no, I can't."

"If it exists, I'll find it." Max texted a note to himself into his cellphone.

"Anything I can do?" I said, taking another bite.

"You can stay away from that woman," said Max. "If she really did it, she's probably dangerous."

"What about Dan Eckles?"

"Barbara's ex-boyfriend?" said Max.

"More like Barbara's ex-fiancé and current lover." I switched early to dessert, from the stress I suppose, sinking a bite into my bumpy cake Double D. I tried to keep myself from saying "Mm-mm" but obviously failed.

"I'll have to remember that." Max chuckled.

"Remember what?"

"The way to de-stress Bella Blumer is with dark chocolate bumpy cake."

I smiled and took a sip of my iced green tea. "Chocolate never hurts."

I was just about to grab a pad of paper to take notes, when there was a knock at the front door. Boodles went into full alarm mode, yipping at the top of his tiny lungs.

"Want me to get it?" asked Max.

"That's all right." I put down my Double D and opened the front door. Sunlight streamed into my living room, as it was not quite nine o'clock in July, giving us the benefit of full sunlight and heat.

Standing on my front porch was none other than Detective Hottie himself, Bill Krieger.

CHAPTER 18

Now that I had both men in the same room, I could see why I'd been so instantly attracted to Krieger, and not so much to Max. While they were both in their fifties, Krieger still had the stature of a young athlete, six foot something, straight and tall, a full head of thick gray hair, and one of those sharp military faces that would be right at home in an aftershave commercial.

Max, on the other hand, was barely taller than me and sort of doughy and soft around the corners. His hair was still mostly light brown, but there wasn't nearly enough of it, although he did have a reasonable amount left on top and parted to the side.

"Detective Krieger," I said.

"Can I come in, Bella?"

"Sure, have a seat." I gestured toward the living room.

Max and Krieger introduced each other and shook hands.

"He's my lawyer." I bit both lips.

Krieger sat up straight at the edge of my overstuffed chair. "We just want you to know that we had an anonymous tip, and that's why we have another search warrant." He held up an official-looking piece of paper along with the badge he presented to Max.

"Let me see that." Max reached across me to Krieger.

As Max started reading, there was a knock at the door. A uniformed officer held a small Glock with latex-gloved hands.

"It was just where the call said it would be," said the uniform, slipping the gun into a clear plastic evidence bag. "Buried right in the shrubs on the west side of the house."

I stood up, angry. "What caller?"

"It was a female, claimed to be a neighbor but wouldn't identify herself," said Krieger.

"What was on the caller ID?" asked Max.

"The ID was blocked," said Krieger.

"It's a setup," said Max. "Bella's being framed.'

"That bitch!" I said, quite out loud. Of course, I was talking about Barbara.

Krieger informed me that the next step involved identifying ownership of the gun, and that if the gun was, in fact, mine, it was another piece of evidence against me. I was too stunned to speak, and let Max handle everything.

After Krieger and the uniform left, I felt like a launched rocket with nowhere to go.

"Well, now we know for sure it's Barbara." I paced back and forth in my living room.

"First, Bella, I have to ask you to refrain from saying things like 'that bitch' in front of the police. It just doesn't look good," said Max.

But my motor was on high tilt, and I was in no mood to listen to such reasonable advice. "Well, she *is* a bitch, and I have to prove she's the one who did it, not me!"

Max leaned back on my couch, totally relaxed. "We know it looks like its Barbara, but we can't really be sure."

I stopped in my tracks. "Look, I go to Blumer's and confront her, and the very same evening the gun turns up in my side garden — with an anonymous tip, no less."

"It might look like that, Bella, but it's not conclusive. Remember, we have a list of possible suspects. It could be any one of them."

I threw my hands up in the air. "Screw the list; it's Barbara!"

Max sighed. "I understand. You're upset."

"You bet I'm upset." I continued pacing across the hardwood floor. "I'm under attack. That tends to upset me."

"Hey, don't forget I'm on your side. But you have to remember not to jump to conclusions. That's what the police—and the media—have done to you."

I stopped pacing and faced Max. "What are you saying?"

"I'm saying that it was probably the murderer, or someone involved with the murder, who planted the gun." He paused. "But we still don't have enough evidence—or proof—to know it's Barbara."

The man made sense, but I was in no mood for sense. I wanted blood. Barbara's blood. "But I know in my gut it's her."

"Your gut doesn't mean squat in court."

"But it makes perfect sense. She was engaged to Eckles. She comes to work at Blumer's, turns Robert's head, sleeps with him, marries him, and less than a year later, Robert's dead. All his money goes to her, and in the meantime, she's been sleeping with her original fiancé. Isn't that proof enough?"

"Not in a court of law," said Max.

"Then what do they have on me?"

Max patted the couch beside him. "Sit down, Bella. The police have a lot on you: motive, opportunity, and evidence. The missing diamonds show up in your purse, and now the gun shows up buried in your yard."

"It was a plant. Literally." My words burst out in a shout.

"Calm down, Bella. I know that. The question is how we're going to prove it."

Max wanted to stay and make lists of suspects, motives,

and alibis, but I was entirely too stressed out to be analytical. I told him to go home and take Chester out for a walk, and it worked. He gave me a quick kiss goodbye, thankfully on the forehead. I was way too tired to worry about it or analyze it. I was just glad to shut my front door and keep the world out, at least till morning. That's when the phone rang.

It was Shelley. "First, I need to know: is Max still there?"

"No." My voice was all tense and tight.

"What's wrong?" Shelley could read me like a book — print or audio apparently.

I told her about the visit from the police and the planted gun. "One more thing to make me look guilty." I could hear the catch in my throat.

"Oh, Bella! Do you want me to come over?" Shelley meant it. She'd spent many evenings with me during the divorce, and I knew she'd drop everything if I would just ask.

But I decided to be strong. "Thanks, Shelley, but all I really need is a bubble bath and a soft quiet bed."

"I understand. And I know how tough this is, so I won't tell you to stay away from Barbara tomorrow. And forever."

I heaved a big sigh. "I promise."

After we clicked off, I let Boodles out and waited in the dining room while he did his business outside. The phone rang a second time. It was Vic.

"Hi, hon."

Vic and my mom are the only two family members who

can't read my voice—or maybe they don't want to.

"Mom." I could hear the venom in his voice. "I understand why you did it, but I'm sorry, you were wrong."

"You mean about Barbara?" Was he actually going to defend that woman?

"It's not that she didn't deserve it, but I can't have that kind of drama at work. It's not good for business."

"I understand." I was way too tired right now to speak up for myself.

I think he was thrown off-guard by the lack of argument. "Are you okay?"

I told him about the police. And the gun.

"So you think Barbara did it? Planted the gun, I mean?"

"Either she or Dan Eckles." I opened the back door to let in a silent Boodles. He would bark like a fiend at a passing dog, but would often stand at the back door expecting me to read his mind.

"Why Eckles?"

I sighed. "That was the whole point of my visit today, Vic. I found out that Barbara's been 'visiting' with Eckles, not Loozie."

I could hear him suck in his breath. "She's been cheating on Dad?"

"It sure looks like it. That's why I lost my temper and chewed her out."

"Oh." There was a long silence before he spoke again. "Now I understand."

"Thank you." It felt good to be vindicated.

"But you still shouldn't have done it. I lost a sale. My customer left the diamond room and the store."

"I'm so sorry," I said, and I really meant it. That made me think of the money problems Vic was having at work. "Did you get the bank statement to Aunt Shelley?"

He sighed. "I'm working on it, Mom. I may have to get new copies from the bank tomorrow. I don't know where Janine files them, and I don't want to ask her and let on that we're checking it out."

"Oh, boy," I said.

"Well, gotta go now, Mom."

We exchanged our "love you's" and then we both clicked off the phone.

As I trudged up the stairs to my bedroom, it occurred to me that Friday night was a good time to check in on my mother and ask her to talk to Mrs. Bernstein. They both went to Temple Shalom and would see each other at Saturday morning services.

By the time I reached the top of the steps I had her on my cell.

"Hello, Mom." I skipped telling her about the gun, because I just didn't want to talk about it again. "So, tell me, whose idea was it to get me and Larry Bernstein together?"

"Why, it was Adele's idea." She had a certain air of joy in her voice at the thought of fixing me up.

"Could you ask her if it was her own idea or Larry's?"

I asked.

"Of course, dear, but why do you want to know? I thought you didn't like him."

I explained the history between Robert and Larry and why this might have motivated Larry to kill Robert.

"Oh my!" she said.

"It's a long shot, Mom, but the more we can find out, the better."

My mother cleared her throat. Uh oh! "While I have you on the phone, Bella, I know we agreed to wait, but I have another young man I'd like you to meet."

Oh boy. Don't ask me why I did it. I was pretty sure it was a mistake before I even opened my mouth.

"I'm seeing someone, Mom."

This stopped her mid-sentence. "What?" She was clearly shocked.

In for a penny, in for a pound. "I've been seeing my defense attorney." It wasn't technically a lie; I was "seeing" him. Hearing him, too.

"Is he Jewish?" My mother's generation doesn't have to worry about being politically correct.

"Yes, he's Jewish, and there's nothing to talk about yet. But I'd rather not get fixed up under the circumstances."

I could hear my mother smiling through the cell phone.

"You have a good night, dear."

At least one of us would sleep well tonight, and it wasn't me.

I decided that, under the circumstances, it was a good idea to get nice and relaxed before I went to bed. I trudged upstairs to take a nice, long, hot bath.

The master bath upstairs has a delightful jetted tub, courtesy of the previous owners. I turned on my Barry Manilow CDs, poured in some bubble bath, slipped off my outfit, and settled in for a relaxing soak. I was sure my Glock would be on the eleven o'clock news, but I didn't care to watch.

Barry hadn't had a chance to finish the first song on the CD, when I heard a commotion outside the bathroom. Boodles started barking just as someone knocked on my bathroom door.

CHAPTER 19

I was expecting a roving news reporter, ready to stick a microphone in my face, but fortunately Boodles stopped barking as soon as the door opened. Heather slouched in and leaned against the pedestal sink. Her cowboy boots were still on, but the Stetson hat was missing. Her face was smeared with makeup from what looked like a good cry.

"I think I lost my job." She burst into a fresh batch of tears.

Oh, boy. This was supposed to be my stress-free down time, but oh well. If I didn't have a heart attack before morning, I figured I must be in pretty good shape.

"Have a seat." I gestured toward the toilet, dripping soap bubbles from my arm. "Tell me what happened."

Heather put down the toilet lid, sat down and was about to bury her face in her hands when Boodles landed on her lap. She half laughed, choking back tears.

I soaked quietly, waiting for her to talk. I knew it wouldn't take long.

"I let Jason have it." She choked down a sob.

"You yelled at Jason, at Billy Bob's, while you were working?" I started to smile.

"It isn't funny!" Heather's voice cracked, and her red-rimmed eyes threw me daggers.

I realized Heather didn't know where I was coming from, but I said it anyway. "Like mother, like daughter."

"What are you talking about?"

"I haven't talked to you all day, so you don't know anything about it." I leaned my head against the tub.

"About what?" She wiped her wet face with her already dirty hand, making her makeup smear even worse.

"I went to Blumer's today and chewed out Barbara. It was quite the scene. Vic is furious with me."

Heather giggled, but it came out sounding more like a hiccup. "But why today?"

"You mean, other than the reason that I found out she's been cheating on your father all along?"

"I know, you told me that when you were at Billy Bob's tonight. But how did you find out—I mean, for sure—that she did?"

I sat up straighter in the tub. The bubbles were starting

to diminish. Either we'd finish our conversation soon, or Heather was going to see more than she bargained for. "I went to Barbara's rendezvous with Loozie today, and there was no Loozie. Just moonstruck Dan Eckles waiting for his Barbara."

"I knew it!" Heather stood up and balled her hands into fists. "She married Dad for the money."

"That's what it looks like." I slid further down into the tub.

Heather sat back down on the toilet lid. "Are you sure it was always Dan Eckles and not Loozie? And what about Monday? Were either of them there on Monday?"

I sighed. This was supposed to be my downtime. But at least Heather was perking up a little. "No, but good idea. I'll ask around Double Ds tomorrow."

"Maybe I can help." Her smile looked out of place on her tear-streaked face. "So you really went to Blumer's and made a scene?"

"Like mother, like daughter. So, are you going to be okay?"

It was Heather's turn to sigh, a deep, dark, gut-wrencher of a sigh. "I don't know. My boss was pretty upset. Told me to knock off early and calm down a bit."

"That doesn't sound like he's ready to fire you."

Heather shook her head. "You didn't hear how he said it, Mom. He wasn't happy."

I decided to switch subjects and tell Heather about the

gun and how it was planted in the side yard to make me look guilty.

"You think it was Barbara?" Her reddened eyes opened wide.

"It makes perfect sense to me."

Then Heather decided to change the subject herself. "So what's the deal with you and the lawyer coming into Billy Bob's like you're a couple or something?"

"Just talking business. But, what do you think of him?"

Heather pursed her lips. "As a lawyer or as a potential boyfriend?"

"Both." Might as well get this out in the open.

"He seems like a fantastic lawyer, but I don't think he's your type."

I would have asked her what that meant, but I was sure it would be a sore topic, what with her father dying less than a week ago, so I let it go.

"Why don't we both get some rest, and see what happens in the morning."

"Good night, Mom." She gave me a quick kiss on the top of my head and left me alone to soak in what was now lukewarm water.

It TURNED out Heather's boss wasn't as angry as she thought, or maybe he was just really shorthanded, because he gave

Heather an early Saturday morning call, and he expected her to get to work by ten. Which meant I was on my own if I wanted to snoop around at Double Ds. Although I was really anxious to get to work and start in on some more pieces for Sunday's Art Fair, I made my way to the cupcake shop, my shoulder fortified with Boodles and my lime bag.

Because it was practically on the way, I stopped in at Ben's at about eight o'clock. Ben walked me over to an empty table and shook his head. "It's so sad. You know, I was never close to Robert, but we were family, and *you're* family, not that little Barbie doll he married."

"I'm sorry it hasn't been me at your mother's," I said, and I meant it. I loved Ben. He would always be my brother-in-law, divorce or not. "How's Myrna?" I'd been so caught up with my own drama that I hadn't thought of my poor mother-in-law. This was surely a tough time for her.

"She's holding up." He smiled. "She loved your little visit on Friday."

I felt myself blush. "I'm too impulsive sometimes. That's probably why some people actually believe I killed Robert."

His hand flew to his heart. "Not me!" He said it just a little bit too loud. A few of his patrons turned to watch us.

I gave him an extra hug. "Thank you, Ben. You'll always be family to me."

He stood up. "Let me get you a cappuccino."

"Can I take a rain check? I have to go to Double Ds and check on Barbie Girl's alibi."

"You go, Bella. Keep trying, and you'll figure it out."

He kissed me on the cheek, and I headed over to Double Ds with only tiny Boodles as my posse.

The smell of chocolate and fresh-from-the-oven baked goods was overwhelming. My Minnie Mouse watch said it was only eight-thirty, but I picked out a vanilla chocolate-chip extra zaftig cupcake with dark chocolate frosting and the signature maraschino cherry. It was big enough for two people who had no intention of dieting. I promised myself to wait till at least ten o'clock to eat it. "And a large cappuccino," I said, eyeballing the cashier who looked to be somewhere around Heather's age.

He pulled the mammoth cupcake from the display case.

"Do you know Barbara Blumer?" I asked, thinking I was being cagey, a regular private eye.

He blew a stray strand of hair off his nose and looked me straight in the eye. "You mean your ex-husband's wife?"

I felt myself blush. "I wasn't aware I knew you."

"You don't." He turned to the cappuccino. "But your face is all over the news. Hers too."

I decided I had no time to get upset about my notoriety. Too much was at stake. "But, did you ever see her here with a dark-haired guy?"

"You mean that sexy one in a business suit?"

"That's the one." I figured this guy was probably gay, or he'd be talking more 'hot Barbara' than 'sexy Dan.' "Are they in here a lot together?"

He hesitated. "I really don't pay that much attention. You know, after a while all the customers look alike. But that guy's a real looker. Yeah, I've seen him in here with her."

"Did they just start meeting here? Or have they been meeting here for a long time?"

"As long as I've worked here," he said, "and that's been about six months."

I tapped him on the arm. "Thanks so much." Then I grabbed my cappuccino, my purse and my dog, and headed over to Bella's Baubles. Halfway to my shop, my cell started to play "I'm bad, I'm bad," but I didn't have enough hands to answer.

When I finally unlocked the door to Bella's and put down all my things, including Boodles, I checked the phone. It was Vic. I opened my safe, took out a few trays of beads, and called him back on my speakerphone, so I could work on some stock for the Art Fair and talk at the same time.

"Hi, Mom."

"You just called." I fingered some lapis beads that were extraordinarily veined with gold. I had to be careful—my tendency was to make all my necklaces blue. I checked out some breath-taking amethyst that reminded me of lilacs in early spring.

"How are you doing?" he asked.

That was unusual. Vic always assumed everything was all right with me. This was sometimes annoying, yet reassuring on the other hand. As long as he wasn't worried about me, why should I be?

I guess he noticed my silence. "Have you seen the papers today?"

"I take it they're making a big deal about the gun." Despite the July heat, I felt a chill go down my spine.

"It *is* a big deal, Mom. It has your fingerprints all over it."

"Of course it does!" I didn't mean to yell, but this was ridiculous. "It's *my* gun, remember?"

"Oh."

"What, you're worried I killed your father?"

His silence indicated to me that the thought had crossed his mind. "You do have a temper, Mom."

I put down all beads. "Look, Vic, if I killed your father, I would tell you. I would turn myself in and pay the price. I wouldn't lie to my family and ask them to help me find the killer. I'm not friggin' OJ, okay?"

There was a long silence, and I was in no mood to fill it.

"I'm sorry, Mom." I could hear his voice crack. "It's been a hard time for me, too." He went silent again, and I could only imagine that he was crying.

"I'm sorry, Vic." I quashed the urge to hang up on him, only because he was my son. "I didn't mean to yell at you. I know you miss Dad."

Vic managed to keep his voice steady, but it sounded low and unnatural. "My father is dead, the books are probably cooked, and I'm going to have to figure out how to save this business on my own. I'm not sure I'm ready for this."

Sometimes words fail you, and sometimes you know just what to say. "Vic," I said, with all the conviction in my heart, "you can do it. It can be done. I'll help you any way I can."

Another silence, and then, "Thank you, Mom, I needed that."

"I love you, Vic."

"Love you, too, Mom."

"Now get those bank statements to Aunt Shelley, and look for that pre-nup, and we'll take this one step at a time."

We both hung up, and I felt a little drained, but went back to work on the amethyst pendant. I like to get into the Zen of jewelry making. Time stands still as my mind focuses only on my work. Jewelry is always patient, beautiful, and precious. I like to be a part of making lasting things of beauty. I think that's why I find my work so calming.

By eleven o'clock, I was finishing up the amethyst pendant. It was a knockout, paired with cultured seed pearls and a mother-of-pearl drop pendant that I'd wrapped with amethyst and silver wire. I made a list of all the materials: amethyst, mother-of-pearl, seed pearls, silver wire, silver fishhook clasp, stringing thread, and the hours I spent working on it, and put the list with the pendant on Shelley's desk for her to determine a price.

I stood at the safe door, going through some amazingly

lovely, green malachite beads with the most beautiful, natural striping of many different greens. These beads deserved fourteen-karat yellow gold, I decided, and they would get it. I put the malachite on my bench and started sketching the possibilities, ironically grateful it hadn't been busy.

Of course, that was the exact moment the door jingled open and in walked Heather, her eyes once again red rimmed, her forehead strained.

I put down my sketchpad and glanced at my watch. It was eleven-twenty. "What's wrong? Why aren't you at work?"

Heather made her way to Shelley's desk and plopped into the task chair. Her hair was still yesterday's bright green, as she'd went into work too early to change it.

"Joel sent me home when Tina came in. Late." Joel was her boss, and Tina was another waitress at Billy Bob's. Heather's face showed no emotion, but her knees were knocking, and I could tell she was a bundle of nerves.

"But I thought he called you in this morning?" I said it as more of question than a statement.

"He did, and this is his way of giving me a fuck-you for last night." Her voice cracked.

"So, do you think you still have a job?"

"Who wants a job like this? If this is how he's going to treat me, I might as well quit." Heather dropped her face into her hands.

"Why don't you start looking today and take all the hours you can in the meantime?" This seemed to be a practical suggestion.

Heather lifted her head. "I don't know if I can stomach it," she whispered. She shook her head slowly, and her voice got a little stronger. "But I'll try. I really need the money, and there aren't too many jobs around."

"Why don't you look online?"

She dropped her head once more, and I could barely hear her voice.

"I don't know. I'm so depressed."

I'm an occasionally patient woman, but I do have my limits. "Well, you can hang out here, if you like, but I really have to get to work."

As I returned to my sketchpad, Heather slumped in Shelley's chair. I noticed a browser at the front window, the old-fashioned kind who is actually a human that checks out a storefront window.

"Say, Heather, I'll pay you hourly to work here today. Shelley can't make it because of Elena today, and I really have to work on stock for the fair."

"Really?" She sat up straight in the chair, the beginning of a smile on her face.

I looked at her bright green hair and her chartreuse cowboy shirt. Underneath the shirt was a metallic silver tank top. "Take off the cowboy thing and put on one of those jadeite pendants to match your hair. Maybe some earrings, too."

Heather did the quick change, just as the customer, a man in his late fifties and quite a bit more beefy than Max, walked in.

"What's that necklace you just put on?" he asked.

Heather, all smiles, got him to explain he was about to celebrate his fifth anniversary.

"Cool!" said Heather. "Tell me all about her."

And before you know it, the two of them agreed the necklace and earrings that she'd happened to put on would be just perfect for his wife.

As she entered a receipt into my cash register, the man turned in my direction. "Say, aren't you the one on TV who killed her ex-husband?"

His jowls shook when he talked. I have to tell you, it wasn't pretty. Add to that the fact \ he thought I was a murderer, and the man was not racking up brownie points.

However, he was a paying customer, a new one at that, so instead of lashing out at Mr. Jowls, I took a deep cleansing breath and, God help me, I smiled.

"Yes, I have been on TV, but you should be very relieved to know I'm not a murderer." I left out the part about how he wouldn't be safe if I were, in fact, a gunslinger on the loose.

"Oh, uh, sorry." He grabbed his wrapped gift from Heather, who was all smiles.

"Thanks for stopping in," she said. "I'll call you before

your wife's birthday and let you know if we have anything she might like."

"Great," he said, but he cast a nervous glance in my direction as he headed out the door.

And so went the afternoon. Heather sold jewelry and took phone numbers and emails from every human that walked in while I worked on creating new stock for the Art Fair. I was in the zone, stringing some particularly beautiful, golden amber gems into a twenty-four inch necklace, when in walked Max and Chester. Heather stood at the counter, completing a sale of a seed pearl necklace to a diminutive man who resembled an elf, without the pointy ears.

Boodles knew something was up. He hopped off his warm spot on my bench top and raced over to greet Chester and Max. After a quick sniff of Chester, Boodles rolled over onto his back, effectively begging for a belly rub. Rather than bend to the ground to accommodate Boodles, Max scooped him up and held him in a snug hug. Boodles' curly tail flipped back and forth against Max's side. Not wanting to be left out, Chester nosed his way behind the counter and put his sizeable head on my lap.

"How's the jeweler doing today?" Max asked.

For a not-that-attractive guy, I must say, his smile was really appealing. *Not that he's my type.* But I could see how someone else might actually go for him.

I smiled right back at him. "Thanks to Heather stopping by, I've had all day to work on new stock." I gestured toward the new necklaces lined up on Shelley's desk.

He leaned toward my bench to take a good look at the amber beads, studying the prehistorically trapped ants. Boodles' tail grazed my face.

"Fascinating," he said.

"Want to buy it for someone special?"

His face clouded over. Thinking of his ex-wife, perhaps? "No one special," he said, his voice somber. Then he smiled at me and added, "just yet."

As the door jingled shut with Heather's customer safely out on Fourth Street, I finally felt free to talk — and to change the subject. "Any progress on my case?"

"Yeah," said Heather, "do the police tell you what's going on?"

Max smiled. "Only if I ask, which I do every day. Other than the gun planted in your mother's side garden, they're not saying."

"Do they believe it was planted?" My voice cracked. This was an exciting possibility.

"They didn't say it," said Max, "not in so many words. But I get the feeling they're a little suspicious about the 'anonymous' nature of that call."

"That's awesome!" said Heather.

"I'm not awed just yet," I said. "In fact, I'm not celebrating until the real murderer is convicted and behind bars."

"That's the spirit!" Max laughed.

I sighed. "Spirit, schmirit, what's our next move?"

Heather wiped the counter. "You mean, how do we prove Barbara did it?"

Max put Boodles back on my bench top and chuckled. "Like mother, like daughter. Now, don't forget, the new Mrs. Blumer is *not* our only suspect."

"It's the only logical conclusion." Heather's voice held more than a tinge of annoyance.

Max held up both hands. "Hey, don't shoot the messenger."

I pulled a yellow legal pad from Shelley's desk drawer. "Let's make a list of what we need to do."

"To nail Barbara," Heather finished my sentence perfectly.

Max sighed. "It's bad enough with one of you, but two?"

I couldn't tell if he was serious or not, and I really didn't care. "You're the lawyer, Max. So what do we have to do?"

Mr. Touchy-Feely put his hand on mine. "I know you feel that finding Dan at Double Ds instead of Loozie is proof positive, but it's not."

I pressed my lips tightly together. Enough was enough. "Are you going to dump on me too, for putting Barbara in her place?"

Max leaned against the counter. My store is too small for extra chairs. "Explain to me what you're talking about."

"When I saw Dan Eckles at Double Ds instead of Loozie, something just snapped." I leaned back into my bench chair. "Sue me; I was angry. It was one thing if she fell in love with

Robert and ruined my life. But it looks to me like she never even loved him at all. It was a calculated plan to marry him and stick with it long enough to murder him and pin it on me!" I rubbed my temples. "That's why I went straight to Blumer's to tell her off."

Max put his hand on the edge of my bench. No more touchy-feely guy. His voice wasn't angry like Vic's, but he didn't exactly sound friendly either. "Okay, Bella, you're still jumping to conclusions. All you know for certain is that Barbara sometimes meets her ex-fiancé at a coffee shop. You don't know if they're lovers. You have zero evidence that either one of them committed murder."

"But they've been meeting at Double Ds for at least six months. I have a witness."

"That helps," said Max, "but it's still not enough. You can't go public until you have the facts."

For once, I was silent. The man was right.

"So what do we do next?" asked Heather.

"We could hire a private investigator to follow them," said Max. "If they're really a couple, it won't take long."

"Another expense!" I slumped onto my bench.

"They're not as expensive as lawyers," said Max. "Maybe ninety to one hundred fifty dollars an hour."

"But for how many hours?" I could hear the whine in my voice. "This is going to ruin me."

"You could ask Gramma for the money," said Heather.

Max smiled. "I'm assuming you mean your mother's

mother."

I sat up straight again. "Actually, I'd rather ask Myrna than my own mother. I can't ask my mom; they've already put up the entire one hundred thousand dollar bail money to save me the ten grand I'd have to pay a bondsman."

Max whistled through his teeth. "I didn't know that."

"So I'll have to do it myself."

"Do what?" asked Max.

"Follow Barbara and take some time-stamped photos of her and Danny-boy."

Max folded his arms in front of him. "As your lawyer, I can't recommend you do this." He winked. "But if you did, I would make sure your camera or cellphone is all charged up and you don't get caught."

"Let's do it in my car," said Heather. "It's hard to go incognito in your Escalade."

Max hooked Chester's leash to his collar, and they both headed toward my shop door. "I didn't hear that, and I won't hear anything else unless usable photos come out of this."

Just as he was ready to walk out the door, in walked my mother, all flushed with spiritual radiance from her visit to Temple Shalom followed, no doubt, by lunch at The Club.

"Bye, Max," I said, quickly, and added, "Mom! What brings you here?"

"Max?" she said, turning to get a look at Max, who still had one hand on the door.

"Mom?" Max released the door and extended a hand to my mother for one of his warm, heartfelt shakes. "I've heard so much about you."

My mother accepted his handshake, along with the grasp of her arm with his other hand. Chester's leash fell to the tile floor.

"Well, I've barely heard a word about you," said my mother.

Max shot a look at me. "I thought you kept your mother in the loop about your case."

"I'm not talking about the case!" said my mother, and once those words left her mouth, I was ready to slide right under my bench and dig a hole to China. "I'm talking about how you two are an item."

CHAPTER 20

Oh boy. Never lie to your mother. It never works out. Here I was, fifty-four already, and hadn't learned the basics.

"What?" squawked Heather.

"Is it something important that brought you here, Mom?" I asked. "Because we're having an important talk about my case right now."

"I thought your young man was leaving." Damn, she was astute.

"We can finish our talk later." Max winked in my direction.

I could feel my face turn ruby red.

"I don't want to interrupt," said my mother. "I just stopped in to get some of those delightful cupcakes you have around the corner for dinner tonight, and I thought I'd come over and tell you that I talked to Adele Bernstein, you know, Larry's mother?"

Max stood at rapt attention. Heather, looking either nervous or angry, started furiously cleaning the countertops with glass spray and paper towels.

"Well?" I was in no mood for a long conversation with my mother.

"You were right, dear. It was Larry's idea after all. He asked his mother to fix you two up." She glanced at Max. "Sorry dear; that was before you two hit it off."

I stood and started ushering my mother out the door. "Thanks, Mom. That was very helpful. Now we need some time to discuss what to do about that."

"Thanks, dear." As she walked out the door, she said her goodbyes to me and to Heather, with an extra special, "Hope to see you again soon," to Max.

"I'm so sorry," I said to Max, and to Heather, once my mother was on the other side of the door. "I just told her that we were dating so she'd stop trying to fix me up every day."

"Geez, Mom," said Heather. "You shouldn't lie to Gramma."

Max smiled. "Well, she did come up with some intriguing information. It's possible Larry Bernstein is behind all of this and you are both just fixated on Barbara."

I was too flummoxed by my mother to say anything, but

grateful Max had changed the subject.

Heather put down the glass spray. "How do we check him out?"

"Bella, why don't you visit him at work and see if you can find out if he has an alibi for Monday morning."

"Why at his work?"

"Because you might learn a little bit more about the guy, good or bad. We don't know a whole lot about him beyond what I knew in high school."

"I have no idea where he works." I could feel my teeth stand on edge; I had no desire to visit Larry Bernstein. You could bet a year's salary that he'd assume I was finally really into him.

"He's an insurance agent," said Max. "He works in the Traveler's Tower near the Southfield Library."

"How do you know that?"

"It's a small Jewish community in Detroit. Word gets around."

"I'll go there Monday." I could hear the reluctance in my voice. Remind me never to go into acting.

"Cheer up." Max slid a finger under my chin. "You have a boyfriend now. Your mother said so."

I bit my lower lip, and my voice was surprisingly low for how upset I was. "Please stop it. You're embarrassing me."

Max chuckled as he headed out the door. "Goodbye, Heather." He looked at me. "And Bella, don't be so embarrassed. You could do worse."

AT NEARLY five-thirty, when the store was empty and had been for an hour, Heather walked over to my bench. I had just begun to string together an onyx and blue topaz pendant, set off nicely with highly polished silver beads. Lovely.

"Mom, Blumer's closes in a half hour. Why don't I go now and pick up something to eat and get my car, or maybe Kara's, so we can do a stakeout at our house." Kara, Heather's best friend, drove an outdated Ford Taurus. It doesn't get any more incognito than that.

"You mean Barbara's house." While true, the words stuck in my throat.

"Whatever. You know what I mean. I'll pick you up before six. Make sure you and Boodles are empty." She had a point.

"Could you walk him to Noir Negligee and back before you go? Otherwise, it could be a problem."

Heather rolled her eyes. We'd never had a dog in the house when she and Vic were growing up. Robert didn't want the mess — or the responsibility. So Heather saw Boodles as an attractive nuisance. She didn't mind petting him while she watched TV, but that was about the extent of her commitment.

"Oh, all right," she said, as I handed her his royal blue leash, a perfect match to his sodalite-studded collar. Okay, so I'm a little crazy for the runt. He's been my soul mate since the day the divorce was final.

Even after Heather returned Boodles, there were no more customers. Later, while packing away all the most valuable merchandise in the safe, I heard an unfamiliar honk outside. I took a peek. Heather waved from the passenger seat of Kara's car. I opened the shop door and put up one finger to let her know just one more minute.

I shut the ancient safe door, spun the lock, and emptied myself out in the tiny bathroom. By the time Boodles and I reached Kara's Taurus, Heather was looking and sounding a little impatient. "What took you so long?"

"I went as fast as I could, Heather." I slid into the back seat with Boodles. "Oh, hi Kara, are you coming along?

She grinned. "You think I'd miss a for-real stakeout?"

If Heather was semi-Goth, with the wild colored hair and army boots, Kara was the real deal, the illustrated girl. Her arms were covered with brightly colored tattoos, as were her shins, exposed beneath crisscross slave sandals. She wore earrings on her ears, her nose, and her lips.

Heather, thankfully, had earrings on her ears and belly button only. The only tattoo I knew about—or cared to know about, for that matter—was a butterfly just above her behind.

"Here's your dinner. I didn't have time for anything but

Mickey D's." Heather handed me a bag with a McDouble and fries, along with a large Diet Coke, as if the aspartame could counteract the toxic grease. "Oh, and I picked up some extra fries for Boodles." Given Boodles' size, it was the equivalent of me eating a bucket full. But oh well, at least Heather was warming up to the little guy.

"Where are we going?" asked Kara, as her Taurus lurched into traffic on Fourth Street. She made a hard left turn on Washington just in time to see Barbara heading out the front door of Blumer Fine Jewelers. It might have been the end of the business day, but she was looking pretty snappy, her luxuriously long brown hair bouncing around her shoulders, her legs shapely above her four-inch spikes.

"She's heading south—probably parks in the structure on Lafayette," said Heather, taking a quick draw on her Diet Coke.

"This is fun!" Kara stepped on the accelerator, and her Ford roared, once again, into traffic. She turned right on the next side street to get to the Lafayette parking structure.

"Take it easy with the driving," said Heather. "You're drawing attention to us. We're supposed to blend in with the scenery, Kara."

I was so glad Heather said it, so I didn't have to.

Kara held tight to the steering wheel at the regulation ten- and two-o'clock position. "Oh, all right. But it's more fun driving that way; makes me feel like a cop." She pulled into an open parking spot that faced the Lafayette parking structure exit, and we waited for Barbara's red Corvette—no doubt a gift from Robert, as was my big pearl-white Escalade. He had believed in the gift of cars, a Motor City boy through and through.

I popped in the last bite of my McDouble by the time Barbara's red Corvette showed up at the parking exit.

"There she is!" said Heather.

Kara gunned the engine.

"Stop it!" Heather and I said in unison.

"Oh, all right," said Kara, "but you're spoiling all the fun."

I cleared my throat and nervously chewed on a cold French fry. "This is serious business, Kara. We're trying to get evidence that Barbara murdered Heather's father."

"And save your bacon too, Mrs. B." She glanced over her shoulder. "I'm sorry. I promise not to do that anymore."

I wanted to tell her that I didn't feel much like 'Mrs. B.' anymore; that we were instead following the real Mrs. B. at this very moment. But I kept my mouth shut and watched from the back seat as Kara deftly made a U-turn to follow Barbara's Corvette south on Lafayette to Lincoln, where Barbara made a right turn and headed toward her home on Hendrie, on the other side of Woodward. We followed until Barbara pulled into the attached garage and the automatic door closed behind her.

Kara slipped into a parking spot across the street, facing the house about three houses down, in front of the Kravitz's, assuming they still lived there, which was highly likely. This part of residential Royal Oak had a very low turnover.

At six-fifteen, Boodles and I were done with our fries. I observed Melvin Kravitz's Lexus glide up his drive and into his open garage. I slid down in my seat, in case he'd take a look at Kara's Taurus. After it appeared that Mel was safely in his house, tending to his own life, I sipped the last of my Diet Coke and started to slurp air from the melting ice cubes.

By six-thirty, the stakeout started losing its luster. Kara leaned back against the headrest of the driver's seat and stretched her arms against the windshield. "How long till she goes somewhere? This is boring!"

"I have no idea." I caught a look at my Minnie Mouse watch. "It's only been fifteen minutes."

We kibitzed. We talked. It felt like an eternity, and still, it was only seven o'clock.

Heather nervously scratched her green hair. "What if she decides to stay in tonight?"

I thought about it for a second of two. "If Barbie and Dan are an item—and they are—either she'll go there, or he'll come to her."

"But what if he has a meeting tonight or something?" Heather sounded a little whiny.

"We have to give it at least until nine."

"Nine?" Heather's voice went up a notch on the hysteria scale. "I already have to pee! How do cops do this anyway?"

I let out a quick nervous laugh. Now that she mentioned it, I had to go, too. "Probably they didn't start out with gigantic Diet Cokes."

Kara swiveled her head back to me. "I have to go too. Hey, could we maybe knock on the door of one of your old neighbors?"

"Sounds tempting." I tried to keep the sarcasm from my voice. "But don't you think that might blow our cover?"

"Who cares?" said Heather. "I've got to pee. Now."

"How fast could we make it to McDonalds and back?" I asked.

"About ten minutes, round trip," said Heather. "I was thinking the same thing."

"One of us has to stay here with a cell phone in case she takes off while we're making our pit stop." I was already squirming in the back seat. I swear, the more you talk about it, the more you really have to go!

"It has to be you, Kara," said Heather. "All the neighbors here know me and Mom."

"That's not fair!" said Kara. Was she bouncing in her seat out of anger, or was the urge overwhelming? "Why should I be the last one to go?"

I glanced over at my old house. "It doesn't matter anymore. The garage door is on its way up!"

All eyes turned to the Blumer garage door, now nearly three-quarters open. The Corvette backed slowly out of my former garage, and Barbara headed south toward Lincoln.

"As long as I see what direction she's going, I'll follow." Kara's hand hovered over her ignition key.

"Man, oh man, I've got to pee!" Heather bounced in the front passenger seat.

"That subject is closed!" I said. "Kara, don't forget to drive normally — no screeching tires!"

"I don't want to lose her." Her hands gripped the wheel, her unblinking eyes focused on the bright red Corvette.

"But don't give us away, either." I couldn't help but wonder what trouble I'd get in with the police if we were caught.

I brushed the potential headlines out of my mind and focused on Barbara's red Corvette. Once she passed Woodward, she started to speed, just as Kara, staying safely behind at my request, hit a red light.

Heather bounced on the front seat. She handed her cellphone over to me in the back seat. "Look up Dan Eckles. I think Marcy said he lives in Royal Oak. Either she's going there or we're going to lose her anyway."

I took the phone and opened the browser. Just as I started typing in 'Dan Eckles,' and before the light turned green, Heather opened the car door.

"You go on ahead without me. I'm going to the gas station."

"Heather!" I said. But she slammed the door shut before I had a chance to say 'don't go!'

"Where to?" asked Kara, entering the intersection.

I looked at the phone. "It looks like Dan Eckles lives in the Lofts on Eleven." Metro Detroit is filled with Mile Roads. Anything south of Eight Mile is in Detroit. Anything north of Eight is the suburbs.

Kara's heavy foot hit the accelerator. "Can't see her car now, so let's just get there." She made an illegal left on Woodward, her tires singing on the pavement. Boodles and I rolled sideways.

"Don't get us killed!" I double checked my seat belt and held on to Boodles for dear life.

"Stop being a worrywart," Kara snorted. "I drive this way all the time, and I'm still here, aren't I?"

She had a point, so I tightened my grip on Boodles and we sailed north on Woodward till Kara made what felt like a two-wheeled turn on Eleven Mile.

"There she is!" said Kara.

I couldn't believe it. Her crazy driving had paid off. Barbara's red Corvette was a few car lengths ahead of us on Eleven Mile. I fished through my lime bag for my camera and turned it on.

"Who's going to follow her and take the shot?' asked Kara.

Control freak that I am, I really wanted to do it myself. But I knew it would be risky. Barbara's car turned into the Lofts on Eleven parking lot. These lofts were only three stories high, and instead of a parking structure, there were open-air parking spaces; some marked for residents, some for guests. Kara pulled into one of the guest parking spots and unlocked the doors.

"She doesn't know you." I handed her the camera. "That gives you an edge. See if you can follow her and get a shot of her with her boyfriend."

"Nope." She waved it away. "No time to learn your camera now. I'll use my phone."

With that, she leapt out of the car, leaving me and Boodles to wait. I couldn't call Heather because I had her cellphone. Her phone was smart; mine was stupid, didn't have an Internet browser. Apparently, I was too old to consider it a necessity.

I watched the seconds tick away on Heather's phone. From where I sat in the back seat, I had to turn all the way around to see what was going on behind the car. Kara caught up to Barbara, walking about five feet behind her. It was about twenty after seven when I noticed motion coming from the brick wall. It was Kara, running, with Barbara about a car length behind. Oh boy. I wasn't sure whether to duck so Barbara wouldn't see me, or get behind the wheel to give Kara a quick getaway.

I checked the ignition. The key was in it. That made my decision for me. Don't ask me how I did it, but I threw one arm over the front seat, and the rest of my body followed. I'm no athlete, but I managed to get into the driver's seat, and I quickly turned the motor, with Boodles already on my lap. I backed up and faced the car toward the parking lot exit. Kara caught on and jumped right into the passenger seat.

Barbara yelled something I couldn't make out, and I hoped she didn't recognize the back of my head. She managed to pound on the trunk of Kara's car, but thankfully, I was able to slip back into traffic on Eleven Mile and drive away, my heart pounding like a jackhammer.

Kara was laughing hysterically. Maybe she should consider a career in private investigations. I'm probably more suited to the jewelry trade; I like it better when my heart doesn't feel like it's going to bruise my chest from the inside.

"I got great photos!" Kara clicked through the shots on her cell phone.

Just minutes later, I pulled into the gas station where we'd left Heather. "Let me see it!" I said.

The first showed Dan's lustful face as he opened his door for Barbara. The second showed the two in a torrid mouth-open embrace. The third looked more ominous. Both Barbara and Dan faced the camera, brows furrowed, their open mouths apparently shouting.

"Why didn't Dan chase you?" asked Heather, who had climbed into the back seat and was looking over my shoulder.

"The guy, Dan, wanted to, but she stopped him," said Kara. "Quite a mouth on that Barbie doll."

"Is this time-stamped?" I asked.

"Sure it is, Mom," said Heather. "Let me email it to you right now."

With sudden urgency, I remembered just how badly I needed the restroom. Kara and I glanced at each other. Without a word, we each opened our car door and raced for the restroom. Note to self: don't take a massive Diet Coke to a stakeout. Note number two: try not to need a stakeout.

CHAPTER 21

After we emptied our personal tanks and Kara refilled the Taurus on my dime, the girls dropped me and Boodles off at my house. It occurred to me that my Fourth Street house was starting to feel more like home than the one I'd left a year ago on Hendrie. I let Boodles out the back door and sank into my overstuffed couch. It was all of eight o'clock, and I was drop dead exhausted.

After just a few minutes of blissful quiet, Boodles scratched at the back door, and the phone rang, all at the same time. I glanced at the caller ID. "Hi Shelley." I opened the back door for Boodles.

"Are you sitting down?"

Now that's never a happy question. My stomach knotted

up. "I was."

Boodles bounded in and we both headed back to the couch.

"You aren't going to believe it. " It was hard to tell if Shelley was excited bad or excited happy.

I sank back into the couch, and Boodles leapt onto my lap. I cuddled him, more for my own comfort than his. "Is this about the Blumer company files?"

"You bet it is! I finally got them all from Vic. I've been digging all day."

"So what have you got?"

Shelley cleared her throat. "It's unbelievable! Janine Jenkins has been openly embezzling money from Blumer Fine Jewelers for at least the last six months."

"Oh my." I was thoroughly delighted to be sitting. I could feel the blood pounding in my head with what promised to be a monumental headache. "But how can you be certain it's Janine?"

"Her name's on the credit card bills — on the bank statement itself, for God's sake!" Shelley sounded angry. "Didn't Robert or Vic ever look at the statements?"

I sighed and gave Boodles an extra hug. "Robert was always a great money manager, but I think he was more of a bottom-line kind of guy."

"What does that mean?" said Shelley. "You can't be a good money manager if you don't take the time to look at your own statements!"

I sighed. "I never looked at the books either when I worked there. That was Janine's job—and there never was a problem with it."

"Oh my God." She was practically screaming. "You didn't look either? This could have been going on forever!"

This time, my sigh was so loud I could hear it myself. "I was always busy with the creative end, just like now—making and selling jewelry. Sometimes I went to the counter. You know how much I hate paperwork!"

"That's no excuse!" In my mind's eye, I could see her shaking her head. "It's downright irresponsible."

Boodles licked my arm, a pleasant sensation in contrast to my conversation with Shelley. "But Shelley, there was never a problem with money. The bank account was always in great shape, or I would have heard about it." I sat up straight in the couch, the better to pique my memory. "In fact, the first time I ever heard of a money problem was the day Robert was killed."

"So Ms. Janine has been doing the books since Myrna and Lou left the business with Robert, ten years ago?" She already knew the answer to that question, so I didn't respond.

"You think she's been stealing from us for all these years?"

Shelley hesitated. "I only have the statements from January through June of this year. Let me call Vic, and I'll get last year's statements."

"I can help you on that one. We, I mean, Robert, keeps, I mean kept, all the bank information in cardboard boxes going back seven years, in the storage closet by the bathrooms in the back. Every year we shredded the oldest box."

"This is at work?" Shelley sounded anxious. "That's perfect." Of course, if they were at Barbara's house, it would create an issue.

"Yes, at work."

I could hear her relax over the phone. Her sigh was palpable. "Why didn't you tell Vic this before?" she asked.

It was my turn to sigh. "I honestly didn't put it together, Shel. Like I said, I was never involved in that part of the business."

"I'm calling Vic this minute." She promptly clicked off the phone.

I have to tell you, I was stunned. After ten years, Janine was practically family. We'd never really been close, but still. Stealing like that? Even though I wasn't part of the business anymore, I felt violated. I had been there with her for nine of those ten years, and who knows for how long she'd been dishonest. And deceitful. A thief is a thief.

I was wondering if I should call Max about it, just as my cell phone started up with the "Bad" theme. I was starting to believe in telepathy because it was Max.

"Hello?"

There was a brief silence. "What's wrong, Bella?"

Geez. I knew my face was an open book, but my voice, too? On the phone, even? "A lot happened since I saw you last."

Max chuckled. "That was just a few hours ago. You lead a very interesting life."

"I want my old life back," I said, flopping sideways onto the couch, my head on a throw pillow. Boodles climbed onto my chest and snuggled down for a nap.

"From what I read in all the police notes, you weren't all that fond of your old life."

I felt my face turn hot. I was tempted to click the phone off, but instead remained silent.

"Bella?"

I was silent for another count or two. "What?"

"Hoo boy, now I've gone and insulted you."

I was very glad this was a phone conversation because I could feel hot tears sliding from the side of my eyes into my ears. I took a deep breath to steady myself. "I think I'm going to go now." I was more than ready to click off the phone.

"Bella, wait, I'm sorry. Really sorry," said Max. "I've been through it, too."

"Been through what?"

"A divorce. It wasn't exactly like yours, but it was painful nonetheless."

"Did she cheat on you?" I couldn't imagine anything worse than the pain of rejection I felt when I saw that Robert preferred another woman to me. I wiped my eyes and ears with my shirt.

He hesitated. "No."

"You cheat on her?"

"Absolutely not. I am a loyal man."

"So what happened?"

Now it was Max's turn to be silent. "I usually don't discuss these things with clients."

I laughed. "But Max, I don't think you've been treating me like you'd normally treat a client."

He made a noise that was half laugh and half sigh. "I suppose that's true."

I wasn't sure why I said that, and now we were in dangerous territory. I needed him as a lawyer, and I wasn't really sure of what I wanted from him beyond that. So I decided to respond to his first comment instead. "You're right, I complained a lot about Robert. And Barbara. It felt like they destroyed me. I guess venting helped."

"I still haven't recovered from my divorce either."

"How long did you say it's been?"

"Eight months." His voice was pained.

"That's right. So we're pretty much in the same boat."

"I liked being married," he said.

I curled into a more comfortable position on the couch. Boodles hopped on my lap and snuggled in. "Me too. So what happened?"

Okay, I know. If I wasn't interested in him as a person—

as opposed to as a lawyer—I shouldn't ask. But I was curious, and the question just popped out.

"I guess I wasn't a very good husband. At least, that's what Darla had to say."

"Okay, you said you didn't cheat, so what gives? What made you a 'bad' husband?"

Max sighed. "I wasn't there for her much. I put everything, all my time, all my effort, into my practice, first as a law student and clerk, then as an Assistant District Attorney, and later in my practice with McGriff. She was virtually a single parent for all the years the kids were growing up."

Kids. I hadn't thought about Max having kids. Just like it's hard for school kids to imagine their teacher having a life out of school, I hadn't thought of Max much beyond the confines of my contact with him.

"How old are your kids?" I asked.

"Let's see...Matt, he's a lawyer in Chicago now, he's twenty-six. Michael, my middle child, is a big-shot investment banker in New York at all of twenty-four. And Jennifer, my baby, is learning how to be a social worker and going to NYU, near her brother. She'll be twenty-one next week."

"Oh, so they're all out of town," I said.

Max sighed. "Yeah, you're the lucky one with two kids in town."

I laughed. "I haven't thought of myself as anywhere

remotely lucky for a long time now."

"For at least this past year, from what I've read."

I was ready to steer the topic away from my life and back to his. "If you liked being married so much, why don't you try getting back together with Darla?"

Again there was a silence. The bad question made the air thick between us, even across the phone lines, making it hard to breathe.

"It's too late now," he said. "I'm a changed man. I know exactly what I did wrong and how I hurt her, but it's too late." I could hear an edge of pain in his voice

"There's someone else now?"

"She's engaged." His voice caught on the word. "Getting married this fall. It pretty much broke my heart when she told me. I'd been hoping we'd get back together."

Oh. "You'll find someone else." I don't know why I said it. I don't know how other people can go through life saying just the right thing and not putting their foot in their mouth. But it was out there, and he didn't waste it.

"I think I have," he said.

I didn't know what to say. I was pretty sure he was talking about me but not positive. Either way, for once, I was speechless.

"Sorry to put you on the spot." He finally spoke. "This is probably not the right time."

I found my voice. "I'm going through so much, Max. I don't know how I feel." That wasn't a lie.

He cleared his throat. "Well, Mrs. Blumer, let's stick to the case for now. Tell me what happened in the exciting life of Bella Blumer after four o'clock this afternoon."

So I told Max about our successful stakeout, the incriminating photos, and the very daring Kara Kostas.

"Fantastic! Get on your computer and send those photos to me right away."

"Will do, but there's more," I said, sounding more like a Ginsu commercial than a client.

I told him about Shelley's call and how Janine was paying her personal charge bill with Blumer's online bank account.

"It's probably the tip of the iceberg," said Max.

"What do you mean?"

"If it was that easy and quick to find, there's probably more."

"Shelley's looking back through last year's statements tonight."

"You know, this could change the whole outlook on your case."

"What do you mean?" I was now sitting straight up on my couch.

"She's going to claim Robert knew all about it," said Max. "At least she will if she gets herself a good lawyer."

"No way!" I could hear the outrage in my voice. "Robert would never let Janine do such a thing. We always did everything by the book."

"He cheated on you, Bella. That's not by the book."

"What are you saying?" I gripped the couch cushion.

"I'm just not sure you know as much as you think you know about Robert."

I stood up. I could feel the nubby area rug beneath my bare feet, but I could barely see the wall in front of me. "Explain yourself."

Max was silent for a moment or two, maybe considering what he was going to say. "I don't have all the answers, Bella. Let's wait and see what the facts are."

"What do you mean?' I asked, for what felt like the tenth time in this conversation.

"Embezzlement is a crime, and if Shelley's right, then Janine had a lot to lose."

"What are you saying?" It felt like the room was spinning.

"People have killed for less."

"You think Janine killed Robert!" This was beyond belief.

"I didn't say that. I'm just saying that it's possible. If Robert caught on, and Janine knew it, depending on the amount she'd been embezzling, it could very well be a motive. Did Vic hire a forensics accountant yet?" he asked.

"What's a forensics accountant?" I asked, thinking of that Jack Klugman show, *Quincy*, where he played a forensics medical doctor. "Do we have such an animal in

Metro Detroit?"

Max laughed. "Of course we do, Bella. We're not exactly in the outback. Tell Vic to ask his accountant for a referral. If they don't know one, I'll get a name for him."

"But will he be able to afford it?" I was suddenly nervous for my son.

"He can't afford not to. Oh, and tell him to put Janine on paid administrative leave."

"Oh my," I said. "When?"

"You don't want her back in the office anymore. That would give her the chance to steal even more—and there's the other thing."

Boodles was dancing around my ankles, trying to get my attention, but I ignored him. My heart was beating a little too fast, and I couldn't concentrate on anything past this conversation. "What other thing?"

"If she's an embezzler, and if she's the murderer, we don't want her having access to anything in the store. That includes computer files, Robert's records, anything."

"Oh my!" As if it wasn't bad enough to know that Barbara had been cheating on Robert, probably from day one, now there was this, too.

"Are you okay?" Max sounded concerned. "You want me to come over?"

The truth was I really needed someone, and it would have been wonderful to say yes. But I didn't think it was fair. It was getting too personal between us. "No, thanks. I'll be fine, and I'd better call Vic right now."

I clicked off the phone, feeling very much alone and wishing I'd said yes.

CHAPTER 22

I stayed on the couch, just Boodles and me. No TV. Not a light on in the house. It was nine-thirty and getting dark, making my normally vibrant and colorful living room dark and eerie. I could make out some shapes from the light filtering in from the corner streetlight, but everything felt odd and out of shape, like my life. It was too early to go to bed, and I was just trying to unwind from all the stress.

There was Robert's murder, my arrest, the gun planted in my yard, being stalked by Larry Bernstein, the discovery Barbara had been cheating on Robert, not to mention the stakeout. Then there was the revelation of Janine's embezzlement. It was enough to make a normal woman want to curl up into the fetal position.

My cell phone startled me with Michael Jackson. I had to change that thing. The caller ID told me it was Shelley. I said a curt hello.

"Bella, what's wrong?" I must be the most transparent woman on earth!

"What's right?" I could hear the dull tone of my voice.

"Bella, there's no time to be depressed. We have the Art Fair tomorrow, and now there's this thing with Janine."

Well, that was a jolt of adrenaline! I wasn't about to admit to Shelley that the stakeout and the conversation with Max had pushed the Art Fair right out of my mind. And it was tomorrow morning! I knew I needed a vacation, or at least a true day off, but there wasn't anything like that on the horizon.

"Bella? You there?" Shelley sounded concerned.

I pulled myself together and decided to stick with Vic's problems. "Do you have last year's statements yet?" I turned on the floor lamp that I'd bought at last year's Royal Oak Art Fair. It was decorated with multicolor glass beads.

"Vic said he'd bring it all over tonight, and here's the thing. I can't do both the show *and* audit Vic's books."

I could feel myself starting to cry again, and believe me, I'm not a crier. This was too much! I couldn't do the show without Shelley. It was impossible. "I can't do it without you, Shel. The audit has to wait."

"No can do," said Shelley. "I already promised Vic. I have to get this done ASAP. Vic needs to know what's going on."

I sighed. "But none of the new pieces are even priced yet. I can't do that *and* set up the show."

"Oh," said Shelley, "I forgot about that. But here's the deal. I already talked to Heather, and she's happy to work the show with you, instead of me. By the way, great job on the stakeout!"

Heather was a great idea. Why hadn't I thought of that? Too much stress crowding my brainwaves, probably. "What about the pricing?"

"Can't you do that yourself, Bella? I've told you the formula about a hundred times."

Shelley sounded annoyed. I figured this audit thing for Vic was putting her under a lot of pressure, so I didn't snap back at her.

"Shelley, I don't ask much, but please just do the pricing, and I'll take care of the rest with Heather."

She sighed. "You want to meet me at the shop now, or in the morning?"

I looked at the clock. It was nearly ten. "Tomorrow would be better. I'll be loading the car up at about eight. The show starts at noon, but shoppers will be there by eleven, I think. I want plenty of time to set up." My garage was filled: with the table, the sign, and the tent we'd purchased online weeks ago for this event. Boodles and I were going to wear matching collars.

"Fair enough," she said. "I'll meet you at the shop at

eight."

Before we could say our goodbyes, Vic's call cut in on my cell. "Gotta go, Shelley. It's Vic."

"Hi, Mom." Vic's voice was crisp and businesslike. "I'm on my way to Aunt Shelley's. Just wanted to check in. I talked to our CPA, and he set us up with a forensic accountant."

"Oh, Max just told me about that. Do you have an appointment yet?"

"They're working on it."

"It's hard to believe Janine would do that." The feeling of betrayal was similar to how I felt about Robert.

"This is a nightmare," said Vic. "We don't need any more bad publicity."

I knew what he was talking about. First Robert was murdered, then Vic's mother was implicated, and now his bookkeeper was about to be arrested for embezzlement. "I don't want to go to the police."

"You may have to. Why don't you ask the accountant what to do?"

"I think I need to talk to a lawyer," he said.

"What about Max?"

"He's a criminal lawyer," said Vic. "I need an employment lawyer."

Oh boy, bring on the lawyers.

"You know one?"

"I'll call Marcy's brother and ask if he knows any."

Apparently, lawyers meet in law school, just like criminals meet in prison.

"This is sounding expensive."

"You're telling me," said Vic.

It occurred to me that Janine's alibi on the morning of Robert's murder was that she'd had a dentist appointment. While it was possible she could have switched, she'd been using Dr. Saperstein's dental office, where Marcy worked, ever since Marcy married Vic.

"Could you ask Marcy to see if Janine really was at the dentist's office the day Dad was killed?"

"You're checking on her alibi?" Vic sounded surprised.

"Well, we know she's a thief."

Vic told me to hold on while he asked Marcy.

"She doesn't remember seeing Janine last week, but she'll look it up at work on Monday."

I felt like I was the chief detective of the Bella Blumer Detective Agency.

"Yes, please have her do that." If Janine's alibi fell flat, then she would absolutely be as hot a suspect as barbarous Barbara.

"I'm pulling into Aunt Shelley's drive right now."

"G'bye, hon. Don't worry, this will all work out." I don't know why I said that. I was a nervous wreck myself. It was probably a mother reflex.

I looked at the clock. It was ten-fifteen. I needed to unwind a bit. I quickly texted Heather to let her know

I needed her up in time to be at the shop by eight-thirty. Then I fastened Boodles' collar to his leash and headed out the front door for a calming walk around the block. Boodles danced around my ankles with joy. You have to love him; such excitement for so little!

I sucked in a deep breath of Royal Oak air. My house was just far enough from downtown that there was little traffic on Fourth. Boodles stopped to anoint just about every tree on the block. The air had cooled a bit, and the mugginess had lifted.

As we rounded the last corner to head back to my house, I had an uneasy feeling that someone was watching me, and it made me think of Larry Bernstein. I swiveled my head to check behind me. No one was out—no neighbors on their porches, no one coming in or out of a car. The parking structure across the street was filled, but I saw no one walking between the cars. I looked at the row of parked cars. With the tinted windows in the shadows, it was impossible to see if anyone was inside. Watching me.

I picked up my pace, nervous now when Boodles stopped to lift his leg. What was I doing? It had only been Friday, two days ago, that someone had planted that gun in my yard. Barbara? Dan Eckles? Larry? Janine?

I shivered and started to run to my front door, happy I'd locked it. I turned my key, ran in with Boodles, and quickly slammed the door shut. I turned on the porch light, and then every light on the bottom floor, before heading up the stairs for an uneasy night of sleep.

SUNDAY MORNING, my alarm went off at the ungodly hour of 5:00 AM. I needed plenty of time to tend to myself and to Boodles. I was going to do what Myrna calls a "complete" overhaul: shower, wash my hair, shave my legs, moisturize, and then carefully work on my hair and makeup. All that plus breakfast, a quick walk for Boodles, and then a trip to my garage to load up all the paraphernalia for the Art Fair.

I felt somewhat overdressed in my almost designer blue jumpsuit and matching blue flats. I was loading up the Escalade in my damp and musty garage when I once again had the uneasy feeling I was being watched, but I preferred to believe I was just scaring myself. I looked toward the street and scanned my neighbors' houses. There were a few cars in the parking structure across the side street, but nothing looked more ominous than usual.

I walked to the front of the Escalade to make sure there was no one hiding in my garage, that's how strange I felt. I saw nothing but a few garden tools left over from the last owner: a hoe, a manual edger with a wheel, a few snaggle-toothed rakes, an ancient push broom, and a shovel. They all looked old and nasty, which is probably why they'd been left behind.

I don't know why I took a second look at the shovel, but

I did. It still had some dirt on the tip. It was moist dirt, as if someone had used it recently. A chill went up my spine. I never locked my garage. Despite the hellacious reputation of Detroit, sleepy Royal Oak, just two miles north, was notoriously safe. Well, except for the Robert Blumer thing.

It occurred to me that whoever planted the gun in my side yard might very well have used this shovel and brazenly returned it to my garage. Complete with fingerprints! I ran into the house for a plastic garbage bag, threw it over the shovel handle, and put it aside in the corner of the garage, looking over my shoulder again to make sure no one was watching.

Heather staggered out the back door to the garage just in time to help me load up the car. Together we hefted the tent into the back of the Escalade. As we were lifting one of two tabletop glass showcases, Heather asked, "Why did you wrap up the shovel, Mom?"

Boodles jumped out of the car and ran to Heather for some affection, his blue-beaded collar a match to my lapis lazuli beads.

"And why are you and Boodles matching? Isn't that silly?" she added.

I leaned against the Escalade, already tired and it was only seven-thirty. "First, I think it's possible that whoever planted the gun in our yard used this shovel."

Heather gasped. "That's creepy. Are you going to call the police?"

"No," I said. "At least not yet. I think I'd rather call Max and have him call the police instead. The less I have to do with the boys in blue, the better." Actually, I was thinking of the intriguing Detective Krieger, who saw me as more of prime suspect, while I saw him as prime beef, medium rare.

"Okay," said Heather. "But make sure you lock the garage then, when we leave."

"That makes sense," I said, banishing my libidinous thoughts of the unattainable detective. "And back to your other point. I like to match Boodles, especially for something as important as this Art Fair."

"I don't remember ever wearing mother-daughter dresses when I was growing up," said Heather, sounding hurt. Was she actually jealous of a dog?

"I thought they were tacky," I said, and this was true. I thought those mother-daughter match-ups were a throwback to the fifties.

"And a woman-dog match-up is classy?" She turned to walk into the house.

"Heather, what's the matter? Is this really about Boodles' collar? Which is, incidentally, adorable, a conversation piece, and a good piece of marketing for that matter."

"Oh," she said, apparently mollified. Good thing. I didn't want to tell her that I just enjoyed the kitschy match-up. Sue me!

"So what's going on? I thought you enjoyed working at the shop," I said. "I'd think you'd be happy about helping me at the Art Fair."

She looked at me and then at Boodles, who bless his tiny heart, had two little paws up, asking her for an alley-oop. She scooped him up despite herself.

"You don't have to be jealous of Boodles," I said. "I love him, but he's just a dog."

"But you dote on him like you never doted on me," she said.

I sighed. And Boodles started licking Heather's arm and then reached up to swab her neck. She giggled.

"You see," I said. "Boodles just isn't complicated. Here you are complaining about my relationship with him, and all he wants is a little love and attention."

"Are you saying I'm complicated?" Heather's voice returned to an edge.

"Heather, we're both complicated," I said. "My mother annoys me. I annoy you. That's what makes the world go round."

"So you *do* love this dog more than me!" she said. But I noticed that she was still holding him. I understood why. Holding Boodles feels great.

I answered her honestly. Again. "Heather, you're making me repeat myself. Of course I don't love him more than you! He's a dog! He's just less complicated." I turned to look into the back end of the Escalade, and then at my watch. "We have to be at the shop at eight o'clock to meet Aunt Shelly. You going to be ready?"

"I'll get dressed." Heather gently put Boodles back on the ground.

AT EIGHT o'clock sharp we pulled into the alley behind Bella's Baubles, directly behind Shelley's Chrysler minivan.

As soon as we walked through the door, Shelley handed me a list and some price tags. "I've gone over all the new pieces," she said. "Here are the tags."

I gave her a hug. "Thanks, Shel," I said.

Heather gave her a hug too. Talk about complicated — Heather always found it easier to talk to my sister than to me. "Thanks, Aunt Shelley," she said. "You can go home and back to bed now."

Shelley laughed. "Fat chance. I have a whole cardboard box of bank statements and records to go over for your brother. It'll probably take up most of the day."

"You think you'll make it to the Art Fair?" I asked.

Shelley smoothed her straight brown hair. She got the straight locks from our dad. I had Mom's wavy mess, only I didn't choose to drown it in lacquer. "If I get done in time, I guess," she said, walking to the door and heading back out onto Fourth Street. "I'd better get going."

Heather and I started packing up all the beads in special trays. I spotted another lapis necklace and handed it to Heather. "Here, Honey, put this on," I said.

"What are you talking about?" Heather's short spiky hair was still bright green. She giggled. "You think it goes with the green?"

I smiled. "Who cares? Now the entire Bella's Baubles team matches."

Heather put on the lapis pendant, which was dripping with opal teardrops. It actually looked nice with her hair, and I suspected she would sell it off her neck before the afternoon was over.

We methodically packed up a considerable amount of my inventory, along with several of my leatherette counter pads, bracelet bars, earring trees, and busts for displaying special pendants.

By the time we reached the field for the Art Fair up on Thirteen Mile by the park and the northern Royal Oak Fire Station, there was already a lineup of cars. It was eight forty-five. I had a nagging feeling in the back of my mind that something was bothering me, something I'd forgotten, but I just couldn't figure it out. The Escalade had been in idle so long, I put it in park.

"Hurry up and wait," said Heather, sliding sideways on her seat to catch a little nap.

Turns out, she had about a half hour before it was our turn to set up. It was a trial schlepping the tent and the heavy showcases, not to mention the tables and the merchandise. We were set up on terra firma, the green grass directly beneath our feet. I made a mental note to bring a carpet remnant next year. And two chairs.

"I'll go get chairs right now," said Heather, ever reading my mind.

And that's when I remembered what was niggling at the back of my mind. "The garage! I don't think I locked the garage door!"

CHAPTER 23

"Oh Mom!" said Heather. "Stop being such a worrywart. No one's going in our garage."

But I remembered the way I'd felt the night before when walking Boodles, and how it felt as if someone was watching me when I was in the garage, loading up by myself. "I hope you're right," I said. "But check that it's locked anyway. And hurry back. It's already eleven."

Heather headed off toward the car. And true to my memory of last year's Art Fair, when I was just a wandering shopper, the aisles were starting to fill with the early birds. The sun was shining bright, and the air was just muggy enough to destroy my hair. I was glad to have a tent over my head, even if I was lacking a chair. Boodles was curled up in a corner where the sun shone in, enjoying a brief sunbath. I wasn't at all surprised when my booth started to get busy.

The first customers to approach my tent were the Schultz sisters. "Hi, Bella," said Golda.

I was surprised that she was still talking to me after the way I'd treated her at Robert's funeral.

"Hi Golda," I said. "I made a lot of new pieces for the fair." I took a quick appraising look at her off-the-shoulder cinnamon-colored sundress. A bit inappropriate for her age, but that wasn't my business. "Take a look at this cinnabar pendant. I've had the design in mind for years and just completed it yesterday." No one likes to think that you whipped up a design on the fly. So even though that's what I do half the time, I tell my customers the design took years. Yeah, right. If that was the case, everything I made would be out of style by the time I fastened the clasps.

"It's beautiful!" she cried, holding it up to her creamy-white neck.

I have to admit, it did look good on her, especially with that sundress.

"How much?" she asked.

Before you know it, there was the first sale of the day. I made a mental note to never aggravate potential customers again.

I'd been waiting on the fifth customer of the day, and it still wasn't noon yet. I kept an eye on Boodles, who'd been napping beneath one of the storage tables in the back of the tent, inside his carrier. Just as I'd been thinking that I should have brought one of his beds, in walked Heather toting two chairs and a tiny Boodles bed. I gave her a peck on the cheek and took one of the chairs.

Right on cue, the customer said, "thank you," and walked away.

"Sorry, Mom," said Heather. "I wrecked the sale." She put the dog bed under the table, and Boodles immediately took up residence, circling the tiny bed until he plopped into a cozy ball.

I sat on the unfolded chair. "You didn't wreck anything," I said. "If she wanted to buy, she would have."

Heather pulled her chair closer to mine, and it occurred to me that there was more seating space in this tent than in my tiny store. "Mom, you won't believe it," said Heather.

"Believe what?" I asked.

"The shovel's missing!"

"What?" I felt my eyebrows rise to the top of my forehead.

"You were right," said Heather. "Someone took it."

"Oh my God," I said. "It has to be the murderer — or whoever planted the gun in our yard." My heart was pounding at the thought of someone dangerous floating around my house on two occasions now.

"Chill out, Mom," said Heather.

I didn't get a chance to bark at her because once again a flotilla of customers sidled up to the showcases at the front of the tent. After that, we were busy for what felt like hours.

When I finally had a chance to look at my watch, it was two-thirty. "I'm starved," I said.

"I'll go get us some Coney Dogs," said Heather. American Coney had set up a trailer just one aisle over and was doing a brisk business in Coney dogs and cheese fries. In case you don't know, Detroit is also home to a great number of Greek restaurants, all of which specialize in these hot dogs topped sometimes with cheese, and always with their own special "Coney-style" meat sauce.

I handed Heather a twenty. "Get us some fries and Cokes, too," I said.

Just as Heather walked off, my mother and Albert showed up at my tent.

"Hello, dear," said my mother, giving me a perfunctory kiss on the cheek. She and Albert were loaded down with bags, and Albert carried a large metal sculpture that looked something like the offspring of a lion and a giraffe. Don't ask.

"It will go perfect in your backyard, dear."

Oh boy. "Thanks, Mom." I was mentally finding a place for it in my garage—close enough to the yard to put in place before her visits.

"I'm so glad you like it," she said, and I could see the pleasure on her face. She sure loves to shop, and Albert loves accommodating her.

"Thanks, Mom. Thanks, Albert," I said.

A crowd of three pulled up to peer into my showcases,

so Albert and my mom politely disappeared back into the crowd.

LATER, WHEN I was chewing the last of my cheese fries and crumpling my lunch papers into a wad, up walked Frankie Zerkin, one of my high school friends, but never a customer. Oh, well. "Hi, Frankie, how are you?"

"That's not the question," she said, her brow furrowed, her eyes looking sad and helpless. "I'm so worried about you. I mean, now that they found your gun and all. I'm so glad you're out on bail."

With friends like these, I thought. "Yes, Frankie," I said. "Whoever murdered Robert used my gun."

Frankie gasped, her hand at her throat. "You're saying you didn't do it?"

I didn't know whether to defend myself or smack her one in the mouth. I was pretty sure that the mouth thing would be assault, so I just stood there for a moment, stunned. Then I decided to respond.

"Frankie, dear," I said, affecting my mother's voice. "It was so nice of you to stop by, but I really have to tend to customers." Thankfully, there was a young mother with a toddler in tow, eyeballing my jewelry.

Amazingly, Frankie took the hint and walked off in a huff.

The toddler-mom looked up. "Good for you," she said.

I didn't say anything, but apparently my face said 'huh?' because she explained, "What a rude person! Trying to talk to you because you're in the news."

"Thanks," I said. "It's been a rough week, and for the record, I didn't kill him."

She touched my hand. "You don't owe me an explanation either," she said. "Could I see that pendant?" She was pointing to a seed pearl and onyx combination, perfect for her tiny frame. She bought it on the spot and went on her way. It was a relief to make a sale, but I wasn't sure it was a good idea for me to be out here in public, right after my gun hit the news.

My cell phone made Michael Jackson noises. It was Vic.

"Hi, Honey," I said. "Are you and Marcy coming to the Art Fair today?" Blumer Fine Jewelers was more of a jewelry store, and less of a one-of-a-kind boutique, like Bella's Baubles, so they never participated as a vendor at the Art Fair.

"No, Mom. Marcy and I are too busy pulling files and searching records." His voice sounded tense.

"Too bad, it's a lovely day," I said, thinking that it was, if you could ignore the hair-destroying humidity. Oh, and the issue of being the number one suspect in Robert's murder. (Oh that!)

"The reason I'm calling," he said, "is that I talked to the forensics accountant again, and she's willing to see us tonight."

"Us?" I repeated.

"Aunt Shelley already said she would come, and I thought you would, too," he said. "Marcy's coming... Look, I'm really over my head here. I never did the books at all. I really need your help."

"What time?"

"Oh...it's at eight o'clock."

I silently sighed, looking at the front of the showcases. Heather was waiting on one customer and there were two more waiting. "Not sure that I know any more than you do, but I'll be glad to come for moral support."

"Thanks, Mom," he said, his voice brightening. "I'll text you the address."

"I better go sell some jewelry." I gave him a quick buss on the cheek and joined Heather at the counter. I might prefer making the stuff, but selling it is equally important.

About ten customers and three sales later, who walks up to my booth, but Glenda Gleason. I walked to the other side of the showcases and gave her a big hug. She clung to me like a mourner at a funeral. It was intense. When she finally released her grip, I held her at arm's length and took a look at her tear-stained face.

"Glenda, are you all right?"

She pulled a ratty-looking tissue from her pocket and wiped her nose. "I've decided to divorce him," she said, choking on her words.

There was no one else at the booth. I caught Heather's eye, and she waved me away.

"Oh, Glenda, I'm so sorry." I put my arm around her. "Are you sure this is what you want to do?"

Her wet face turned into a scowl. "You got rid of your cheat. Now it's time for me to get rid of mine."

I turned toward her. "Robert sued me for divorce," I said. "I had no idea he was even cheating on me."

"That's, that's even worse!" she practically wailed. "How could you stand it?"

"It was unbearable." That was God's truth. It *was* unbearable. "That's why I complained so much to anyone who would listen."

We started walking down the center aisle and finally stopped when we saw some chairs and tables by the American Coney concession.

"I'll get us some Cokes." I looked at her blotchy, wet face. "And some extra napkins."

After a few sips on our drinks, we sat quietly for a while. I patted her hand. "You'll be okay, you know. Eventually."

"It doesn't feel like that now." Glenda's voice was monotone, but at least she wasn't crying any more.

I'm sorry if it makes me shallow, but it was hard for me to imagine loving someone as fat and unattractive as Ollie Gleason. But here she was, his soon-to-be ex-wife, absolutely devastated by the prospect of life without him. Go figure.

"So you really love him?" I knew it was a stupid question. Thankfully, it didn't cause an eruption of fresh tears.

Instead, Glenda sat straighter in her folding chair. "You know, I think I want to buy a new necklace."

"Glenda, you don't have to do that for me. I'm just fine." I was thinking that she was just trying to be charitable.

Glenda opened her eyes wide and gave me a strange look. "I'm not buying a necklace for you. I'm buying one for myself. I've been hinting for the past year that I'd like one of your designs, and what does that old galoot do? He buys a diamond for that gold-digger! I'll show him! I'm buying my own necklace from you, Bella. What's the most expensive thing you've got?"

I stood up and laughed. "Let's go, Glenda."

We headed back to my booth, arm in arm. The most expensive thing I had on hand was an opal and malachite pendant with diamond-set beads and clasp. I'd bought those already set, but the rest of the piece I'd designed and crafted myself.

Glenda refused a box, insisted instead to wear her new jewel home. I have to say, it looked stunning on her yellow silk blouse. It set Ollie back several hundred dollars — but not nearly as much as a three-carat diamond. Or a divorce.

"What's with Mrs. Gleason?" asked Heather, when Glenda was several tents away and out of earshot.

I told her Glenda was planning to divorce Ollie.

"Men suck." She was spritzing the showcase glass and

giving it a good wipe between customers. Heather was a retail natural.

"I don't know about that. Not all men suck, at least not all the time." I was thinking about Max, who seemed to be perpetually nice and caring, even if he wasn't my GQ ideal.

"Well, they all suck enough." She punctuated her thought by wiping the counter with gusto.

"Don't give up on finding someone special." My voice was a little softer. "Don't let Glenda and me ruin you for romance."

"Romance?" Heather chuckled. "Don't say that word in front of anyone else, Mom. It makes you sound like you're from the Stone Age."

"Maybe we had more fun in the Stone Age," I countered, acting glib, but feeling a little stung by her critique.

"How's that working out for you?" she said.

I didn't quite know how to answer that, so I was relieved when, once again, our showcases were crowded with curious customers.

It's amazing how fast time goes by when you're totally busy and engaged. By the time I had a chance to glance at my watch it was three thirty, during the peak heat of the day. I felt as cool as possible in my lightweight outfit; the thermometer topped ninety sweltering degrees. I poured some water into Boodles' little bowl. He hopped out of his carrier to take a few licks and then a quick leak on the grass floor. Note to self: maybe forget about bringing a rug next year. That would be one less thing to worry about.

"Mind if I take a quick break?" asked Heather.

I shooed her off, along with her promise to return in fifteen minutes. As soon as I was alone, the chief creep himself, Larry Bernstein, walked up to my booth. After our last conversation on Fourth Street, at my shop, I'd thought I was through with him.

He leaned over the counter, resting his elbow on the glass. "I hear you're asking about me, Bella," he said, his eyes all come-hither.

Now, you don't want to be mean to a guy, because even the worst of them have feelings, and Larry was the worst. And then there was the matter of him being a suspect. No point in pissing him off big-time in case he was actually the murderer and, gulp, the one scouting my house making me feel creepy. And stealing my shovel!

I decided to play it straight. Kind, but straight. "My lawyer thought it was a good idea to find out who initiated our fix up — my mother or yours," I said. "And once we knew it was your mother, it was important to know whether it was her idea or yours."

"Why are you talking about lawyers?" He looked alarmed. "What? Am I a suspect or something?" No more smarmy lean across the counter. The man was standing straight and ready to run. This gave me strength.

"Well, everyone's a suspect until they're not. Where were you on Monday between nine-thirty and eleven?"

"You've got to be kidding! Why would I be a suspect for killing your husband?" I noticed his hands were balled into fists.

"Um, I heard Robert wasn't your favorite classmate in high school." I was glad this conversation was out in the open air of the Royal Oak Art Fair and not in the small confines of my tiny shop.

"You've got to be kidding." He repeated as his face turned a nice shade of flush. "That's ancient history. It's almost time for our fortieth reunion!"

"Better late than never," I said. Okay, so I was getting a little smarmy myself. Can you blame me? If anyone deserved my worst, it was Larry Bernstein.

"I didn't kill your husband." He pursed his lips.

"My ex-husband," I corrected him. "And I probably believe you, but just for the record, where were you Monday morning?"

"I was at my desk, at Michigan Insurance. You can ask any of the ladies who work there."

I just might, just to be sure. "Well, thank you, Larry. No hard feelings."

Wrong word choice. With that, Larry once again leaned against the counter. His parents must be Elsie and Elmer. The guy was pure glue.

I was hoping for Heather to return, or a bevy of customers, when out of the blue, Max appeared, along with beautiful curly Chester.

"Max!" I squealed.

Max let loose of Chester's lead and Chester rushed inside my tent. He put two paws up on my midsection. Boodles hopped out of his carrier and did his little dance. Two paws in the air as he jumped in a circle in front of Max.

"Hi, Larry," said Max, extending a hand.

"You two an item?" he asked as they shook.

Max shot me a questioning look.

"Of course we're an item." I put a proprietary hand on Max's arm.

"But he's your lawyer." Larry turned toward Max. "You told her to check up on me through my mother?"

Max held up both hands, a surrender gesture. "All's fair in love and law."

Larry stuffed two hands in his pocket. "Well for the record, I didn't do it. You're probably defending a guilty woman, but that's your problem." With that, he thankfully walked away from my tent.

Max turned and gave me his signature hug. "Are you okay?"

I couldn't help it; I put my head on his shoulder. "It's been a tough day. So many people think I'm guilty. And then came Larry."

Max chuckled. "You working here alone?"

I told him about Heather and how she happened to take a break just before the appearance of Larry. And then I told him about Vic, and how the appointment with the forensic accountant was moved up to tonight.

"What time?" he asked. I already knew the way his mind worked. He wanted to come.

"Eight o'clock, but I can't afford to pay you."

"It's on the house."

"Even if I'm not sure about us?" I bit my lower lip. I didn't want to take advantage of him, but it would be nice to have his help — as a friend.

"My father owned a deli; did you know that?" asked Max.

"No, you've never mentioned your dad." What did that have to do with the price of tea in China?

"Well, he did, down in the west side of Detroit, over by Seven Mile and James Couzens. He used to give away food all the time, a taste of this, a nibble, a nosh. It drove my mother crazy."

"I don't blame her," I said. "You can't give away the merchandise and make a living."

"But you're wrong. That's what brought them back. That's why they came and ordered trays for Bar Mitzvahs and brought all their friends in. That's what makes the customers love you."

I narrowed my eyes. Was he trying to make me love him?

"Bella, stop with the face. I just want to be there to make sure Vic gets a fair shake. No strings attached. We're just friends."

"Friends," I repeated, and part of me felt deflated. I really needed a shrink.

"So what time do I meet you there?"

"Vic said eight o'clock. He's going to text me the address." I looked at my phone, and Max looked over my shoulder.

"Oh, it's in the building next to the Traveler's Tower," he said. "How about I pick you up at about twenty to eight? It'll give us enough time to park and get there on time."

We said our goodbyes, which included another of Max's uber-friendly hugs.

THE REST of the day at the Art Fair sailed by. I was talking to customers, unlocking the showcase, watching women try on my pieces. Usually, once they go that far, they buy. There is something tantalizing about a well-made design. I don't mean to be full of myself, but especially mine. Shelley does a good job pricing them—and I try to be careful when buying my gems and findings to keep costs as reasonable as possible.

The crowd thinned out at about a quarter to five, and Heather and I started packing things up. Boodles hopped out of his bed and shook his little white curls and made a full stretch. How could you not love that tiny thing?

"I think he needs a walk," I said to Heather. "Would

you rather walk him or help me pack up?"

Heather chose the walk. I handed her a couple of plastic bags. "Just in case."

She screwed her face up at me, but grabbed the bags nonetheless.

As the two of them walked off, I called out, "And don't let him pee on anyone's tent." Heather pretended to ignore me. I was sure she heard, so I returned to my pack-up duties.

By the time she returned, all that was left to dismantle was our tent. "I can't believe the small minds in this town," said Heather.

"What are you talking about?" I asked, my voice halting from the strain of working on the tent pole.

Heather was folding up the huge white tent fabric. "They're all talking about you, saying you have a lot of nerve showing your face here after what you did to Dad."

I felt my face flush. With a surge of energy, I gripped the pole and the rest of the frame came down, crashing into one of the packed showcases, smashing into the glass. I stood there, stunned. "Damn it all to hell!" I screamed. I was so tempted to sit down and weep, but I didn't want to give any of those cretins the satisfaction.

Heather lifted the offending pole off the broken showcase, and turned to look at me. "Sorry, Mom, I shouldn't have told you."

"You think?" I ignored the tears stinging at the back of my eyes. "Let's get out of here. I'll go get my car." With that,

I put Boodles in his carrier and hurried off to the parking area, until it occurred to me that Heather had driven it to lunch. "Where's the car?" I called back to her.

"I parked it over by the baseball concession. It's closer to Thirteen Mile than to Woodward."

By the time we packed up the Escalade and drove off, it was six thirty-five. We picked up some McDonald salads on the way home, and I was delighted to find a set of leftover Double Ds in the fridge, both bumpy-cakes, each with the signature maraschino on top. Blame it on the stress—I skipped the salad and went straight for the bumpy cake. The more chocolate the better, to manage the stress ahead.

CHAPTER 24

The office of Margo Levinson, forensics accountant, was surprisingly un-lavish, considering that she charged three-hundred fifty dollars an hour. She looked about forty-six or so, with carefully dyed brown hair and ridiculous round Harry Potter glasses. Nothing adorned the room, save a few university certificates.

"Maybe we should move into a conference room," she said, as Max and I walked through her office door. I could see her point; Vic, Marcy, and Shelley were already squeezed into the less-than-spacious room.

The five of us followed her and filed into a more appropriately appointed conference room. The offices were on the tenth floor, and the conference room enjoyed a floor-to-ceiling panoramic view of the Southfield skyline.

Southfield is an odd kind of city. It doesn't have a downtown district like Royal Oak, and yet it boasts many more high-rise offices. Where's a city planner when you need one?

Ms. Levinson sat at the head of the inlaid mahogany and white oak conference table, hands poised over a yellow legal pad, ready to work. "Who wants to explain the situation here?" she asked.

Vic and Shelley exchanged glances.

"Why don't you start, Vic," said Shelley, "and I'll fill in the blanks."

Ms. Levinson first had Vic explain who everyone was in the room. Once she was clear about each person's role, Vic explained about the situation with the cash flow problem, how it had been a concern of Robert's in the months before his death.

"I wasn't the one who handled the banking," said Vic, "it was always my dad." He paused.

"Go on," said Ms. Levinson.

"Well, my mom…" Vic gestured toward me. "My mom was sure that Barbara, that's my dad's second wife, was the reason for the cash flow problem."

"The girl's a gold digger," I added.

"Mom, please!" Vic was clearly annoyed.

I consciously pressed my lips together so tight I wondered if they'd bruise. There was so much more to say, but I didn't want to upset Vic.

"So my Aunt Shelley…"

"That's me," interrupted Shelley.

"Is an accountant," said Vic.

"A bookkeeper really," said Shelley. "I'm not a CPA like my husband."

"She offered to go through the books to see if she could find any, well, any irregularities."

Ms. Levinson pointed her round glasses at Shelley. "And what 'irregularities' did you find?"

Shelley reached down beside her leather chair, and with a little grunt, hefted a large stack of papers onto the conference table.

"These are bank statements from this year, January one to the present." She stood to lift another stack, nearly twice the size as the first, and then another. "And these are last year's and the year before that."

"What did you find?" Ms. Levinson looked like she was salivating. Perhaps she liked her work as much as I love my chocolate bumpy cake Double Ds.

Shelley ran her palm over the top of the first stack. "It wasn't Robert's second wife doing the stealing. It was Janine," she said.

"Who is Janine? And what is her last name?" Ms. Levinson's eyes were steely blue behind those glasses.

Vic spoke up. "Her name is Janine Jenkins. She's been our office administrator for the past ten years."

"What do you mean by 'stealing'?" asked Ms. Levinson, her eyes on Shelley.

Shelley had a wry smile. "She was paying her personal charge online with the store bank account. That, and later her new car payments."

"How do you know that these specifically were Ms. Jenkins' charge card and auto payments?"

"Her name is on the Blumer statements every month. It doesn't get more specific than that!"

You had to give it to Ms. Levinson. Other than one slightly raised eyebrow, she had no physical reaction.

"When did it start?" Ms. Levinson was jotting notes on her yellow legal pad, her little fingers flying across the page.

"That's the funny thing," said Shelly. "It started nearly two years ago this coming November. Prior to that, I couldn't find anything wrong."

"So she's been at it for a year and a half." Ms. Levinson's eyes were still on her legal pad. She lifted her pen off the page and gazed at Vic. "Can you think of anything that might have been happening in Ms. Jenkins' life at the time?" she asked. "A bankruptcy? A divorce?"

I leaned forward in my chair. "I was still at Blumer's at that time. In fact, I was at Blumer's until a year ago this month, and I don't remember anything in Janine's life that changed." I shifted in my seat, thinking about how she'd been stealing from the business, right under my nose. It made me feel like a fool. "She's married. I just talked with her husband this week. And if they had a bankruptcy, we sure didn't hear about it."

Vic shook his head. "It doesn't make any sense at all. There has to be something we just don't know about."

Ms. Levinson glanced at her watch, maybe counting her big buck hourly rate. "Has the embezzlement been consistent, or did the dollar amount grow with time?"

Shelley pursed her lips. "It started small, with her charge account, a hundred here, two hundred there, like it wasn't her main account."

Ms. Levinson smiled. "She probably opened a special account just for this purpose. And when Mr. Blumer made no comment of it, well, she probably kept on charging more and more each month. We see this all the time."

"You're right on target," said Shelley. "The charge payments grew until she was charging ten times that each month."

Vic burst out, "A thousand dollars a month!"

"Make that more like two," said Shelley, "but it gets worse."

"What do you mean, worse?" I was starting to feel as angry with little Miss Janine Jenkins as I was at Barbie Blumer.

"It got even worse last August when she started with her nine-hundred dollar car payments."

"Oh my God," I said. "That explains her fancy schmantzy car. I saw it at the funeral."

"She's been taking three grand a month!" Vic's face was bright red. I was afraid he was going to have a coronary.

Marcy put a hand on his arm. "Calm down, Vic," she said. "It's already gone. Now we can stop her from taking any more."

Vic put both his hands in the air, like he was ready to clap. "Why didn't Dad know about this?" He choked on his words and stared at the conference table.

"Maybe he did know about it," said Ms. Levinson. "That could be her argument, if this ever goes to court."

Now it was my turn to blow a gasket. "What do you mean Robert might have known about it? No way would he let that, that mousy redhead steal from the store! It makes no sense!" *He fooled around with Barbara, not Janine.* I felt breathless, like I'd been socked in the gut, and it wasn't even my business any more. It was Vic's—and possibly Barbara's.

Following my train of thought, Ms. Levinson adjusted her horrible glasses and peered at Vic. "Are you the sole owner of this establishment?"

Vic looked up from the table. The flush was draining from his face and he was starting to look pale. "I'm not sure."

"You're not sure?" said Ms. Levinson.

I couldn't help it; I jumped back into the conversation, even though Max had put a restraining hand on my arm. "What do you mean 'you're not sure'?" I asked.

"I can't find Dad's will," he said. "I've searched his office, and the safe. It's not there."

Max tilted his head toward Vic. "Have you asked Barbara where it is? Have you spoken to your dad's attorney?"

Vic rubbed his left eye. "I didn't want to go there with Barbara so soon. My dad just died Monday. He was her husband. It's been just a week. I was hoping she'd bring it up. And no, I'm not sure which lawyer my dad used for his will. He was kind of cagey about some things."

I silently chuckled. Now *that* was an understatement. Robert was cagey about everything! Secrets R Us. I started to wonder what the truth really was about that Blumer bank account.

Ms. Levinson broke into my thoughts. "If Mrs. Blumer is part owner of this business, she deserves to be in on this discussion."

Before I knew it, I was out of my chair and banging on the table, a regular Khrushchev. "No way does that little bitch get any say in this at all. She's probably the reason that Robert is dead!"

"Mom!" Vic looked about ready to shoot me, if only he had my gun.

"Bella, sit down." Max, once again, put his hand on my arm.

I pulled it away. "It's not right!" Tears stung at the back of my eyes.

"That very well may be," said Ms. Levinson. "It may not be right, but it may be legal. Until we see the provision made by your ex-husband in his will, there is no way to know whether Barbara Blumer is involved."

Max swiveled the chair in my direction, a silent plea for my cooperation. I sat. But I wasn't happy about it.

"So what happens next?' asked Shelley.

"I don't want her near that bank account again," said Vic. He turned toward Max, "What was it that you called it? Some kind of 'paid leave'?"

"That's paid administrative leave," said Ms. Levinson. "You are within your rights to check out your case against her, but you do have to pay her for those days of investigation. Otherwise, if it turns out that we're mistaken, you're liable for a nasty law suit."

"She can sue me?" Vic's mouth dropped open as his eyes widened.

"You bet your sweet tushie she can sue you," said the ever-proper Ms. Levinson. "She can sue you even if you have all the goods on her. As I said before, she can claim that all her actions were done with the approval of Robert Blumer."

"But it's still illegal," said Vic. "It can't be legal to pay your personal charge out of a business bank account."

"Oh, but she can claim that he forced her to do it, rather than give her a raise," said Ms. Levinson.

"She *had* a raise!" Vic was shouting. "Every year!" My sweet, quiet Vic had been pushed to the max.

"Who handles payroll?" asked Ms. Levinson.

"Janine," said Vic.

"Well, that's just another opportunity for her to skim. Who checks over the hours? Who cuts the checks?"

Vic looked beat up. "We go on the honor system for the hours and Payrite does the checks. All of them are bank transfers."

Ms. Levinson took another glance at her watch. "Here's what we do next. Vic, I need you to give Ms. Jenkins a call tonight and inform her that she's on paid administrative leave for at least three days."

Vic paused, absorbing the instructions. "What if she asks what it's about?"

"Oh, she will," said Ms. Levinson. "You're to tell her that you're conducting an investigation, and nothing else."

"She's not going to take it well." Vic frowned.

"That's not our concern," said Ms. Levinson. She turned to Shelley. "Do we have all the bank statements for this year and the past two years?"

Shelley patted the three stacks of statements in front of her. "They're all right here. I've marked the important pages with sticky notes," she said.

"And what about your records?" Ms. Levinson asked Vic. "Do you use QuickBooks?"

Vic nodded.

"I'll need a copy of all your records for the past three years," said Ms. Levinson.

"I've got it right here on a flash drive." Shelley pulled it out of her purse and handed it to Ms. Levinson. "Just let me know if you need anything else."

"Thanks, Aunt Shelley." Vic's eyes now looked more haggard than alarmed. I was grateful that Marcy put a steadying hand on his arm.

It was a quiet ride home. Boodles was sprawled out on my lap as I sat in the passenger seat of Max's gray Lexus. I didn't say anything to him, but I personally thought it was every Detroiter's duty to buy American, but that was just me so I kept my mouth shut. I had enough going on in my life without sparring with my criminal attorney about his choice in vehicles.

"Penny for your thoughts." Max made a left turn onto Evergreen, heading back to Royal Oak.

"I feel sorry for Vic. He has so much to deal with. His father just died last Monday, and now he has to let a ten-year employee go. That's tough stuff."

"We learn from the hard times," said Max. "He's a bright guy. I'm sure he'll deal well with it."

"Yeah, but he's still my baby, so I can worry about him. It's my job."

"I thought Heather was your baby." Max turned right on Eleven Mile.

I explained that both my kids would always be my babies, no matter how old they might be. Max chuckled.

"So how does this Janine thing affect my case?"

"That all depends on what the police do next," said Max. "If they think her embezzlement may have been a motive for murder, then you might be off the hot seat."

I must have heaved a huge sigh of relief, because Max added. "Don't get ahead of yourself, Bella. First, let Margo Levinson do her job. Then, if Vic is smart, he'll take that information straight to the police."

"Oh dear."

"What?" asked Max.

"I don't think Vic wants anymore bad publicity for the store. And turning Janine in to the police will definitely create publicity."

Max stared straight ahead as we crossed the intersection of Eleven Mile and Greenfield. "Not as much bad publicity as his mother being put behind bars."

There was a pregnant silence.

"I didn't think of it that way." I leaned back on the headrest, feeling weary.

"That's why you pay me the big bucks." Max put a hand on my arm. "Go ahead and worry about Vic. Let me worry about your case."

"You think she did it?" I asked. "It's hard for me to believe."

Max stared at the road in front of him and was uncharacteristically silent.

"What?" I asked.

"Just thinking like a criminal attorney," said Max.

"What do you mean?" I asked.

"She had a motive if he was calling her out on embezzlement."

"Duh," I said.

"But where and how he was murdered seems a lot more personal than that."

I swallowed hard. "What are you saying? That Robert was boinking her *too*?"

"I'm not saying anything." Max looked straight ahead, keeping his voice steady and even. "This is all speculation." By now he'd pulled up my drive, and I was gathering up my purse and Boodles' carrier.

I turned and looked him straight in the face. "What you're saying though, is if Janine killed Robert, they had more between them than money." I was tempted to raise my eyebrows like Groucho and say, 'more likely they had less between them,' but I was in no mood to joke.

"Bella, I'm sorry I said anything. It's probably not like that at all."

It was getting hard for me to talk.

"Want me to stay?" Even without his spectacular smile, the offer was awfully tempting.

"I'll be fine." I resisted the urge to give him a hug goodbye. Forcing my voice to sound more normal than I felt, I thanked him for coming along to the accountant's office. We said our goodbyes, and Boodles and I watched as his car drove off until it turned a corner and disappeared from view.

It was hard sleeping again that night as I contemplated the fact that Janine had been with Blumer's for over ten years and chances were high, knowing randy Robert, that he'd been 'boinking' her all along. She'd been quite the looker ten years ago when Robert first hired her. No wonder she'd hated Barbara so much. It all started to make sense. Janine and Robert had been cheating on me all along, and then came Barbara and ruined everything for her. I'd have to check the dates that Janine started stealing from the company. I had a strong hunch it had everything to do with Robert's infatuation with Barbara.

CHAPTER 25

right and early Monday morning, I was in my shop, putting leftover stock from the Art Fair back into the showcases and safe. Shelley came in to clear up financial issues and go to the bank before she headed out to spend the day at Blumer's helping out in Janine's absence.

"We did great at the Art Fair." Shelley was crunching the numbers on her laptop. "It's a definite 'go' for next year."

I continued putting things away and started swabbing down the showcases. I still couldn't get the image of Janine and Robert out of my mind. As usual, I guess it showed.

Shelley gave me a look. "What's wrong, Bella?"

"Max thinks Janine killed Robert."

"What?" Of course, my comment took her totally by surprise.

I repeated, "Max thinks Janine did it."

Shelley cocked her head and crunched her eyebrows at me. "So this is good news. Max is finally committing himself to someone being a likely suspect, but still you look upset. Now isn't that a good thing? Doesn't that get you off the hook?"

I could feel the sting behind my eyes, and I pressed my lips together. I was sick of crying all the time.

"All right, what is it, Bella?"

I sat down in my bench chair, grateful that the shop wasn't open yet. My words came out in a whisper. "I feel like my whole life has been a lie."

Shelley put her glasses down on her desk. "Come again?"

"Shelley, if it was Janine, she killed him in his bedroom, in his underwear." I couldn't help it; the tears started streaming down my face, no doubt making a mess of my mascara.

Shelley scooted her chair next to mine and put her arms around me. "Oh, Bella, I see what you mean."

I started to sob, my nose almost instantly dripping gunk.

Shelley handed me a tissue. "It might not be what it looks like. Maybe the embezzlement is a totally different issue."

I wiped my face. It took about ten tissues, and I was anticipating a complete face redo in the store bathroom. "You think that's possible?"

"Just because she 'possibly' has a motive, it doesn't

mean she did it," said Shelley.

"But Max was right. " I hiccupped and wiped again at my nose. "Whoever shot Robert knew him personally."

"Which brings us right back to Barbara. We know for a fact she was intimate with him. We don't know that at all about Janine." Leave it to Shelley to use the word 'intimate' instead of 'boink.' My sister is a class act.

"So, let Ms. Levinson and the police deal with this before we jump to conclusions." She put her arm around my shoulder and gave it a squeeze.

I took a deep breath. "There's one more thing." I told her my theory about Janine starting her embezzlement when she was angry and hurt about Barbara and Robert.

Shelley frowned, concentrating. "Those dates do line up." She looked at my face. "But that really doesn't prove anything yet. They have a lot of circumstantial evidence on you, too."

We were interrupted when Heather arrived, buzzing at the back door.

"We're going to have to give her a set of keys for the store," said Shelley, walking over to open the door. "It might be a while before Vic gets someone to replace me. In fact, I think it's time for me to head over to Blumer's."

I WASHED my face and totally reapplied my morning

makeup, thanks to my oversized and well-stocked lime bag. Heather's hair that day was an intriguing shade of aqua. I went to the safe and handed her a turquoise pendant and some contrasting onyx earrings to go with her skinny black jeans.

"Have you heard from Vic yet?" she asked, checking out how she looked in our countertop mirror.

I looked at the clock. It was ten o'clock, and no, I'd not heard from him yet. Blumer Fine Jewelers opened at nine, so certainly Janine had already been informed.

"Not yet," I said.

"Want me to call Aunt Shelley?"

Right on cue, my phone broke into Michael Jackson's "Bad." It was Vic.

"How did it go?" Of course I was curious about his situation with Janine.

"Not well. I'm calling from my office for privacy."

"What happened?"

"She didn't take it well."

"What do you mean?"

Vic cleared his throat. "She was screaming at me, asking me what I was investigating. But, of course, I couldn't answer. I had to be a backboard and just keep repeating that she was going to be paid, and that we were doing an investigation."

"It sure makes her sound guilty," I said.

"But there's more, Mom, much more."

"Okay?"

"Well for one thing, Marcy called, and Janine was not at Dr. Saperstein's office the morning Dad was killed. So unless she recently changed to a different dental office, she doesn't have an alibi."

"That's huge," I said. "Be sure to tell the police."

"There's even more."

"What? What else?" I was positively curious.

"It's about Barbara." His voice took on an edge.

"What about Barbara?"

"She went ballistic when she found out I was giving Janine paid administrative leave."

"What did she want you to do? Let Janine keep stealing?"

"It's not that. She was upset she wasn't included in that decision, or even told about the embezzlement."

I didn't immediately respond. I absolutely detest that woman, but I had to admit she had a point. "So what happened? Did she calm down yet?"

"Well, she wasn't happy about Aunt Shelley being here either, being that she's *your* sister. She stormed out of here, yelling about Dad's will, and how she owned the place and was going to kick me and everyone else right out of here."

I gasped. "That's not possible. Dad couldn't have left it all to Barbara. That would be insane!"

Vic sighed the sigh of a beaten man. "I hope not, Mom. But we can't be sure until we see that will."

"Dad never showed it to you?" I was shocked.

"He was awfully secretive about anything that had anything to do with Barbara."

"And probably more." I sat in my bench chair, hands in my lap. "I guess unless she comes back with it in hand, there's not much we can do about it right now."

"I could call an attorney," said Vic, "or you could call Max, and see if there is a way to find a copy."

I shook my head. "You have enough on your plate. Let Barbara come up with the copy and get a lawyer after that. Right now, we have to wait and see what Levinson comes up with."

"Okay, Mom." He paused. "And thanks for loaning me Aunt Shelley. She's really quick. I think we won't miss a beat without Janine."

After we hung up, I decided to take a few cleansing breaths and get started on my day. In through the nose, out through the mouth, back straight, eyes closed. If stress was a health hazard, I was already halfway to Hades.

I tried not to think of it that way and opened my eyes. Boodles walked the few steps across my desk and gave me a nice kiss on my newly applied makeup. I gave him a little squeeze, and he settled for a nap in my lap while I pulled out my sketchbook to review some new designs for my earring collection.

Heather was waiting on a thirty-something office worker that stopped in on her coffee break. I could hear an animated conversation that sounded like it was going to result in a sale. This made me feel the Zen of peace that comes when you concentrate on the positive. I could almost imagine my body lifting up in the lotus position, sketchbook in hand, when the door jingled open, and in walked Tom Jenkins looking flushed, as if he'd been running. But he didn't look so much out of breath as angry.

I stood up, lotus position totally forgotten, feeling suddenly frightened. I'd never seen Tom as anything but friendly. And he definitely wasn't looking friendly.

"Hi, Tom," I said, and for lack of anything better to say, "Are you all right?"

"What do you mean, 'all right'?" he asked, and it was obviously a rhetorical question, because he answered it on the spot himself. "Your son puts my wife on leave and puts her job in jeopardy after ten years of working for your wonderful family."

The way he said 'wonderful' indicated that it was anything but. I had to think fast. I decided to go for the politician thing. Deny, deny, deny. "What are you talking about?" I tried to affect a puzzled look.

"Don't play stupid with me!" He banged on my glass countertop, making my merchandise jump.

"Hey! Easy on the counter," I said, actually a little angry with this guy. And that's why I blew it. "Why are you coming here and yelling at me? Get out!"

He leaned over the counter. His voice was a menacing hiss. "My wife gives you rich ingrates the best years of her working life, and this is the thanks she gets? An investigation? She's told to leave? That store is nothing without her!"

I could feel the blood pounding in my ears. "I was always perfectly nice to your wife. If she's on leave for an investigation, then I'm sure Vic had good reason, or he'd never do it."

He gave a bitter laugh. "You're such a liar. I know you went to the lawyer with your little boy to see how you could screw my wife out of her job."

The hair went up on the back of my neck. How on earth did Tom know that I'd gone with Vic to the forensic accountant? I assumed that's what he was talking about. Was he my stalker? And not Larry Bernstein?

"Mom, you want me to call the police?" Heather's hand hovered over the store phone.

I turned to Tom. My voice was amazingly calm, but I'm sure my face was blood red. "I think you better go now."

Miraculously, he turned toward the door. But as he walked out, he said, "Don't think you've heard the last of me. I'll be back."

As soon as he walked out the door, my hands flew to my mouth. My fingers were ice cold.

"I think we'd better warn Vic." Heather tapped his number on her cell phone.

Forgetting my makeup entirely, except for my mascara, of course, I rubbed my face with my cool fingers, giving my temple an extra massage. When this was all over, if I didn't end up in prison, I really, really needed a vacation.

"It's okay, Mom," said Heather. "Vic ordered a security guard at the store. That's probably why Tom came here."

I was just about to take the phone from Heather, when in walked Detective Hottie himself, looking like a million dollars' worth of crisp fifties, neatly rolled in a banker's wad and carefully placed in a pocket.

"Who ordered a security guard?" he asked. "Who came here?"

I quickly told him the story of Tom Jenkins and how he'd overreacted to Janine's paid leave. I also had to explain the whole paid leave thing, how we suspected Janine had been embezzling and how Vic might be coming to the police with the information that afternoon.

"Well, maybe it's not an overreaction," he said. "It sounds more like Mr. Jenkins has something to worry about."

My head was still whirling from that frontal assault. "What do you mean?"

"It's simple," said Krieger. "If he or his wife has nothing to hide, he wouldn't be going around harassing people." He took a second look at me. "You okay?"

"I'm fine," I lied. I hadn't been fine for over a year. Who was I kidding?

"Why don't I take you out for a cup of coffee? Let's go to Ben's. It'll give you a chance to calm down."

I looked at Heather and shook my head. "I can't leave my daughter alone; that lunatic might come back here again." There was that, and the fact I wasn't at all certain I wanted to get personal with Krieger. I liked him too much. I was attracted too much. Let's face it, it was a year after my divorce, and I was still majorly screwed up.

"Go ahead," said Heather. "I'll just lock the door and let in people I can tell are okay." She paused. "I don't think he'll be coming back today anyway."

I looked at Krieger's open collar. I could just imagine my cheek resting against his skin. It looked inviting. It looked terrifying.

"Come on, Bella." His voice was intoxicating. "It's just coffee."

I grabbed my purse and put Boodles in his carrier.

"You're not taking that dog, are you?" I swiveled my head to tell him that 'that dog' goes where I go, when my attention was captured by my mother walking through the jingling door.

"Hi, Mom." I felt as awkward as a teenager trying to sneak out a bedroom window.

"Heading out, dear?" She was playing innocent, but I could tell she was out for the kill

Krieger spoke up. "I'm taking your daughter out for coffee."

My mother's mild demeanor took a plunge to the arctic. "You're going on a date with another man?"

"It's not a date. It's just coffee." I sounded positively whiny. And embarrassed.

Krieger cracked a smile. "I promise you, Mom, my intentions are honorable."

"I'm *not* your mom." She turned to address me. "He doesn't even look Jewish. You finally have a Jewish boyfriend, and already you're two-timing him with this, this… other man!"

"You have a boyfriend?" Krieger still looked amused. "How come I never heard about a boyfriend? A Jewish one." He paused. "Oh…it must be Fosner. Are you two going steady?" He was obviously mocking my mother, and while it should have been satisfying, it was really annoying. I decided to ignore it.

"Mom, this is Bill Krieger. He is the detective on Robert's case, and we are really just going out for coffee." With that and Boodles and my purse on my shoulder, Detective Krieger and I headed out the door.

"Bye, Mom," he said.

When we were safely on the other side of the door, I said, "Boy, you're really not making brownie points with my mother."

"She's a pistol," he said. "And I know all kinds."

"She's been trying to fix me up even before the divorce ink dried. She just doesn't feel complete unless she and her daughters are safely married."

"Don't you mean 'happily'?"

"My mother's into safety." My words were glib, and I hadn't thought of it until he asked, but that was actually a dead-on observation. My mother still saw marriage as a way to security. Albert's bank account certainly made her happy. I guess she expected the same for her daughters.

We walked over to Ben's. I was so relieved that my former brother-in-law wasn't there. I really didn't want to have to explain Krieger to yet another family member.

He ordered an extra-strong plain black, I ordered my cappuccino, and we sat in one of the black leather booths. After I put his carrier on the seat, Boodles put both paws up on the rim and took a look at Krieger, with a low tiny growl in his throat.

"Do you take that dog with you everywhere?" asked Krieger. The question wasn't open and curious. It was a judgment.

I put Boodles into the bottom of his carrier and rubbed his deliciously silky ears. I turned to Krieger, licking some of the chocolate and cream off the top of my drink. "I take it you don't like dogs."

"I like dogs, all right. But, Bella, you have to admit, that thing is more of a cat. What does he weigh, anyway?"

"About five pounds. Otherwise, it would be hard to carry him around."

"That's the point. Most people walk dogs; they don't carry them."

This was starting to get annoying. I decided to change

the topic. "So what did you want to talk about?"

"What?"

"Why did you come into my store? What did you want?"

"You called me first, remember?"

"I did?" I honestly couldn't remember calling him. "About what?"

He took a sip of his plain black and held the cup up near his mouth. The steam on his lips made me feel steamy. He put down the cup.

"Okay. Maybe it was your boyfriend who called me about the shovel missing from your garage."

"It wasn't 'missing,' it was definitely taken. And he's not my boyfriend."

"What is he then?" asked Krieger.

"He's my lawyer." I sounded defensive, and I was mad at myself for it. I didn't have any reason to be defensive. "And he's my friend. He's actually a great guy." I hadn't planned on saying that; it just came out. There I was, finally on a semi-date with Detective Hottie, and I was talking nice about Max.

"Why does your mother think he's your boyfriend?"

"That sounds so junior high." I was glad I found a way to deflect his question. I really didn't want to answer.

"What, 'boyfriend'?"

"Yes, boyfriend," I said, starting to sip at the rest of my cappuccino. "We're grownups now. There should be a different name for that."

"So what is he?"

"Why do you care?" I asked. Gee, this was not going like I thought it would go on a date with Krieger. Thankfully, he finally changed the topic.

"So, what happened to your shovel?"

I explained about the shovel and how it had what looked like fresh dirt on the tip of it, how it might have been used to bury the gun in my yard. I told him about the plastic I covered it with, and how I forgot to lock the garage. Oh... and how I had that weird feeling you get when someone's watching you — and how the shovel disappeared as soon as Heather and I left for the Sunday Art Fair, because it was missing when she returned home later that morning.

He'd taken out a small notebook and scribbled away while I talked. After the shovel information, he questioned me about my encounter with Tom Jenkins. By the time we were done, my cappuccino was nearly empty, and his coffee looked cold.

"I think I'd better get back to work." I stood.

He reached over and put a hand on top of mine. "For what it's worth, I don't think you're guilty."

I pursed my lips and scrunched my eyebrows. "I appreciate that, but you sure haven't acted like it."

He stood, pulling at his wallet for a tip. "Just doing my job. Look, when the dust clears, I'd like to get to know you better."

Just like a girl in middle school, I felt my knees go weak.

Maybe the term, 'boyfriend,' was as accurate as any.

"I'd like that," I said, trying not to think about Max.

I heard an official buzz go off. It wasn't my conscience; it was Krieger's phone, which he instantly put against his ear. He made a few agreeable sounds into the speaker before saying, "I'll be right there."

"Some kind of emergency?"

He slid his finger beneath my chin. "It's good news." He spoke quietly into my ear. "For you, anyway. I just got word that your son has turned in an employee for embezzlement. We both know that it's Janine Jenkins."

I nodded, mesmerized by his touch.

"You know this could be great for your case." By that time we were out on the sidewalk and no one was around, so he spoke openly. "Better tell your boyfriend there's a good chance the charges against you might be dropped."

"You mean she's automatically a suspect?"

Krieger laughed. "Let's see. Her boss is killed a week ago, just when he was starting to look into why his bank account was looking so flimsy...I think we have a motive there. It's a long way between that and conviction, but I think we definitely have another person of interest."

I checked my watch. It was eleven-thirty. "I really do have to get back to my shop. It's not fair to leave Heather there alone."

Krieger grabbed my arm, the one without Boodles. "I'd really like to go to dinner with you," he said. "How about tonight?"

I was floored. This guy went from stone face flatfoot to hot-to-trot in sixty seconds flat. "Isn't there a conflict of interest? A code of ethics?"

"I'm not sure you're a prime suspect anymore." His face was so close to mine that I could smell his aftershave. It was intoxicating.

I fought the intoxication. "So when do I get that bail money back?" I was thinking it would be nice to return the money to Albert. And my mother.

"That's between you and the court. It's not time yet — that's another question for your boyfriend."

"He's my *lawyer*." I once again felt annoyed.

"So what about tonight?" His voice sounded husky.

"I don't think so. People will recognize us."

"I was thinking of a restaurant in Ann Arbor."

What can I say? It sounded like a terrible idea for his career, for my relationship with Max (whatever that was). But I really wanted to go. "Pick me up at seven-thirty."

"At your shop or at your house?"

"I'll be at home."

As he walked away, he turned. "Oh, and Bella, leave the mutt at home."

I was so enchanted by the prospect of a romantic dinner with this unbelievably hot guy that I forgot to be upset about Boodles. For his part, Boodles emitted another low growl until Krieger was out of sight.

CHAPTER 26

It's odd to admit, but I felt guilty, like I was cheating on Max. This was ridiculous, of course, because I hadn't ever even kissed Max, and I had promised him no allegiance. Still, as I unlocked my shop door and heard the jingle as I walked inside, I had that familiar feeling I used to get when I was holding something out on my mother in high school. I'd told Max I wasn't ready for a relationship, and then I jumped at the chance to go out with Krieger. Krieger, who'd done nothing but harass and persecute me, while Max had done nothing but look out for me and my family. I was a tramp, a slut, a nafka. Ask my mother; I'm sure she'd agree.

I decided to leave the front door to my shop unlocked, with the theory that Tom Jenkins wasn't likely to return. He was just upset about his wife. I figured it was an aberration. Heather was waiting on one customer after another. I sat at my bench, happy to lose myself in some blue-green amazonite beads. About an hour and a half later, the store phone startled me from my work. It was Max, all flush with great news and unaware of what I was doing to him.

"Bella, it's unbelievably good news! Vic turned Janine in, and the police are already on her case. They've brought her in for questioning. Krieger implied there's a good chance they'll be making an arrest. I don't think you're their number one suspect anymore!"

I could feel a growing pit in my stomach. "That's great." I got the words out, but I knew my voice didn't match my words.

"What's wrong, Bella?"

I couldn't think of anything more original; did I ever tell you that I'm a crappy liar? "I have a headache. Just took some Tylenol."

"Well, rest up and get better because we're going out tonight. My treat. I'm thinking some place special."

Oh boy. "I can't go," I didn't have the heart to be honest. And like I said, I'm a crappy liar, and evidently a coward. "I promised Shelley we'd have a girls' night out tonight. I want to thank her for all the work she's done for Vic."

"Can't a guy come along?"

I felt like such a heel. But then, it didn't even occur to me that I could have canceled my date with Detective Hottie.

"Not this time, Max. Can I have a rain check?"

"Okay, how about tomorrow?" I could hear the disappointment in his voice.

"You got it," I said, trying to rev up some enthusiasm.

"You sound terrible. Maybe you should go home and lay down."

"I can't, but I'll be okay."

"We need to talk again, about your case."

"Can it wait until tomorrow?" I asked, noting that there were two customers waiting for Heather. "Got a customer, Max. I'll talk to you later."

WHEN MY tiny shop cleared of customers, Heather flopped down in Shelley's desk chair. "I'm bushed," she said. "Is it always so busy?"

I gave a tight laugh. "No, I think all the notoriety is good for business."

"You mean Dad's murder?" She sounded upset.

"Well, yeah," I said. "It's not that I would plan it that way. But you know the expression: any publicity is good publicity."

"People really suck," she said.

I hated that word, but decided she was too old and too upset to be corrected.

"I miss Shelley's laptop," I said. Shelley had taken it

with her to Blumer's and mine was still with the police. "I would really like to see what's going on in the news, with Janine, I mean."

Heather opened her oversized orange purse, a garage sale find no doubt, and pulled out a tablet. She tapped at the screen and presented me with the headline from Channel Four News: "Blumer Jewelers Employee Held on Suspicion of Embezzlement and Murder."

I clutched my chest. "Oh my God! I can't believe it happened so soon."

Heather looked upset. "You really think she killed Daddy?"

"Well, the police think so," I said. "I hope they're right this time."

The phone rang. It was Vic. "You hear the news yet?"

"Yeah, Heather looked it up on her tablet. Amazing." I was feeling upset and was trying to figure out why. It was kind of like how it is when you wake up the day after someone dies and you know something is wrong, but you just don't quite remember what. And then I remembered. "Oh," I apparently said out loud.

"What?' asked Vic.

I was thinking about how this meant that Janine had probably been sleeping with Robert, right under my nose, and probably for years. It wasn't a good feeling. "Just thinking about stuff." I wasn't lying, but not really telling the truth, either. Why bother my kids with that? It was too personal.

"I wonder if they'll actually charge her," said Vic. "They have to have more than circumstantial evidence."

"I don't know, but we'll probably find out." I didn't want to tell him I had a dinner date with Krieger that night, and that would be my first line of questioning, to use police jargon. Krieger would have to spill.

"Why don't we all go out for dinner tonight?"

Oh boy. Another one. Exactly how much did I want to go out with Detective Hottie? I had about a split second to find out. One...Two..."How about tomorrow?" I asked. "Tonight's not good for me. I just told Max the same thing. Maybe we can all go out together."

"I think this means Albert will get his bail money back," said Vic.

"That'll be a load off my shoulders." I sighed. "He didn't make me feel bad at all about it, but still...it was one hundred thousand dollars. I owe him big."

"What about Ms. Barbara?" My mind flashed on her threat to throw everyone out of Blumer Fine Jewelers.

It was Vic's turn to sigh. "Haven't seen or heard from her yet."

There was a silence.

Vic broke it. "I was always trying to give her the benefit of the doubt, Mom."

I knew what he was talking about. I decided to be reasonable. Vic brings that out in me. "She was your father's wife. It was probably the right thing to do." I couldn't believe I'd said it.

"She was pretty awful to you. And it looks like she wasn't the greatest wife to Dad, either."

It was nice to hear, but it was time for me to say something to Vic. "I know I complained too much, and it probably made it hard on you."

I could hear a low laugh. It was Vic's way of telling me I was right on target.

"But the two of them, they ripped my heart out, you know that." I could still feel the raw spot; I wasn't lying.

"I know."

"Well, whatever happens with Barbara, I'll help out any way I can." I certainly held no grudge against my son.

"Thanks, Mom. Let's see what happens. If she doesn't present us with a copy of Dad's will, I'll have to get one from the court."

"You know the procedure?" I was wondering how Vic knew what to do.

"Max called and talked to me about it—no charge, he said."

I was feeling like I was about as good of a person as my ex-husband. Fortunately, Boodles landed in my lap, and I could distract myself with his silky fur.

"I guess we'll see what happens by the end of the day."

"Call me and let me know." As I clicked off the phone, I could imagine lovely Barbara, waving Robert's will in the air, charging around the store like she owned it—if, in fact, she did.

ANY MISGIVING I'd had about keeping my date with Krieger totally dissolved when I saw him at my front door. Wowzer. All decked out in dress slacks and an Armani shirt, soft but crisp, just the way Robert always wore them. I resisted the urge to jump his bones. As I'd told Shelley, it had been a long time since I trotted. But seeing this man dressed up for a date with me made me absolutely hot.

He took my hand, twirled me around, and slid a knowing hand down to the small of my back. "Don't you look good," he said.

I felt absolutely beautiful. For the occasion, I was wearing the royal blue version of the little black dress, a tight sleeveless thing I'd picked up at Patti's Collection on Main, sometime last summer after the divorce. I'd bought it on a day when I'd been feeling sorry for myself and thought it unlikely that I'd ever need such a dress. But look at me now!

His personal car was a classic Corvette, wouldn't you know it. I was so used to seeing him in a squad car that it required a little bit of mental adjustment on my part. He had the top down, and my hair flowed in the summer breeze.

Krieger shot the car across Woodward and took off

down the entrance ramp to I-696 like it was a runway. The Jewish mother in me started to get a little nervous, but the hot vixen was still in control.

"Hang on," he said, shifting the car into high gear. I didn't know men in their fifties could still drive that way. I glanced at the speedometer; he was already going over seventy and he'd barely merged onto the expressway.

"Isn't it worse for a cop to get a speeding ticket than the rest of us civilians?" I asked, hoping he would get the hint.

"Haven't you ever heard of professional courtesy?" He laughed. "Just lean back and enjoy it."

God help me, I leaned my head back on the headrest and felt the thrill of youth. *Sorry, Mom, but I'm out with another bad boy, and I love it!* His hand rested on my knee and started traveling north. I could feel all systems go, but somehow pulled myself out of the moment. Didn't want to think with my hormones just yet, if you know what I mean.

"So tell me about the arrest," I said, slipping my hand under his and holding it in place, due south of his destination.

"You know I can't tell you about that."

"I think you owe me," I said and I meant it. "You and your cronies made my life a living hell this last week."

He was silent for a moment and moved his hand off my thigh, giving me the chance for mental clarity.

"Why did you arrest her? What was the evidence?"

"Promise to keep it to yourself?" he asked, "and not

even tell that lawyer boyfriend of yours?"

Now that was jarring. First he was going for third base, and in the next breath he was still calling Max my 'boyfriend'? I was tempted to call him on it, but I really needed to know.

"Promise," I said emphatically.

"We brought her in for questioning, and her prints were on the gun," he said.

I gasped. "She planted the gun on my property, and she didn't have the sense to wipe off the prints?"

Krieger put both hands on the wheel, arms stiff at two o'clock and ten o'clock. The summer air was whooshing through the car, so we were fairly shouting. "First, remember she's not a professional and people make stupid mistakes. Second, she claims she didn't plant the gun."

"What! That doesn't make any sense at all."

"There's more," he said. "There is another set of prints on the gun."

"Barbara's?" I was hoping maybe it was that witch and not Janine who'd killed my Robert in his underwear.

"No, Barbara volunteered her prints back when we were making a case against you. She said she'd never even touched that gun, and her prints proved her right."

I was silent for a minute, digesting the fact that Barbara was very likely not the killer. Which meant it was Janine, and that meant Robert had most definitely slept with her, too. And to think I'd been a loyal wife all those years. It occurred to me that maybe I wasn't the best judge of character. I took a sidelong glance at Krieger, who looked absolutely GQ, especially with the wind of his convertible in action.

Krieger glanced back at me. "What's going on in that mind of yours, Bella?"

By now we were on the southbound I-275 interchange, heading toward Ann Arbor, where I could safely have a romantic dinner with this man and decide later if he was worth the price.

"My husband cheated on me, a lot more than I ever suspected." The wind was whipping my hair, but he had the windows a few inches up, so we could still hear each other speak.

Once again, his hand descended onto my thigh. He started higher this time. "Well, it's your turn to howl."

Once again, I grabbed his hand and held it in place. Somehow, getting even with my dead ex-husband wasn't at all a turn-on. I held on tight till we reached Ann Arbor.

Chez Shayes is a high-end trendy restaurant on Liberty near Main in downtown, practically part of the University of Michigan campus. Krieger pulled his Corvette into a waiting parking spot, just in front of the restaurant.

"Do you normally live such a charmed life?" I gazed into the lighted visor mirror in an effort to rearrange myself. Apparently, the wind had blown my hair into raw ringlets, and blew the lipstick right off my mouth.

"Just a lucky break." His voice was less modest than

smug.

After I did some minor repairs, Krieger held my elbow as we walked inside the restaurant. "I'm bad" very appropriately started playing on my phone. I slipped it out of my lime bag. There was no Boodles here; at Krieger's request, I'd left him at home. It was eight-fifteen and the call was from Shelley. I quickly hit the 'ignore' button.

"Who is it?" asked Krieger.

"Nothing important," I said, even though I knew that it probably was. I couldn't risk talking to Shelley when I hadn't even told her I was going out with Krieger. She absolutely hates bad boys, and her choice of a husband is a testament to that. Mitch is a certified public bean counter and just about as exciting as a plate of unseasoned garbanzos. I'd talk her through it later.

"Hi there," said the hostess, a young twenty-something, dressed to kill in spike heels the height of the former World Trade Center and a set of boobs to match. Her eyes were on Krieger, who even at his age clearly enjoyed that certain something that draws in women. Is it a smell? Those pheromones scientists like to talk about? The reason oxen get lucky all the time?

Krieger slipped her a five for a good table, and his hand and the five came perilously close to those well-exposed breasts. The girl didn't seem to mind, and in fact touched his hand as she accepted the tip.

She led us to a private booth that even had drapes that

gave a little privacy. They weren't all the way closed, but if you sat back, you were not visible from the adjacent tables.

I slid into the seat, and Krieger slid in right after me, hand right back on my thigh, fingers lightly moving. This time, I did not protest.

The waitress showed up, this one maybe more stacked than the last, but a bit shorter, even in her three-inch heels. Her hair was platinum blond and swirled provocatively around her ample breasts, where a simple pendant happily rested. Krieger's grip on my thigh loosened, and he smiled at the girl.

"Would you care for some wine?" She handed us the wine menu.

We ordered two glasses of zinfandel, and as soon as she left, we resumed the mating dance. Waitress be damned, I felt a rush of joy shoot up my leg. I turned toward the man and enjoyed a slow, deep kiss, the likes of which I hadn't felt in years. I could feel my body melt and was very glad we were in a restaurant and not my house, because if we were, I'd be ripping off my clothes by now.

My phone rang again. I tried to ignore it, but you know, we're pretty well trained to answer the damned thing. It was Shelley. Again. I hit 'ignore,' shut off the ringer, and turned once again into a woman of lust.

Other than the phone calls silently piling up, the night was perfect. I was feeling a light buzz from my second glass of wine, which made Krieger even more irresistible. I was acting like an irresponsible teenager and loving every minute. We kept our hands on each other through dinner and enjoyed a few slow kisses before dessert.

By that time, I'd shut my phone completely off, as I had zero desire to be interrupted by Shelley again. There really wasn't much talk. It was as if we were both very hungry, even after we'd eaten our fill.

"Want to go for a walk?" he asked.

I didn't actually relish a walk in my three-inch heels, but how could I say no? I was fairly floating across the floor until we were nearly out the door of the restaurant. That's when reality hit and hit hard.

We were one table from the door when Ms. World Trade Center approached. It could have been the wine, but it really didn't matter. When she wished us a good night, I saw it. Krieger made a passing gesture at her, and his hand grazed her behind, slowing enough to hold a quick handful. She returned a lustful smile, and at that moment, it was like a switch turned off. I was through.

We walked into the mild evening air, and I decided not to wait.

"I want to go home." My voice was both strong and flat.

Krieger was clearly surprised. "Why? What's the matter?"

If he hadn't been the detective in charge of my case, I would have bluntly told him. No problem. This night was supposed to be about me, about us. It wasn't supposed to include a twenty-something and her fabulous ass.

"I think I made a mistake," I said, and boy, did I ever mean it!

Krieger opened the door to his Corvette, and I practically fell to the ground as I slid into its low interior.

"I thought we were having a good time," he said. I couldn't tell if he was confused or annoyed and, honestly, I didn't care.

The truth was, I was having an old familiar feeling. Being with Krieger in that restaurant, his hands on me, enticing me, reminded me of how it felt to be a young thing in love with Robert Blumer. I'd been wild for that guy. Crazy, even. My parents had warned me against him. My mother said I could do better. Shelley called him a playboy, but I didn't care. My desire overcame reason, and we all know how well that worked out. I was tempted to ask Krieger how many times he'd been divorced. I was certain it was more than once.

"I don't think it's smart to get this involved when my case is still open." While this was partially true, it was certainly not the real or only reason.

"You're practically off the hook," said Krieger, and I was happy to see his hands were on the wheel.

"It's only been a year since my divorce, and I'm not sure I'm ready for a relationship."

"Who said anything about a relationship?"

Well, that takes the cake. Here Max had been dropping

hints about wanting to be with me, liking marriage, and acting like one of the best friends a woman could ask for on earth, and I was pawing at this loser. I decided then and there that I truly needed a shrink to find out why I was attracted to these skunks.

I took a look at his patrician profile, and decided there was a lot more to a relationship than a GQ kind of guy. What a dolt I was, waiting until I was fifty-four to figure this out.

I really didn't want to fight with the guy, because it might have an effect on my case. So despite my strong desire to be sarcastic, I was uncharacteristically nice. "I don't think we want the same things," I said. "I think you have me confused with my ex-husband. *He* was the one who took relationships lightly. I was faithful for nearly thirty years."

"You've got to be kidding," he said, and I believed he meant it. He obviously couldn't relate to fidelity.

"No, not kidding," I said. "So you probably don't want to get started with me. Like I said, we're not really looking for the same things."

The rest of the ride home was silent. After a while, Krieger turned on the radio and listened to a Tigers game. It was a welcome distraction. When he pulled up my driveway, I put my hand on his. "I'm really sorry it didn't work out. I obviously find you unbelievably attractive. I hope you won't hold this against me."

He was back to wearing his immobile tough-guy face, so I wasn't surprised at all, when all he said was, "No hard feelings."

"Thanks," I said quickly, and ran into my house, eager to see my little Boodles. After about a thousand tiny wet Boodle-kisses, I turned my phone back on. I could feel the hairs on the back of my neck stand up. There were about twenty messages, and they were all from Shelley.

CHAPTER 27

According to my diamond-set Minnie Mouse, it was after eleven, but still...rather than wait until morning, I decided to call her back. There were so many calls, I was certain there was some kind of emergency.

She picked up on the first ring. "Bella, where have you been all night?" It wasn't a friendly question; it was said more the way you'd ask a teenager who broke curfew.

I decided to go with the 'answer a question with a question' routine. "Why? What was going on? Why are there so messages on my phone?"

"It's about Max. Mitch and I ran into him at the Beirut Bistro and he told me I was supposed to be with you!" It felt like a black drape went over my eyes. What were the chances?

"Oh," I said.

"And that you turned down a celebratory dinner with him to be with me."

"Uh, huh."

"Bella!" She sounded like she was ready to blow a fuse. But I was really too upset to answer.

"What?"

"*Where were you?*"

I took a deep breath. "I was on a date with Krieger."

She went silent for a few seconds. And then a few seconds longer. Finally she spoke. "So why didn't you tell him you were going on a date?"

"Because I didn't want him to know. Because I think I like him, you know, *that* way." My voice was pretty dull; I was keeping it low key because I was afraid I was going to start with the waterworks again.

"If you think you like him, then why did you go out with the Krieger guy?"

It was my turn to go silent. "I don't really want to talk about it right now."

"Why didn't you tell me you used me for an excuse?" She still sounded angry.

I leaned back on my couch. "Shelley, I'm really sorry. I obviously had no idea that you'd actually run into him tonight. Why did you eat out anyway?" Shelley usually cooks at home because she thinks restaurant food is inferior to anything that comes out of her kitchen.

"I don't know. Mitch came home late, and I did too. There's so much to do at Blumer's. So we decided it would be fun to go to the Beirut Bistro." Then her tone changed from angry sister to curious sister. "So how was the date with Krieger?"

Boy, that was the question of the night. "Wonderful and horrible."

"What do you mean?"

"He's gorgeous and sexy and he was really into me, and we were even necking at the restaurant." I left out the part about his roaming hands. Some things are best left to yourself, especially when the date didn't work out.

"So what's the problem?"

"He had his eyes and hands on the waitress *and* the hostess," I said.

"Oh."

"And when I told him it wouldn't work out because of that, he told me he wasn't looking for a relationship anyway."

"Bella, you don't believe that."

"What do you mean?"

"He just said that because you were rejecting him."

I thought about it for a second. That would make some sense and would explain why he had such a stony face when he dropped me off. Somehow, that didn't matter anymore.

"So you think I ruined things with Max?" I didn't really

want to hear the answer, but I had to ask the question.

"Truth?"

Oh boy. "Of course I want the truth!" My voice sounded a little snappish.

"He's really hurt you lied to him. I could tell."

We both fell silent.

"So what are you going to tell him?"

"I don't know," I said, and I really didn't.

WHEN I woke up on Tuesday, my feelings were classically mixed. I dove into the work on my bench like a starving woman finally presented with a feast. I was so relieved that I was no longer suspect number one. Now it was Janine's turn. Her name was all over the news, and not in a good way. I didn't feel the least bit sorry for her; she absolutely deserved it all. I was trying hard to not think about the fact that, in all likelihood, she'd been sleeping with Robert for years, possibly in my own bedroom. I needed a shrink for more reasons than one. I had to get over my attraction to disloyal, cheating, dirt bag jerks. I was trying hard not to think about Krieger. Or Max.

As a customer walked out the door with a bag of Bella's baubles, Heather, resplendent in bright green hair and malachite beads, pulled out her tablet and showed me the cover story from the Royal Oak Times. There was Janine, who'd suffered a really bad photo at the hands of the local paparazzi. It looked like one of those horrible selfies that show off a multitude of chins. She'd been held overnight for questioning and hadn't as yet been arraigned.

I know I should have been elated, but I wasn't. I was most definitely, as Krieger had put it, off the hook. Yet there was a dull, empty feeling at the pit of my stomach, and I knew it was because I had probably blown it with Max. He was a perfectly fine man who adored me and treated me like a queen. Someone I enjoyed being with every single moment we were together. But I'd held him off and pushed him over the very first chance I had a shot at the very handsome — and romantically useless — Krieger. I was devastated, but doing my best to just concentrate on my work.

My phone started with Michael Jackson's "Bad." I reached for it in an over-eager jerking motion, hoping it was Max. It wasn't.

"Hi Vic."

"You won't believe the good news."

"I know. Heather already showed me the Royal Oak Times."

"Not that." I could hear the smile in his voice. "It's about Barbara and the store."

I'd been so self-absorbed with my little Krieger-Max drama that I'd forgotten about Barbara's threat to Blumer Fine Jewelers.

"It's good news?"

A customer came in, so I switched my phone from speaker and held it directly to my ear, while Heather took care of him at the counter.

"So tell me what happened."

"Barbara came in at eight o'clock this morning and slapped a copy of Dad's will on my desk. You know I've always been nice to her, even when it wasn't easy." Now, that was an understatement.

"Go on." I stopped all work at my bench. This conversation deserved my total and undivided attention.

"And she tells me that I should read the first part of the will, the part that says that Dad left the entire business to her."

"That stupid son of a bitch!" I couldn't help myself. I just blurted it out.

Heather and the customer swiveled their heads in my direction.

"I'm so sorry," I said, realizing how inappropriate that sounded in a business setting.

"Mom, I told you it was *good* news."

"How could that be good news?" I was really upset, but I was trying to keep it clean.

"I told her to give me a chance to read the thing, and she left my office," said Vic. "I decided I needed a lawyer, so I called your Max."

Your Max. Those words put a stake directly in my heart, and I totally deserved it.

"So what did he say?"

"He told me to fax it over, and I did. He called me back less than a half hour later and told me that the young Mrs. Blumer...oh, sorry, Mom...doesn't read very carefully."

"What do you mean?" I was painfully aware of the fact that it was nearly two o'clock, and that prior to yesterday, I would have heard about this from Max first. Still, I was anxious to hear the rest of the story.

"Well, Dad *did* leave the business to her, but really only part of it. Barbara *didn't* read carefully."

"What part?"

"He left the business name and all the merchandise to Barbara. But he left the building, which he owns without mortgage, and all the store fixtures and furniture, to me."

I gasped. "Why on earth did he do that? Why make it so complicated?"

"Max thinks it's because he wanted to make sure that we'd continue to work together, but it didn't work out like Dad planned."

"Why not?" Boodles, noting that I was no longer engrossed in my work, jumped on my lap for a little attention.

"When Dad had the will drawn up, the merchandise in the shop was of equal value to the store and the fixtures."

"But not anymore?" I could feel Boodles' tiny warm tongue licking the base of my fingers.

"No," said Vic. "Our cash flow was so bad and our

reputation so good that we have ninety-percent of our merchandise from designers and manufacturers on memo. Aunt Shelley ran a report for me."

"You mean, because Janine was stealing, and the bank account was always too low, Dad was only buying on consignment?"

"That's pretty much the story."

"So that leaves Barbara with pretty much nothing." I suppressed a giggle. It was just too rich.

"Well, she owns our name, and Dad left her the house," said Vic. "The rest he split between Heather and me."

I thought of Heather and her desire to go back to school. "Is there enough for Heather to go back to school?"

"I don't know. But Max suggested I freeze all the accounts and get records of all activity since Dad was killed."

"Good idea."

"Well, you probably already heard about all of this." Obviously, Vic had no idea that Max was apparently not speaking to me.

"Not yet," I fibbed. "He's probably busy."

"I think we're going to need a new name for the store," said Vic. "I have some ideas, but we can talk about it later. I have to get back to sorting out what belongs to Barbara."

"Is she still there?" I envisioned the lovely Barbara, her eyes flashing, her claws fully extended and now out for Vic's blood.

"Oh yes. But I haven't explained the whole consignment

situation just yet. I promise she'll know about it by the end of the day."

"How do you think she's going to take it?"

"The first thing I'm going to do is revoke her lease and kick her out," said Vic. "And she can take the merchandise with her. Most of it is the loser stuff we have a hard time turning over."

"That'll go over well." I held Boodles tight, imagining the nasty scene.

"I can take it," said Vic. "I've got more plans, but we'll talk about it later, maybe tonight?"

"Want to come over at eight? Or would you rather talk over dinner?"

"I'm thinking nine. I'm really sorry that dinner won't work tonight. But I'll come over with Marcy."

"Tell Aunt Shelley to come too." It would have been nice to have Max there, too, but now that was probably impossible.

The rest of the day went smoothly. I tried calling Max a couple of times, during the lulls, but he never picked up my calls. I seriously doubted he was that busy, and I was pretty much sure he was checking the caller ID and ignoring me. I guess if he had a flaw, other than his rumpled and pudgy look, it was that he was unforgiving. Too bad I didn't know that earlier. Who's kidding who? I wouldn't know I'd feel this way unless I went on that date with Krieger. If I hadn't, I would always feel like I was settling for Max. Now that I knew I really wanted him, it was too late.

Business was still brisk, thanks to the now indirect publicity; people were now asking us about Janine instead of giving me sidelong glances. What a relief. We closed the shop at six, and Heather and I ate al fresco at Mister Z's, with Boodles sitting innocently on the chair next to me, nibbling daintily now and then at the scraps I dropped his way.

I told Heather about Vic's meeting at our house at nine o'clock.

"Am I invited?" asked Heather.

"What are you talking about? Of course you're invited."

"I wonder why Dad left the building to just Vic, and not half to me." She sounded a little hurt. My ever-emotional Heather was feeling slighted by her dead father.

I didn't really want to defend the skunk, but I decided to do it for Vic's sake. "It probably made sense to Dad. Vic works there; you don't."

"If I stay at Bella's Baubles, will you leave the business to me?" she asked.

I smiled and dropped a bit of bread to little Boodles. His tiny tongue flicked it immediately inside his mouth.

"It's not worth too much yet. But if you stay with me and it's something worth giving, the answer is *yes*."

Heather grasped my hand across the table. "Thanks, Mom. That means a lot to me."

I looked at my brightly colored daughter and realized she probably thought of herself as a screw-up.

"You're very capable, you know." I gave her hand a squeeze.

She released her grasp. "I love business. I didn't realize how much I'd like selling."

"That's wonderful. But don't you miss your art?"

Heather sat back in her chair. "I've been thinking. With my whole family in the jewelry business, maybe it would make sense for me to go back to school and learn how to design and make jewelry."

"I could teach you."

"Thanks, Mom, but I was thinking about working in metals, like gold and silver. I'll leave the beads to you."

"That's wonderful. Maybe Dad left you enough money to go back to school."

"I hope so. But whatever it is, I'll stretch it. I'll keep working and go to school part time. It helps to keep expenses down, living with you I mean."

"You're welcome to stay as long as you need to." My romantic prospects were dim; I didn't anticipate needing any privacy in the near — or far — future.

"Thanks, Mom. Want to go with Kara and me to hear Deb Baker speak at the Royal Oak library? It starts at seven-thirty, so we'd be able to get home by nine." Deb Baker is a novelist who grew up in the U.P., what we call the Upper Peninsula of Michigan.

"Thanks, hon, but I'm bushed. I need to go home and unwind a little before everyone shows up."

We parted ways at about seven-twenty. Heather took off for the library, her lovely green hair bouncing merrily in the evening sunshine. There was no humidity in the air. I was having a good hair day, but I was too upset about Max to enjoy it.

Boodles walked about half the way home when I could tell he was getting tired. He was holding back against his faux diamond-studded leash so I scooped him up and put him in his carrier for a rest. By the time we reached my front door, I was exhausted and ready to fall apart on my comfy couch.

I felt an unexpected tap on my shoulder as I turned the key and opened the door to my house. For a split second, I felt a sense of relief, as I was positive it was Max. But I turned my head, and there, just an inch from my face, was Tom Jenkins. Boodles started his low growl as Tom forced his way into my living room and shut the door behind us.

CHAPTER 28

I had about a split second to decide how to act. There was no pretending this was a social visit. The man had just forced his way into my house. I tried to think of something to say, but I was uncharacteristically speechless. What do you say to a home intruder?

But he spoke before I had a chance to open my mouth.

"Sit down at the table." His voice was no-nonsense. I could see he was carrying a small handgun. "It's time to write a note."

I started walking to the dining room table, my eyes darting around, trying not to stare at the gun, which was most likely loaded for my benefit. I sat down.

"I don't have any paper." My voice barely registered. It

didn't sound like me at all. I was terrified. Boodles picked up on the tension and started barking at Tom.

"Shut the mutt up!"

I scooped Boodles into my arms and tried to comfort him. I didn't want him to get shot by this crazy man. The barking stopped, but Boodles was shaking.

"I told you, I don't have any paper." Holding Boodles made my voice calmer.

Tom waved his gun in the air. "Go get some!"

"Do you have to wave that thing around? I'll go get some paper from the kitchen."

He followed me into the kitchen, the gun now dropped at his side. I took a panicky look around while I reached into my junk drawer for a legal pad and a mechanical pencil. I was trying to find a weapon I could grab, but there was nothing that could compete with a loaded gun. There was my wooden block filled with knives. Gun or no gun, the thought of sticking a knife into a living person made me nauseous. I saw my cast-iron frying pan sitting conveniently on my stovetop—made to order for concussions, but no match for a loaded gun. I ran my hands through the drawer, pretending to look for a pencil, thinking that I'd likely be dead before the frying pan hit his head.

"Stop stalling!" His voice made me jump.

I grabbed the pencil and pad. "You're making me nervous!" This was a ridiculous understatement, but it sort of made sense at the time.

I sat back down at my table with little Boodles on my lap. The air conditioning blew in my face, but I really didn't need it; my blood ran cold with fear.

"What do you want me to write?"

Tom reached into his shirt pocket for a folded piece of paper. "Here, copy this."

It was a computer printout of a letter. It read:

Dear Heather and Vic,

I can no longer live with myself after killing your father, Robert Blumer. Now that Janine Jenkins, your father's loyal employee for over ten hard-working years, has been wrongfully arrested for his murder, I have no choice but to take my own life. I can no longer live with the shame and guilt of having an innocent person jailed for my crime and cannot bear the thought of going to prison.

I am sorry for the pain I have caused you. I hope you will forgive me.

Love, Bella Blumer

It was a horrible letter. If I copied it exactly the way Tom wanted, everyone would know I wasn't the person who really wrote it. But it wouldn't help me much if I was dead by the time they read it. I couldn't help it—I looked at him like he was crazy. "You're planning to kill me and make it look like suicide?"

"I don't have any choice. You should have left well enough alone."

"What!"

"You should have kept your nose out of the

investigation."

It hit me with a flash. "So you're the one who buried the gun in my yard? You're the one snooping on me, stealing my shovel?"

He didn't answer my question, but he certainly didn't deny it either. "They wouldn't have put you away for long. You would have had a lot of sympathy. Robert cheated on you for years." The pain in his voice was palpable. It occurred to me I hadn't thought of how Robert's cheating had affected anyone but me.

This time, when I spoke, my voice sounded sympathetic. "Tom, why kill me? I was a victim just like you."

"Your husband's gone now. I want my wife with me — and with our kids, not in prison. They'll put her away forever."

"You don't know that!"

"C'mon! She cheated on me with him when he was married to you and probably while he was married to that other bitch." His voice cracked. "She's been stealing from him for years now."

"You knew?" I was surprised.

"You think I'm stupid?" He started pacing through my living room, the gun clasped firmly in his left hand. "First she started coming home with special gifts, things we couldn't afford. I was suspicious, thought she was having an affair."

"When was that?" I was curious. And buying time.

"Years ago, when she first started working there."

"Maybe Robert *was* buying her gifts then." I tried to make it sound like Janine was innocent. Besides, that was likely the case. When he'd first started cheating with Janine, he probably *had* bought her gifts.

"Yeah, maybe. But it really started up when your husband got engaged to that little whore."

I was thinking that the Robert-Barbara engagement wasn't my favorite time either, but I kept my mouth shut.

"All of a sudden, she had even more money, started going to the spa to lose weight, and decided our kids needed private school, never consulting with me. Oh no, she was too high and mighty for that."

I was tempted to say he sounded angrier with Janine than with me, but I was afraid to confront him. So I decided to ask a question instead, trying my best to stall for time. "You weren't at Robert's funeral. So who took the shot of me fighting with Barbara?"

Tom laughed. "That was Janine. She got a big kick out of seeing the two of you going after each other."

More likely, she was happy to set me up. Again, I kept my mouth shut. I glanced at my watch. It was eight-forty. Just twenty minutes till Vic and the others arrived.

"Why are you looking at your watch?" His voice was mocking. "Expecting someone?"

I looked down. "No, everyone's out tonight. I was too tired and told them to go out without me. I have no idea when they'll be back." I prayed I sounded convincing. No reason to give him a deadline for killing me and getting out in time.

Questions, I wracked my brain for questions. The longer I stayed away from that suicide note the better.

"How did you know I went to the forensic accountant?"

"That little whore called Janine, right after your jerk of a son let Janine go. I guess she was pissed about it, too."

"Barbara?"

He nodded toward my legal pad. I decided to try and get him back on track with his talk about Janine. The more I knew about the truth, the better. That is, if I lived through this visit.

"I didn't know your kids were going to private school." I tried to say it as innocently as possible, and it worked.

He frowned. "All of a sudden, public school wasn't good enough for her; she signed them up for Cranbrook of all places."

Cranbrook is a private school that serves metro Detroit's elite. His gun hung limply at his side. It was hard for me to believe that I used to like this guy. He always seemed so mild mannered and kind.

"Wow, that's expensive." For the record, my kids went to public school. No wonder the Blumer bank account was so low.

"I thought maybe she got them in there on scholarship." He scowled. "But when she bought the Cadillac from

Gleason's, I knew something was up."

"How long ago was that?" I asked.

He thought for a moment, the gun still limp in his hand. I debated making a rush for him, but I thought better of it. I had never been very athletic, and I was still in my heels.

"About six months ago, last February. I asked her about it, and it started a big fight."

"So you knew she was stealing from Robert, but you couldn't possibly know for sure that she was cheating on you."

His hand tightened up on the gun, and his left hand balled up into a fist. "I knew all right. That's when I started following her."

"Following her?"

"I only work four days at Gleason's." His voice was bitter. "I was making less than my wife, even before her tidy little extras. That fat bastard keeps as many of us on part time as he can. That way he doesn't have to pay any benefits."

"Oh, I didn't know that." That *was* pretty horrible for Ollie to do to his employees.

His face broke into a bitter smile. I was acutely aware of the fact that the only thing between me and a permanent checkout was the fact that I hadn't yet written that note.

"There's a lot you don't know. I started following her, and you know, usually she just went to work, like a good little wife. But *that* day…" He paused.

"You mean the day of the murder?"

He looked at me. "I guess it doesn't matter much now if you know. Yes, the day your husband bit the dust."

I didn't want to correct him about the fact that Robert wasn't my husband. Why agitate a crazy man? "What happened?" It was more than morbid curiosity. I *had* to know the truth.

"I followed her all the way to your house, your *old* house. She had the garage door opener and drove right in, like she belonged there, I guess so the neighbors wouldn't talk."

I gasped. She had the remote to our garage!

"That's right. She might as well have had keys to your house. I asked her about it later. She told me she'd had it for about nine years."

"Nine years!" I was horrified. This confirmed my worst fears.

"Yeah, she thought he'd leave you and marry her. That's why she got so mad when he left you for that other one, almost as soon as he met her."

I felt tears stinging at the edge of my eyes, but I wasn't going to cry. "So why did she kill him? Was he onto her stealing? Was he going to turn her in to the police?"

"She didn't kill him." He stood proud. "I did."

"What?" I was truly shocked and horrified.

"I parked my car a few houses away, and I walked around to the back of the house, to see if there was an easy way to break in—and there was."

"But we had an alarm." Robert had always been security-conscious because, as a well-known jeweler, he felt like a target.

"The alarm was off, so that son-of-a-bitch could let in my wife!" He calmed himself down. I think he was enjoying the release of telling his story. "The door to your garage on the back side of the house was unlocked. I just turned the handle and walked right in. There was my wife's Cadillac, parked right next to your husband's, just like a happy little couple."

I was silent, mesmerized, visualizing the end of Robert Blumer.

"From there, it was easy. The door to the house from inside the garage wasn't locked either. I walked right in. I was so angry, crazy really, that I didn't even try to be quiet. I barged right up the steps. I could hear them."

I wanted to ask if they were making love, but it was still too painful to put into words.

He laughed. "I guess your rich hubby was more ready for action than she was, because there he was, looking pretty stupid in his underwear, and she was more than half dressed. They were arguing."

"Arguing?"

"He was telling her that she took too much. I guess he meant from his fat bank account."

I was in no mood to tell him Janine had taken enough money to put the store in financial jeopardy. It was definitely not his business.

"He was ready for some action, and she was still giving it to him for marrying that Barbara babe, instead of her." His voice cracked.

"That must have been painful for you." I imagined this was true.

"Painful all right. But then that bastard did it."

"Did what?"

"He laughed at her, said he would never have married her and to get over it." Tom's eye's flashed with anger. "That's why I killed him. I had to."

I stood up. "You didn't have to kill anyone!"

Tom's face was drained of blood, and his eyes opened wide, not blinking. "He wrecked my life, and for him it was a laugh." Tom took a deep breath. "The wall safe in the room was open, and there was your gun. I didn't know it was yours, I just knew it was a gun. I took it and shot him, again and again, until there weren't any more bullets. He fell back on the bed, and that was that."

This brought back the image of Robert bleeding out on our mattress, and I was horrified.

"Why didn't you just get a divorce like a normal person? Why did you have to kill him?" I was being pretty irrational myself. It's not too smart to start yelling at a man with a gun.

Tom sagged against the table, and finally sat down. I took a nanosecond glance at my watch. It was eight fifty-nine.

"I don't want a divorce," he said, quietly and firmly. "I love my wife."

This was chillingly absurd and logical at the same time. He loved her no matter what, and I was in the way.

He pointed at the paper and pencil with his right hand, the gun now loosely on the table in front of him. "Start writing." His voice was dull, flat, and no-nonsense.

Hoping that time was now on my side, I started slowly to write.

"Hurry up," he said, catching on to my slacking. "Let's get this over with."

I continued to write, praying for some action at the front door, hoping against hope that at least one of them would get there on time. When I was just about to sign my name to the page, the doorbell rang.

"Who's that?" Tom looked upset.

"CALL 911!" I screamed at the top of my lungs.

"Shut up!" Tom swung the gun to hit me in the face, but I flinched and ducked, luckily getting out of the way by less than an inch or two.

"GO GET HELP!" I screamed, once again.

Tom ran to the door. Whoever was there was now both knocking and ringing the bell. I didn't think. I wasn't about to let him kill one of my children! I dove into the kitchen, grabbed my iron frying pan, and ran behind him to the front door. Just as the knob started turning with one of my kid's keys in the lock, the heavy pan connected with the back of his head with a sickening thud. He slid to the floor at my feet, and his small gun skittered across the hardwood floor. It stopped at the feet of Boodles, who had been barking the entire time.

As Vic edged his way into the door, I could hear the sirens coming down Fourth Street. I didn't bother picking up the gun. Tom Jenkins was out cold.

CHAPTER 29

he rest of the evening was a blur. The cops arrived. I was so relieved that it was two uniforms, rather than Krieger and his sidekick. Tom was taken away in an ambulance, along with a police escort, to Royal Oak Beaumont Hospital, presumably with a concussion. Vic, Marcy, and I were all questioned separately. The police were getting to be a familiar commodity, but I was so grateful to be alive that, for once, I had no complaints.

Vic called Max, who immediately came on the scene and saw to all our rights. He then disappeared without a personal word to me — positive or negative.

It was hard sleeping that night, even if Tom Jenkins was likely on police guard and there was no one snooping around my house, watching me from a distance. I should have felt safe and happy, but I was miserable.

The good news was that the time spent awake listening to Boodles' sweet little snore, was not time wasted. I had some unfinished business, and I spent most of the night visualizing and rethinking every word I was going to say. Sometime in the wee hours of the morning, I fell into a deep, soundproof sleep.

I SAY it was soundproof because I woke up Wednesday morning with a jolt at exactly 9:45 AM. This gave me just enough time to get dressed and run to work—if I skipped breakfast and, worse yet, my makeup.

Boodles and I literally ran the five blocks to my store. Imagine my shock when I unlocked the back door and there, resplendent in fire-engine-red hair, with blown-glass red beads to match, was my Heather.

"You look awful, Mom." She appraised my plain, unmade face and disheveled hair.

"Thanks, I needed that." I ducked into our ultra-tiny john. "So what are you doing here so early?" I didn't say it, but if I had known she was going to be there, I might have taken my time coming in.

Heather stood behind me as I carefully applied my mascara. "Didn't you see the note I left for you?"

"What note?" I picked up my scissor-handled lash curler.

I have to say it was better doing this in front of Heather rather than Shelley. Shelley, bless her I-have-a-natural-look-and-I-don't-give-a-damn heart, puts on colored lip gloss and calls it a day. For Elena's Bat Mitzvah she broke down and wore some blush. Let's just say that my sister and I don't relate too well on the makeup front.

"I taped the note on the microwave." Heather handed me a tissue to blend my cheeks. "You slept through that alarm of yours that could wake the dead, and I thought I'd open and stay here for you today."

I slipped my eye shadow back into my purse and turned to give Heather a super-duper hug.

"Gee, Mom, you had a pretty tough night last night, so I figured you needed a rest." She pulled back and took a look at me. "Max was acting pretty weird last night."

I turned back to the mirror and started in on my hair with the curling iron, pretending ignorance. "What do you mean?" I just wasn't ready to talk about it.

"C'mon, Mom, Aunt Shelley told me all about it."

I felt my muscles tighten. Shelley and her big mouth. Sometimes I like how close she is with Heather. This was not one of those times.

I turned back to Heather. "I can't talk about that now. You think you can hold the fort down for about an hour?"

Heather pressed her lips together. "Sure." I knew she was dying to ask where I was going. But, thankfully, she didn't. I'd have to remember to return the favor.

I plugged in the flat iron to continue the process of hair repair. Less than ten minutes later, Boodles and I were on Fourth Street, heading for the law offices of Fosner and McGriff.

I made a quick stop for some Double Ds. It was mid-July-hot in Royal Oak, but the humidity was still at bay. So I expected to remain reasonably irresistible for the rest of the morning.

The door to Fosner and McGriff was not locked. When I entered, McGriff sat at what should have been the receptionist's desk. He looked up from his paperwork. "Oh, it's you."

"Nice to see you too." I decided that sarcasm was my safest bet.

He took off his glasses, and I could see he was probably about ten years younger than Max. "What did you do to him?"

"Pardon me?" I just couldn't see how this was any of his business.

"He's been miserable for more than a day now. That hasn't happened since the divorce. I figure it has to be you."

I felt my lower lip jut out into a pensive frown. Realizing that this was definitely not my best look, I immediately drew it back in. "Is he in his office?"

"He's working on a paying case," said McGriff, obviously no stranger to sarcasm himself.

I hoisted Boodles and my purse onto my shoulder and

marched right past him, and was halfway into the office hallway when he said, "And where do you think you're going?"

I shrugged Boodles' carrier higher on my left shoulder. "I'm here to pay him now, so I'm sure you won't object." My voice was more vinegar than honey. And just before I totally disappeared to the other side of the door, I added, "I hope your wife liked her anniversary gift." I couldn't see or hear his reaction. No harm in being a good retailer and a smartass at the same time.

I took a few steps toward Max's office. So much had happened since he'd first met me, and it had only been a week! I knocked on his closed door.

"Come in," he said.

I guess he was expecting McGriff, because he didn't look up till I deposited the bag of Double Ds on his desk.

Boodles hopped out of his carrier, walked across the desk, and plopped into his lap. Chester jumped off Max's leather couch with heavy feet and positioned himself so that his curly head was directly under my right hand. Apparently, no one told the dogs there was any problem between us.

I put my lime bag on his desk, which was covered with several stacks of files of varying heights. "I'm here to pay my bill," I lied. I was still pretty much broke, but all the things I'd planned to say the night before had gone poof. My mind was blank.

"It's not ready yet." Max sat back in his chair like he was relaxed, but he wasn't. His face was flat in tone, not at all like the Max I knew.

"Well then, have a Double D." I tried to sound like I didn't notice his mood. "I brought a lemon torte—your favorite."

No smile. "It's a little early for dessert, but thanks. Maybe later."

I was feeling a little stung, but I persisted. "Should I come back?" I thought maybe there was an opening here, a chink in his armor.

"That won't be necessary." He glanced back at the paperwork on his desk. "I really have to get back to work."

My heart sunk down to my toes. Boodles hopped back into his carrier. Maybe he was catching on. Chester settled with a decisive thump on the area rug in front of the couch.

"Max?" I said his name; even though it was obvious he was ignoring me.

"What?" He snapped, but he didn't look up.

I sat down in one of the two chairs that faced his desk. "Listen, I was up all night thinking about what I wanted to say to you." I left out the part about over-sleeping, even though it was probably relevant. I could see he really was, in fact, busy, and I had to get to the point.

"Max, I'm sorry." I could hear the catch in my voice. "I really screwed up."

He looked right through me. "You don't owe me a thing.

Well, except for the bill."

"You've been a wonderful friend, and much, much more."

"Apparently not." His voice was all business.

"Max, I'm telling you I made a mistake. I'm sorry!"

"It's not that simple, Bella!"

"What do you mean?" Okay, so my voice got a little screechy here. This wasn't going the way I planned it.

Max sucked in his lower lip. "You lied to me. How can I ever trust you?"

"It was a white lie, Max. I just didn't want to hurt your feelings. How was I supposed to know you'd run into Shelley?"

He snorted out something that sounded like 'huh.' "So you're really just upset that you got caught."

He had a point there, but I didn't feel like letting him have it.

"That's not the point."

"So, where were you, Bella?"

I paused. I didn't want to lie, but neither did I want to tell the whole truth.

"I was out to dinner with Detective Krieger. It was just dinner."

"If it was 'just dinner,' why didn't you tell me? Why the lies, Bella?"

"I knew you'd be upset, just like you are now. I didn't want to hurt your feelings."

"Of course you hurt my feelings! You told me you weren't ready to date, and the first bozo that asks you out that isn't *me*, and off you go." He looked so angry it sort of scared me. "That was the bigger lie, Bella. Telling me you weren't ready, when you really just weren't interested in me."

A silence hung in the air between us, so thick I wasn't sure I could breathe. I think I counted to ten before I found my voice. I could have told him it was 'just dinner' with Krieger, but we both knew that wasn't the truth.

"You want the truth, Max?" It felt like the room was starting to spin. I held onto his desk for support.

"That would be refreshing." He still sat in his chair, and as I stared at his face, it seemed to fade in and out of shadows.

"The truth is, I really wasn't ready for you. I was all mixed up." I stopped for a moment to concentrate on breathing and was grateful that he didn't interrupt. "Krieger asked me out, and it felt just right. I felt like I had when I was young and dating Robert."

Max tightened his lips. "Why are you bothering me? Go back to Krieger. I'm busy, Bella."

"I'm not done." I put both hands on his desktop and spoke directly to him. "The truth is he was just like Robert. Attractive, suave." I didn't add 'hot' or 'great-looking,' even though I was thinking it; why hurt Max any more than I already had? "The only thing was, he really was a lot like

Robert: his eyes and hands were on every woman in the joint."

"So you're saying you want an ugly guy now?" He still didn't look happy.

"Don't put words in my mouth! Stop being a jerk." Now I was angry. "One-half of a date with him was enough to show me that I deserve a quality man; someone who is as loyal as I am. I was hoping that was you. But if it's not, I guess I'll have to live with it." I started gathering up Boodles and my lime bag, glad for my anger; I knew I was going to be miserable when it petered out.

My hand was already on his office door when I heard him say, "So I'm a quality guy, huh?" His voice slightly choked, but it sounded more like my Max.

I put down Boodles and ran to his side of the desk. I wasn't in the mood for a wimpy hug, so I gave him a full-body bear hug.

"I could get used to this." He drew me in so close I had to wonder if it was his wallet I felt, but I didn't ask. After two deep kisses that left me wanting for more, I whispered that we both should probably get back to work. After promises to meet that night for dinner, we shared one more kiss, after which, I fairly floated across the sidewalk all the way back to work, with little Boodles in tow.

*C*HAPTER 30

*L*ater that night, we all met at Armaggio's on Fifth. I invited everyone—Vic and Marcy, Heather and Kara, Shelley and Mitch, Elena, Ben and Stella, my mom and Albert, and of course, my Max. I even included Myrna for good measure. No point in leaving out my kids' other grandma.

I insisted that this time it was my treat. My plan was to put it all on my charge card and worry about it later. Probably not a good plan, but I wanted to thank every one of them and be grateful that I was still alive and out of jail permanently.

After about the seventh toast to everyone's health and happiness, Vic raised his glass. "I have a proposal for you, Mom."

"Hey, that's my line," said Max, who'd been eating one-handed the whole night, so he could keep an arm around my shoulder or waist.

"Barbara is officially out of the business." This he said with a big smile, making all those trips to the orthodontist years ago so worthwhile.

"I'll drink to that!" Heather's red hair reflected off her wineglass.

Vic put down his wineglass. "Not only is Barbara gone, but she's taken our business name with her."

I knew that already, and I wondered what he was going to say next.

"Tell her, Vic," said Marcy, who was looking positively radiant in her little black dress.

"Tell me what?" I asked, curious, yet pleasantly aware of Max's hand on the small of my back. He hadn't let go of me from the moment he'd picked me up at the house. I felt bad leaving Boodles at home with Chester, but this night was a people-only event.

Vic couldn't stop smiling. "We need to get a new name for the business, something with name recognition. Something familiar, but maybe different."

"Okay." I had a clue as to what he was driving at, but I was afraid to ask in case I was wrong. It would be really embarrassing.

"Aunt Shelley tells me you're paying one thousand a month rent for that hole-in-the-wall you call a store."

"That's right." I could tell my guess had been right on target.

Vic savored a slow sip of red wine. "Well, first I should tell you that Albert is loaning your bail money to me, once he gets it back from the Court."

I smiled at Albert. In the dim light of the restaurant, if you squinted, his horrible toupee almost looked real. "That's really wonderful, Albert," I said, and I meant it. "You really treat us all like family."

Albert smiled back at me. "You *are* my family."

Vic cleared his throat. "Now back to your rent, Mom. If you could pay rent to the business and move it into our building, already we'd be way ahead, both of us."

I had to admit that this was tempting. The Blumer Fine Jewelers building was a palace compared to my tiny shop.

"Where would I put my bench?"

"You could take over Dad's office." Vic's voice choked a little still, at the mention of his dad, and I felt for him. But Robert's office was huge, nearly twice the size of my whole tiny shop—and it would be all for me and my work!

But I couldn't be totally selfish here. "What about Aunt Shelley? And Heather? And how would we all be paid?" My head was swirling with the possibilities.

Vic smiled, and I could tell he was dead serious. "Aunt Shelley is a perfect bookkeeper and I.T. person. Better yet, I can trust her with my life, let alone the books." He turned to his sister. "You tell me Heather is great in sales." He hesitated. "Even though I'm not so sure about that hair."

A balled-up napkin hit him on the side of the head, but Heather was smiling. "I'd work part time there while I go to school."

"But what do you want to call the place?" I was silently hoping I could make good use of my beautiful Bella's Baubles sign, but I was afraid I was hoping too much.

"I thought you understood," said Vic. "I'd like to capitalize on the name recognition. I'm thinking Blumer's Jeweltown. And we can be the home of Bella Blumer Designs."

"That's perfect!" I said, and I meant it. This would keep the flow of my business name, but made it just right for Vic, too. "We could use my sign, maybe over Dad's office, and have the sign guy change it up a little."

"Exactly what we were thinking!" said Vic. I hadn't heard him talk in such an animated way since the day we'd found his dad. "Dad was always such a Motown fan. He left all his memorabilia to me. We can put it all up in the store. And technically, we're in Motown, or just a few miles away. Jeweltown would be a take on that. I'm sure Dad would love it!"

I was kind of surprised the mention of Robert Blumer didn't bring up any passionate feelings. No love, no hate. I was just sad for my family's loss.

I looked at my two children and at my sister. "Am I the last to know?" I glanced at my former mother-in-law. "And what about Grandma Myrna? Are you okay about all of this?"

Myrna looked a little misty-eyed. After all, just a little more than a week had passed since Robert's death. But she was a fair and practical woman. "I think that after all my son put you through it's time to come back and work with the family."

I slipped out of Max's arm and gave Myna a hug. She felt more bony and frail than I remembered. She'd probably aged a few years this past week.

Then I went around the whole table and hugged every person there, including my mother, who looked like she was about to have an orgasm, just watching me with Max. I wondered what she would pester me about next. Her eyes wandered over to the temporarily unattached Heather. I smiled. Oh that.

I returned to my seat.

Max whispered in my ear, "I don't think you have much of a choice." Then out loud he said, "I'll draw up the papers. On the house."

Albert laughed. "Have you gotten a penny from this woman yet?"

Max put one arm around my shoulder and the other on my waist. "Not a penny. Not a dime."

I jabbed an elbow into his squishy side. "He hasn't sent a bill yet," I said in my defense.

"And I never will." Max kissed the side of my head.

It was a perfectly wonderful dinner that night, even though I can't remember a thing that passed through my lips besides the wine. It was the people around the table, and the fleeting feeling I hadn't felt in so long that it was hard for me to place it, until I realized what it was.

I was happy.

$\mathscr{A}$CKNOWLEDGMENTS

Writing Deadly Diamonds has been a long, extended blast! But it would not have been possible without the help of many people. So I'd like to extend a big 'Thank You' to Beta Reader extraordinaire, Mari Cooper, as well attorney Alona Sharon, Esq. and her husband, Mark Jeross, who lent some thoughts and suggestions on the legal contents of the book. I take sole responsibility for any legal errors, omissons or misconceptions.

A big shout out of thanks to my army of Beta Readers, including Patti and Dan McCarty (if you want to buy a house in Royal Oak, contact the McCarty Team), Liz Zerwekh, Connie Huber, Ann Little, as well as David and Beth Rodgers. Kudos to Developmental Editor, Claire Ashgrove of Finish-the-Story.com, as well as copy editor Judy Beatty. And I continue to be dazzled by the work of cover artist, Michelle Preast.

Of course I have to add a big thank you for the support of my family, especially my one and only, Peter Rodgers, who's heard more about this book than he ever cared to hear about anything! (Sorry honey, there are many more books to come.)

$\mathscr{A}$LSO $\mathscr{B}$Y
DENISE RODGERS

Coming soon . . .
Murderous Emeralds

It's fall in Royal Oak, Michigan, just two miles north of the infamous Eight Mile Road, and jewelry designer Bella Blumer is ready to live the good life and leave the drama of last summer behind her. But the good life is not quite ready for Bella. In addition to jumping head first into another murder investigation to help a long-time friend, Bella has to deal with the fact that her fabulous boyfriend wants to marry her — even if the thought of marriage makes her more than slightly nauseous. Add to that the fact that her newly sullen daughter is ignoring her, and her dragon-lady of a stepsister is in town and making life miserable for Bella's not-so-lovable mother. When the murder investigation reveals one sordid secret after another, Bella has to scramble to find the murderer to save both her friend...and herself.

If you would like advance release notice for the next book,
sign up for my newsletter at
www.DeniseRodgersBooks.com

Contact Denise Rodgers
Email:
deniserodgersbooks @ gmail.com
Facebook:
www.DeniseRodgersBooks.com

$\mathscr{A}$BOUT THE $\mathscr{A}$UTHOR

Denise Rodgers is the author of *Deadly Diamonds*, the first of the Jeweltown Mystery book series, as well as the soon-to-be-released *Murderous Emeralds*, and work-in-progress *Poison Pearl*. An established children's poet, Ms. Rodgers is the author of two books of poetry and has been anthologized in two Jack Prelutsky books as well as countless magazine and textbooks for children. The Jeweltown series is her foray into the adult mystery genre. She lives in metro Detroit with her husband and two small dogs. She is the mother of two grown sons and two (soon to be four) wonderfully beautiful, talented, and extraordinarily intelligent (okay, so she's biased) grandchildren. When she is not writing or editing, she is at work at her family business, where she crunches numbers and consults on marketing issues. She also enjoys bike riding, kayaking, and babysitting. (Not necessarily in that order.)

www.DeniseRodgersBooks.com
www.Facebook.com/DeniseRodgersBooks
deniserodgersbooks @ gmail.com

Carolyn – to LAX
* Hurry get your seats.
  But plane was late
* Food choice awful

to Honnolulu
* No TV – very
  irratating
* Dirty bath
*
Lighting
but looks
unstable

47168497R00214

Made in the USA
Charleston, SC
30 September 2015